Lustful Sin

By Robert Wright

ALSO BY ROBERT WRIGHT JR

<u>Young Adult Novels</u>
Witch Way Home
Witch Way Back
Witch Way to Haven
Into Darkness
Walk the Stars
Walk the Earth
Ruby Red and the Wolf
Ruby Red and the Undead
Unwanted
Extinction Effect: Undead Uprising
Lucifer's Daughter

<u>Young Adult Short Stories</u>
Welcome to the Dark World
(with Scott Wright)

<u>Children's Books</u>
Monsters Under the Bed
Dragon in the Woods
Mummy in the Museum

DEDICATION

To all the women who stand on their own. I have been lucky to have
so many strong women in my life. May they always fight for what they
believe.

ACKNOWLEDGMENTS

This book was born out of a challenge I was given–to write a spicy paranormal romance. A book with no filters. Challenge accepted.

Thanks to all who helped in the process. Those who listened while I bounced ideas around. Those who beta read and provided ideas and suggested re-writes. The ones who let me know that a little spice is good.

Now, on to the first book in the Bounty Hunter series.

1

His eyelids fluttered as he woke from a dreamless sleep, woke to—quiet. Silence raged within his head. As the alpha of the biggest Northwest wolf pack, he should be able to feel the power of his pack members. Be able to draw on their power. Even from the lowest of the low among the pack. But even more disturbing than the quiet was the absence of Brother Wolf. The other half of himself that made him a Were, but it was as though his mind was a blank slate, wiped clean. As though there was no pack. No Brother Wolf. Nothing but emptiness. For the first time in the alpha's life, he felt loneliness and even a touch of fear.

He lay in the dark, listless, drained, straining at the maddening stillness in his mind. The feeling of abandonment. Of loneliness. He fought to hear some little inkling of a noise. Not even as a pup where he was the dominant of his litter had he felt this feeling. A feeling—no, not a feeling but a taste of real fear. How many of those who had fallen to him over the years had felt this? Panic set in as he fought against the quiet. Pain soon crept into that empty space. To fill it bit by bit. Pain that encircled his wrists and ankles. Pain that ate into his soul feeding the growing fear within him.

A low growl escaped his lips as he tried to pull away not only from the pain but also from the never before felt sensations that raged through him and bound him to the soft surface where he lay. Even as he fought harder against his bonds, his mind gasped: Silver! But with that thought came some relief. If silver was holding him, causing him this unwanted pain, then he hadn't lost all that made him a Were. All that made him the top of the food chain in his world.

Another rattle of chains from the alpha brought a mocking, throaty, female voice floating from the darkness. "Well, dog, I see you're finally awake."

The alpha choked down the fear now that he had something tangible to focus on. Grasping at his growing fury at the voice in the darkness. At last here was something perceptible. An enemy. This he could fight. This he could focus his anger toward. "Who are you, bitch? What have you done to my pack? My wolf?"

A low chuckle from the shadows. "You can call me Aezriane. Though I am disappointed that there was no 'where am I', dog. For that is the real question you should ask yourself."

Another growl erupted from deep within his chest as he fought against that silky voice. The soft voice that promised to deliver forbidden desires. Wicked pleasures. He shook his head as though to rid his mind of the voice as his mouth whispered of its own accord. "So, where am I?" Hating his weakness even as the words flowed past his lips.

"Yes. Good puppy. Very good indeed. You will do nicely."

He pushed against the pleasures the voice held. Against all it promised. With a will that struggled against the feelings raging in his mind this time he barked out the question. "Where am I, bitch? I demand to know. Or you will pay when I get out of here. Pay with your life. You—you have no idea who you're screwing with."

A sharp pain followed the creature's hand and nails as they raked across the alpha's face. The echo of a slap rebounded off unseen walls as an icy voice hissed in his ear, "My, but we are a feisty one, dog. DO—NOT—PISS—ME—OFF—PUPPY. It's you that has no idea who they are dealing with. We can do this one of two ways, dog. One way you will regret very, very much."

A chill ran down the Were's spine as the voice changed. This time promising, in its tone, not pleasure but a violent death. Or maybe even deep dank holes with slimy crawly things in them waiting to burrow into live flesh as you slowly ran out of air. An involuntary whimper escaped his lips. "Ple—please." Bitterness overwhelming him at a word he had never used before in his life.

The alpha hated himself to his core for that whimper, but deep in his soul he cowered against the wicked possibilities the voice now promised. He knew there were worse things in this world than death and that voice assured a taste of that.

"Yes, puppy, can you feel it? Your life hangs in my hands."

"Where am I?" The hatred raged deeper within himself for showing any weakness to this creature. Hating the feeling of helplessness. A feeling he had never experienced before in his life. He thought he would die before he would ever let a feeling like this overwhelm him. Now, he would do anything to survive his encounter with this creature.

"We are in your dream, dog." The voice's whispered breath, now hot, brushed against the Were's ear, stirring a few strands of sweat-stained hair. The heat of the creature's breath. Her scent sending shivers of pleasure up and down the alpha's body. *"You're lying in your bed. All you need to do is wake and I'll be gone and you will be safe. Be yourself. Be one with your wolf and your pack. So simple if you have the strength that is, dog. I mean, you are an alpha after all aren't you, puppy?"*

The alpha moaned as he willed himself to wake from this fresh hell. To fight himself out of this dream. No, not a dream. A nightmare. He struggled against the chains. Against that unholy voice that held him in this hell until he wore himself out.

He lay panting, sweat glistening on his skin. That low throaty chuckle echoed through the room. *"Poor puppy, can't wake can he?"* The chuckle died as the voice moved away from the Were. *"Well, no matter, dog. Better creatures than you have failed to break my spell."*

"How are you doing this? Why are you doing this?"

He could hear the creature moving about in the shadows that surrounded him. That voice now echoing from across the dark room. *"I need something from you, dog. Something that only you and a select few can give me. A little something that will allow me to complete my mission for my mother and then I will give you your—uh, release from this cruel world."*

He could read the lie in that voice, but clung to the small hope he would somehow live through this nightmare. *"What do you want? I'll give it to you. Whatever it is. Please, I need my wolf."* Hating himself again for sniveling before this creature in the shadows. But not being able to stop himself. Longing for his wild side. His want of Brother Wolf overwhelming any shame he felt at groveling before this stranger.

"Don't worry, dog. I know you will give me what I want. It is such a tiny thing anyway. Besides now we have come to an understanding, we will do this the easy way. You'll really, really enjoy this, I promise."

He lay shackled to the bed trying to get his breathing back under control. Doubting deep down he would enjoy anything this creature did, he heard the flare of a match and a wisp of smoke floated across the room bringing forth his animalistic fear of fire. *"What ... You're going to burn—"*

A tiny light in one corner fought against the dark that threatened to engulf it. A blurry outline of a long, lithe body flowed in and out of the shadows. Hair the color of the sun flickered in and out of his vision. "Oh, don't be silly, puppy. Burn you? Why we haven't even had our little fun yet. I thought I would add a little light to this party. Besides a little fragrance is needed to set the mood, don't you think?"

"I—I don't know what you're talking about."

The only thing the alpha could see was the thin match moving to another point where the long, tapered fingers holding it touched the flame to another candle. The tip flared to life. The tiny flame, like its sister casting shadows as it danced in the dark. Fighting to chase the gloom away. But failing as the darkness fought back and won.

Two more times the creature holding him, touched the tip of the match to a candle before she blew the flame out. The candles flickered at each point of the compass. Dancing as though a tiny breeze blew across the room. "There now. Doesn't that smell divine?"

The Were shook his head as he took a deep breath. His anger reasserting itself over the frightened puppy deep within him. "I don't know what game you're play—playin—" The scent of the candles carried over to the bound Were. His eyes closed for a second in confusion as he gasped before he took another deep breath in reflex. Sucking in the cloying scent that filled the air. A scent that tickled at other feelings deep within him.

The creature moved closer to the bound Were, one candle almost flickering out as she moved past it. "Yes. Yes, that's the way, dog. Breathe in the aroma. I made these candles special just for this little project. Just for you as they probably wouldn't work on other supers, but with you, I'm sure they will work just fine."

"What is that scent? I never smelled anything like that." The shifter's voice started to deepened as fear and pain were rudely pushed aside by a growing animal lust. A lust that pushed what little humanity he carried aside and allowed his animal instincts to surge to the surface.

He felt his body tense as the creature walked out from the shadows and ran a hand across his chest, the nails leaving red streaks of blood where they scored the skin. The pain seemed to deepen his rising lust instead of dampening it. Sending tremors downward where his shaft jerked to its full length as he closed his eyes and groaned. "Oh. You like that, puppy? I guess being a Were you would like the rough stuff. See, dog, I made each candle from the tallow of a virgin human. Along with a few other bodily fluids they donated and, of course, a special little spell I created. So, with your superior sense of smell … Well, you can see the results." She trailed a finger along his hard shaft, making it jump again.

The shifter groaned as the creature ran her hand down the leg closest to her. Again, her nails left a trail of bloody streaks behind. She brought her hand to her lips as her tongue flicked out to taste the blood. "Yes, I taste the lust within you, dog. It has a—certain spicy flavor. Italian, I would say."

He fought against the yearning ravaging his body. "You can't … You're not allowed to—"

Quiet whispers of laughter echoed around the room. She slithered up the side of the bed and leaned down toward the Were's head. "What can't I do? Use humans for my magic? They're just humans. Who will miss a slave or two? Or even a dozen. Besides the fairies and creatures like you use humans every day. Why is that so different from what I do, dog?"

The alpha fought against the desire that was pounding against his senses, now that she wasn't touching him. His anger overriding his want, his voice ringing off the walls. "It's against the law."

Reaching above the Were's head, the creature grabbed a golden bowl and set it between his legs as she straightened up. "Yes. Well, that is your law. Or should I say that is fairy law? Your master's law? Not mine. I answer only to my mother. To a higher power. A higher law. Now we need to see about collecting that little thing I need and then I will give you the release you deserve, dog."

Lifting his head, the Were tried to see what had rattled inside the bowl when the scent of the candles overpowered him once again and his lust surfaced even faster than before. Leaning his head back, he closed his eyes as his shaft jerked of its own accord, the tip emitting a tiny drop of fluid.

"Yes, that's much better. Now let's see how you like my other little surprise." The Were heard her lift something from the bowl. The noise of a cork popping sounded overloud in the room as she poured a liquid over his chest.

Where the scent of the candles had kindled the shifter's lust, the fluid hitting the open wounds across his chest felt like molten fire. He arched his back as sweat poured from his body. His muscles tensed and shook as though the creature was running a steady stream of electricity through him.

"Oh my, that seems to work just fine doesn't it, dog? How about we see what it does here?" With that, she poured the bottle over his crotch. His shaft jumped as the scalding liquid hit it. Growing even harder, if that was possible. Aezriane gazed at the Were's manhood displayed to her eyes. She gave his shaft a tiny pat. "I thought it would be more impressive, puppy. You know, you being a wolf and all. An alpha. Oh well, it will do for what I need, dog."

The Were let out a low growl. A mixture of anger and humiliation that died as the creature wrapped her hand around his shaft. "Yes. Yes, dog. Well, I guess we have to make do with what we have at hand, so to speak."

His eyes closed as the creature's words washed over the shifter. All his attention focused on the fingers wrapped around him. Slowly. Ever so slowly, she ran her hand upward until it rested on the head of his shaft and rubbed it around just barely contacting the taut skin. Another tiny drop of fluid leaked from the tip.

The alpha groaned, his hips bucked involuntarily as she held her hand there. Now, not moving it all. "What's the matter, dog? Do you want release? Do you want me to take what I need? Do you want the pleasure I can give you, puppy?"

The Were was now lost in the animal lust that rode his mind as he tried to ride her hand. The creature slapped her other hand on his belly, holding him flat to the soft surface. "I want to hear you beg, puppy. I want to hear you beg as my sisters once begged for their lives. I need you to beg me to take your seed."

The shifter was lost in the sensations as the creature ran her hand up and down his shaft. Barely touching the skin, as he trembled and tried harder to buck his hips. "Please—pleassse—" He hated himself for begging for what this creature promised. His lust overrode any thoughts of self-preservation the Were might have had.

"Say it, dog. I want to hear you beg. Beg for release and I will give you the end your worthless body craves." Aezriane grabbed his shaft at the base and squeezed hard eliciting another low moan.

The smell of the candles. The liquid boiling within his blood. Feeding his brain with a rutting lust as he had never felt before. Not even with his own mate. The feel of the creature's hand giving another quick squeeze on his shaft before she released him pushed the Were over the edge. "Yes, please, take whatever you want. Please, I need release. I—"

His voice trailed off to a low moan. The creature smiled as she gripped the Were's shaft and started a steady movement up and down. Inch by inch, up and down. As she reached the top, she would rub her hand along the head before sliding down again.

The Were's breathing became ragged as his heart crashed against his chest as though it would burst. She smiled at the Were as she removed her other hand from his belly. The alpha humped her hand without conscious thought as his body sought the release his mind craved. "Yes, dog. That's how you do it. Do you feel it building? Soon you'll have the release you want. Oh, yes, such a good doggy you are. You will soon be the father of a whole new race of my sisters. A whole new creature that will rule this world."

The Were was too far gone to hear any of the creature's words. All his thoughts, his longing, were focused on one point of his body as he fought for the sweet release. For the end of this madness that seemed to be building to a blinding climax.

With her other hand, the creature reached into the golden bowl as she felt the Were getting closer to the point of no return. Drawing out a silver dagger, she placed the point just below the shifter's ribs. "That's a good dog. You're so close—just so close. Can you see the edge? Just let yourself go, dog. Give me what I need and the nightmare will be over for you."

Just as the shifter felt like he couldn't go on any longer, he reached the peak of his explosion. He blasted over the other side and spiraled downward. Loud growls filled the room as Aezriane pointed the Were's shaft toward the golden bowl between his legs to capture her prize. The sound of his release as it filled the bowl bounced around the dark walls of the room.

"YES! YES! That's what I needed, dog." His body jerked as spurt after spurt shot into the golden receptacle as though the Were would never stop. The alpha's hips bucked. His body trembled as his balls contracted further within his body with each shot.

With a low moan, the alpha's hips gave one more shudder. He heard the creature whisper, "Thank you, dog. Now for your release." It was the last thing he heard as she shoved the dagger under the Were's ribs and straight into his heart.

The Were was lying in the afterglow of his orgasm one second, then felt the sharp pain of silver that penetrated his body the next. As his worn-out body registered what was happening, Aezriane gave a quick twist of the knife destroying the Were's heart.

He sucked in his last breath as his back tried to arch away from the intense pain radiating out from his center. As his legs kicked in the Were's death throes, Aezriane grabbed the golden bowl from between his legs with one hand as she shook her other to get the blood flowing through it again. "Oh, we can't waste any of that, dog. I worked way too hard to get it from you to spill it all over your bed."

Aezriane stood and watched as the shifter stopped moving before she set the golden bowl down. She walked over to the body and gazed at it before yanking the silver dagger from his chest. A thin trickle of blood seeped from the wound.

Slowly the Were's room dissolved into another, brighter room. Torches along the wall provided the only light. Aezriane gazed at the black bowl set on a pedestal as a mist deep within it dissolved. Plain but for the tiny statues of creatures lining the edges, she rubbed one of the figures in the shape of a wolf as she let out a satisfied sigh. Turning her back on the bowl, she slinked over to an altar that took up one wall. Putting the golden bowl on the black marble surface, she kneeled and bowed her head. "Mother. Lilith. I, the last of your children, bring you this offering so you may bless it. So you can avenge yourself against all those that have destroyed your children."

A dark shadow appeared above the altar and hovered there as the creature kneeling before it lifted her head and flung out her arms. Shiny eyes filled with tears. A harsh voice filled the shadows. "Very good, my daughter, you have brought me the first of my new children."

The contents of the golden bowl glowed with an eerie green light before fading. The shadow dissolved. "Thank you, Mother, for the blessing. Your will be done. We shall make the fairies pay for the insult they have shown you and your children, I swear."

2

The human waitress, her eyes wide, stood as far from the table as she could. She slid my plate in front of me before scurrying away. Her blue eyes threw a quick glance over her shoulder as she hurried behind the counter. Like that flimsy barrier would save her if a supernatural like me wanted to eat her.

"Touchy little human isn't she, Sin? You would think something was out to get her. Come to think of it, she probably would be a tasty little dish."

"She's young and new, Sebastian. From the info I got on her, she just started working in this sector. Probably just not used to seeing an imp, I'd guess." I chuckled at the bony six-inch winged red imp sitting on my shoulder. One hand was tangled in my red hair as the three claws on each foot dug into the black leather top I wore.

He gave the strands of hair he was holding a tug. "Yeah, I don't think so, Sin. Imps are a dime a dozen. Me, I don't think she is used to seeing a dragon."

I flicked a finger at the imp as I surveyed the rest of the greasy spoon before digging into the raw steaks sitting on my plate. Sebastian was wrong about imps being a dime a dozen, but he was probably right about the dragon part. It was likely most of the humans and supernaturals that ate in this place had never seen one of my kind before. Dragons are a rare breed of supernatural. Even rarer than imps.

Every eye had flicked up at me when I came in to find out if trouble was walking through the door. Once they were satisfied I didn't pose a threat to them, they went back to minding their own business. It was just that kind of place, lying as it did on the edge between the supernatural and human lands. A place where humans and supers could die a quick death if they didn't keep their wits about them.

As most supers know, dragons are nothing like the creatures that humans have drawn for ages. From far away, I could even pass as a human female. A short human female at that since I only stand five feet three in my bare feet. It is just when I get close enough for someone to make out my light green skin and the yellow patch that starts at my throat and runs down my front that most people figure out what they are dealing with. By then, for the ones I have a bounty on, it is too late to do anything. They are either captured or dead depending on the price on their head. And how much trouble they put me through.

"So, is she the one we'll use, Sin?" Sebastian's voice snapped me out of my daydreams and back to the job at hand. I watched the young waitress move around behind the filth-encrusted counter. It pretty well matched the rest of this 'fine' eating establishment. "What's the matter, girl? You getting a conscience? She's only a damn human, after all. Besides, she fits the profile of the humans that the vamp is going after, doesn't she?"

My partner was right. She was only human and, in this world, being human made you the bottom of the food chain. I glanced at the young woman knowing she would make perfect bait for tonight. She looked like the last three girls who had been taken by a rogue vamp operating in this sector. "Yeah, your info was right as always. She'll do, Sebastian. Tell the manager to make sure she is the last to leave this pit hole."

"Ah man. Why do I always get the sucky jobs, Sin? Did you see who runs this place? An orc. You know how bad orc bodies smell. And we won't even go into how bad their breath is."

"Sebastian, just go do it, please. I'm in no mood to listen to your whining tonight. Besides, we need to finish this job so we can take some down time."

The imp fluttered away on his tiny bat wings. "Yeah, you just want some boom-boom time with that damn fairy is all. Play a little kissy-face with the queen's son." I could hear him muttering other things about dragons and their hormones under his breath, but chose to ignore it. The imp may have been a pain in the ass, but he had pulled that ass out of a few fires since we had met thirteen years ago.

I started to pick up the steak on my plate, figuring to wolf down whatever this mystery meat was. Movement at the door caught my attention as three large green creatures bulled their way in from the misty night. Shit. Goblins. Just what I didn't need tonight. I pushed my plate away while reaching under the table and loosened the tie that held my weapon against my thigh, before leaning against the wall behind me.

The three green mountains of fat and muscle strode down the narrow aisle. The smaller two were grabbing food from customer's plates as they stared down anyone who might protest. Supernaturals and humans alike got up and left as they passed, taking the veiled hint that trouble was brewing in this grease pit.

The orc behind the counter rapped a ladle against the kitchen window. "Hey, no trouble in my place." The lead goblin shot him a look that had the owner ducking out of sight. The leader watched the kitchen doors swing shut before they continued down the aisle toward me.

As you can tell goblins aren't the most popular supernaturals. Could be their evil tempers. Could be their rude manners. Or could be that whenever they are around other creatures, said other creatures tend to die noisily, very violently, and not necessarily quickly. My take on goblins is that it could be that they stink like three-year-old horse manure piles. Hell, the orc running this place smelled like a rose next to a goblin.

The three stopped beside my table and stood looking at me for a few seconds as I took in their leader. The light glinted off a gold nose ring and his bald head brushed the ceiling. His beady black eyes stared at me like I was his next meal. "What the hell are you doing on our turf, bounty hunter? I don't remember you coming to ask permission to hunt here." The sneer he wore showed blackened tusks and teeth that had never been near a toothbrush in his life.

I gave the three my best 'I couldn't give a damn what they thought' smile before answering. "I'm not after any of your people, Grumble." Yeah, I knew who this goblin was. Like I said, I do my homework before I go on a job. Or I guess I should say my partner checks things out. "So, I guess I don't need to ask you shit. Which, by the way, you and your boys smell like. You guys ever heard of soap and water? Maybe even rolling in dog shit? Try it sometime it may improve the smell around here."

The two goblins behind Grumble growled as they stepped forward, their hands sneaking toward the knives at their sides. Not that a goblin needed a weapon to kill most humans or supers. My hand came up in a flash holding my nine-mil aimed dead center at their leader. That stopped them in their tracks. It was quiet for a second as three pairs of greedy eyes looked at the forbidden hardware filling my hand. Forbidden for all except me and a few other high mucky-mucks, like elite fairies.

Grumble showed sharp teeth as he nodded at my weapon. "Loaded with iron, Sin?"

"Could be, Grumble. Could be silver. You want to take the gamble? I mean I could plug one of your 'boys' here. See if they die or just get tickled."

The goblin leader stood eyeing my weapon for a few seconds as he considered the alternatives. Behind him, goblin eyes bounced between their leader and my weapon, a touch of fear showing before Grumble shook his head. "Why are you here, bounty hunter, if not for one of us?"

The relief in the goblins' eyes was almost laughable but I had more important things on my mind. I figured it wouldn't hurt to tell them about the contract I was on. Who knows? Maybe I could gather information that would let me collect my bounty quicker and not use the human waitress for bait. "I have a bounty from the fairy queen for a rogue vamp that is preying on humans in the outlying sectors. Know anything about it, Grumble?"

The goblin glanced back at his two soldiers before gazing at me and shook his head. "We don't worry about humans, Sin. Hard to believe queen bitch would care all that much about humans either."

"Yeah, well, this vamp isn't just killing humans. He is turning them. So far he has taken three human females and turned them."

They were silent for a minute or two as they measured the implications. I could almost see the wheels turning in Grumble's mind. I had to bite back a laugh as a goblin's thought process was almost as bad as their smell. "Well, that explains her concern. Still, even if I did know something, I wouldn't help you or that fairy bitch. What do I care if some vamp is making himself a harem?"

"A rogue vamp turning humans could affect all of us, Grumble. Besides you need to watch your mouth. The queen may hear what you're calling her. Last time I heard someone make disparaging remarks about the queen, it took them two years to die. Two very long and very painful years."

Grumble threw his head back and roared with laughter as did his two companions. "We goblins are worth ten fairy warriors. Let that pint-sized whore do her worst. She'll find out she tried to bite off more than she could chew if she thinks she can take on me and my warriors."

I sat quietly, the smile plastered on my face. Yeah and if that is true why is she sitting in her high castle and you're ruling the gutters? I was smart enough to keep my opinions to myself though. Even with a loaded nine-mil in my hand.

When the three stopped laughing, I pulled my plate back toward me as I lay my pistol right next to it. I ignored the greed in the three pairs of eyes as they gazed at my weapon. "Well, since we are all done with the warm and fuzzy visit, Grumble, and you know that I'm not after one of yours, maybe you'll let me finish my meal in peace?"

The goblin leaned down, resting his fists on the table. "Speaking of whores, Sin, when are you going to stop selling yourself out to the fairies? You know, stop being their little bitch and come running at their every beck and call. Or is that the price you have to pay to use forbidden weapons, dragon?"

I heard a low growl that, after a second, I realized was coming from my throat. Sebastian always warned me about my temper, but what the hell. I was a dragon after all and no one insults a dragon and gets away with it. With one hand, I grabbed that golden nose ring, pulling Grumble toward me as I filled my other hand with an iron knife, the point laid across Grumble's throat. "No one calls me a bitch or a whore, Grumble. I work for myself. Not the fairies. Not the Weres. Not for any supernatural. Do you understand me? And for your information, I earned the right to carry my weapons, goblin."

Goblin hide may be tough, but being a dragon, I had enough strength in this small frame of mine to slice through it like it was butter. The two goblins behind their leader stood frozen in place as I pressed that knife into the throat of their leader with each word. A drop of green blood trickled down the blade before I snatched the knife away and shoved Grumble's face away from me.

The goblin stood wiping the blood from his neck as he gazed at me. Hatred bathed his face and eyes as he rubbed his huge hand on his pants. One of the two warriors behind him jerked a knife from his belt. "Grumble should we—"

Grumble spun, a fist streaking out connecting with the goblin's jaw. The loud crack of a bone shattering echoed down the aisle of the diner as the creature dropped like a stone. His foot connected with the unconscious goblin's head and I could hear the unmistakable sound of a neck snapping. "That's for not protecting your king."

The other goblin stood perfectly still. A slight grunt only just heard above the shattering bones his only reaction. Grumble's eyes swiveled toward him as the goblin braced for the blow he thought was coming. After a few seconds, Grumble took a deep breath before nodding at the body at his feet. "Take this piece of crap out of here. Take it back to the kitchens." Yeah, goblins, gotta love 'em.

The goblin scrambled away without looking at his leader or me. Grabbing both feet, he dragged the dead body down the aisle and out the door. Grumble stood still, his eyes following the warrior out the door as I cautiously reached for the nine-mil next to my plate and pointed it at the green super before me.

Turning once his guards were out the door, his eyes flicked to my hand and the weapon before they locked onto my face. "You cost me face before my men, dragon. Plus, one of my best warriors is now dead because of it. For that you owe me."

"Yeah, I don't think so, Grumble. Remember, you started it when you insulted a dragon. You should know better than that. I say we call it even and leave it at that."

Grumble's eyes narrowed to slits. "Gold and pride, dragon—gold and pride. Always the downfall of your kind, Sin. Remember that. For the goblins shall not forget what happened here tonight. You will pay in blood for this one day, dragon." The goblin gestured toward the necklace that hung from my top. "Even your precious fire goddess won't be able to help you if I get my hands on you again. This isn't over. Not by a long shot."

With that little speech finished, Grumble turned and stalked down the aisleway of the diner and out into the dark misty night. I should have shot him right there, but I had enough problems with the bounty we were on without adding any more complications to it.

Waiting a few seconds to see if Grumble was truly gone, I put away my weapons and tucked the talisman of the Celtic fire goddess, Brigit, back into my top. Picking up the steak on my plate, I took a bite before I threw the piece of meat back and pushed the plate away.

Sebastian floated from one of the lights above and sat on the edge of my plate. He was shaking his head at me as he does when he thinks I've screwed something up. "Making new friends I see, Sin. What? You couldn't have handled that any better than you did? Especially since we are on a job right now and don't need the extra hassle from the likes of those things."

"Whatever. Like I'm worried about what some damn goblin says or thinks. Once we are done with this job, we can leave this sector and go home. Besides, I didn't see you around helping me there, partner."

Sebastian stood gazing at me as he slowly ran one finger around the congealed blood the raw meat swam in. "Hey, six-inch imp here. What the hell do you think I'm going to do against a goblin, Sin?" He stuck his finger in his mouth and smacked his lips, frowning. "Oh gross. Dog meat. We could have gone to a nice place that served cat or even human."

Right. My partner may only be six inches tall, but I've seen him barbeque a full-size mountain troll with his magic. "Shut up, Sebastian." I glimpsed frightened eyes from the kitchen. "Just shut up for a few minutes. Let me think in some peace and quiet, okay?"

My partner and friend looked at the plate as he rolled another finger around the raw meat slicing off a tiny piece with his claws, before popping it into his mouth. He chewed quietly as I went over what Grumble had said. Sebastian was right. I should have handled that better than I did. I gave a mental shrug as I figured there was no use in worrying since I couldn't go back in time and change it.

The imp stood after gagging and shaking his head as he gave the 'meat' on my plate a nasty look. He fluttered to my shoulder. "You know that green piece of crap was right about one thing, Sin."

I sighed feeling bad about snapping at my friend like I had. "What was he right about, Sebastian?"

"Why about dragons, of course, and their pride and lust of gold, Sin. Gold and pride have killed more dragons than anything else in this world."

I stood and threw some silver coins on the table. "Did you arrange for the human to get off last, Sebastian?"

"Yeah, I told the orc to keep her here until after everyone else left. He balked till I dropped a bit of silver in his greedy little hands."

"Did he ask questions?"

Sebastian gave another tiny tug on my hair. "Why would he? She's just a human female. He probably figures we wanted something decent to eat. You know, have a little takeout."

"Fine, whatever, Sebastian. Let's get out of here and find a place where we can watch the back door."

"What if the vamp doesn't go after her, Sin?"

This could be a great waste of time and effort, but I had a feeling this job would end tonight. "If it doesn't work, you will figure something out. Seeing as you're the brains of this partnership and I'm just the muscle." I gave one quick glance out the door before we left the diner and faded into the night.

3

Maria tossed and turned kicking off the light blanket revealing her sweat-slicked body to the shadow standing over her bed. Gazing at the nude young woman, Aezriane stood as still as the night. Drinking in the sight of the ripe form thrashing around on the bed, she felt a growing wetness between her legs. A few seconds later, the creature laid a hand on Maria's forehead. "Hush, my dear, it is only a dream. Only a delightful dream where you will receive a wonderful gift from a goddess."

The creature set a tiny bag at the edge of the bed before turning and laying an open palm on the young woman's stomach. She bent her head. Her eyes closed as she prayed. "Mother, receive this vessel so she may carry my sister. Let this child and all the others I plant in your name in these fertile gardens grow to avenge those you have lost."

Maria's brown eyes opened, a slight pain in her belly pulling her from her sleep. The pain not unlike the times her body let her know it was ovulating. Her mind roiled in a fog as it tried to focus on the blonde figure standing above her, knowing it was too early for what she felt. She flushed as the eyes of the creature took in every inch of her bare body. Shame churned through her mind while another smaller part screamed in terror at being under the control of this supernatural creature.

The young woman tried to move, to cover herself. To do anything to get away from the creature. Aezriane reached out a hand and lightly brushed back the damp hair that lay against her cheek. The only thing Maria could do was sob.

"Don't worry, my dear. I'm not here to hurt you. In fact, I'm here to do the exact opposite of that."

Maria shut her eyes as she listened to the voice that promised not to hurt her. She had been living on the edge of the human/supernatural boundaries since she was a little girl and knew you never could take the word of a super at face value. She had seen too many of her friends disappear or die after a super told them to trust it. Her older brother, Robert, had warned her not to live on her own, but she knew better than him. She knew she could take care of herself. Now, it looked like she would pay for her foolish pride.

She felt the hot breath of the creature brush across her hair as it leaned close to her ear. "In fact, dear, you are very, very special. So very special to my plans. You are more beautiful than the others I have bestowed this gift on tonight."

"Please, don't. I—" Her voice choked off as she sucked in a breath while the creature's hands slid from her face, across her neck, and onto her breast as the creature's teeth nipped at her ear lobe.

"Don't do what, my dear?" Aezriane rubbed her palm across the young woman's nipple which hardened to a point of pleasure and pain. "Don't do this?" Tears leaked from the young woman's eyes as her breath caught in her throat. The creature's hand moved over to Maria's other nipple and she pinched the hardened nub. "Or is this what you want me not to do, my dear?"

Maria arched her back as the intense sensation speared to her center. Her breath hissed out as pain shot through her and centered in her belly. "Please, I— I've never—" Maria hoped the creature would stop the exquisite torture it was putting her through even as her body betrayed her. Wetness spread between her legs as the creature's mouth moved toward her breasts while her hand inched down her body.

The creature's tongue flicked out, rubbing against the young woman's nipple making her forgot her protest before the green eyes locked onto hers. "Oh, my dear. I know that you have never been with a man before. Or even felt their touch—" the creature's palm slid across the girl's mound and one long finger slipped inside her. "That's why you are one of the special few that will receive this precious gift my mother is giving you. Besides, you taste delicious, my dear. So sweet and innocent."

Maria gasped. Her breathing grew ragged as the creature rubbed the palm of her hand harder into her. Smashing the skin onto her hardened nub as another finger slipped inside. Sliding deep into untouched areas before moving in a slow rhythm in and out.

The young woman's breathing deepened as the creature picked up her pace moving circles around the top of her mound as she slipped yet another finger into her. Maria lost all thoughts of protest as she began the long ride up the crest that the creature was sending her on. Her back arched. Her hips bucked. Her legs trembled. As the wave built to a dazzling height, her wetness coated her inner thighs and the creature's hand.

Just when Maria thought she wouldn't be able to take any more, the creature shifted her body. Her palm moved from its spot, dropping the young woman off the wave that was carrying her higher and higher. Until the creature's hot mouth sucked in the young woman's hardened nub as her tongue flicked out, caressing and teasing the area around it. All the while her fingers moved faster and faster in and out, in and out.

Maria catapulted over the crest and into the sky. Her nipples stiffened to the point of pain as her legs shot straight out. The creature worked even more quickly. In and out of her wetness, in and out. Her hips bucked against the creature's mouth as her toes curled. "Oooooooooooh... I... ooooooooooooh"

The pleasure kept hitting the young woman in smaller and smaller waves as the creature's tongue whipped across her center and slid into her wetness as the fingers slipped out of her. "Pleassssse... oooooooooh... pleassssse... stooooop."

The creature slowly ran her fingers around the young woman's mound as she sat on the edge of the bed. She smiled at Maria, at the young girl's flushed face. Her breath coming in deep sobs of release. Tears leaked from closed eyes. "Yes, my dear, I see that you enjoyed that very much, didn't you? I was right though; you are the sweetest of all the vessels I have seen tonight."

"Please, please, no more. I—"

Aezriane stood, her face shiny with a wetness that made the young woman blush as another tiny spasm of pleasure rippled through her body and made her legs jerk. The creature reached to the side of the bed and grabbed the bag she had left sitting there. She licked her lips carefully and wiped a hand across her face. "Okay, dear, the fun part is over. Now we need to get down to the business that brought me here."

The afterglow of Maria's climax faded as her face went pale. She had been hoping that all this super had been looking for was a little quickie with a human and then she would be done with her. She hadn't been thrilled with having the creature use her like that, but it could have been worse if it had been a male super. A lot worse. Maria remembered a friend who had been all but ripped in two after being used by a male. "What are you going to do to me? You said you wouldn't hurt me."

Aezriane laid the bag between Maria's legs and pulled various items out as she locked eyes with the young woman. "My dear, I told you I would not hurt you and I meant it. Like I said before, I'm going to give you a gift. A very special gift. I just thought I would make it a little more pleasurable for you to receive it. You know, sort of prepare the way for the gift to be given you."

Maria dragged her eyes away from the creature and glanced at the long tube dangling from the super's hand. "I don't think I want any gift. I—I mean you're not going to—"

Aezriane threw back her head and laughed. She shook her head as she gazed at Maria. "Oh, you humans. After all this time, you should know by now you have no choices in this world. You gave that up when you almost destroyed Mother Earth and the supernaturals had to come out of hiding to save it. You have nobody but yourselves to blame for the predicament you're in."

"But—but I wasn't even born when that happened. How can you blame me for—"

The super laid a hand on Maria's forehead. "Hush, child. I know you personally aren't to blame for everything that happened when the supernaturals took over this world. Or for the reason, we had to come out of hiding to save Mother Earth from you humans, but you are going to help right some wrongs."

"Wrongs?"

"Yes, my dear. See when the supers took over the fairies were jealous of some of us 'lesser fae' and rather than share this world, they destroyed us. Like my sisters, for example. They said we were lesser creatures. Creatures that had to be purged from Mother Earth. They hunted all of us like animals and killed them for no reason. All except for me. They missed me because I was the youngest. Not fully into my potential. So now my mother has given me the task of bringing more of my sisters back into this world to avenge ourselves on the fairies and every creature that aligns with them."

"I—" Maria started to argue with the creature.

Aezriane laid two fragrant fingers across Maria's lips, silencing her protest. "No. No more talking, my dear. It is time for the conception. Now open your legs for me like a good girl." As the creature moved her hand, Maria's lips parted, her tongue snaked out to wet the cracked skin. A tear trickled down her cheek as she tasted herself.

Even as Maria's mind snapped, 'OH HELL NO', her legs shot up and open so that her knees were touching her firm breasts. Rubbing against nipples still sore from the creature's touch. She fought. Tried to push her legs down and closed for a few seconds before giving up, her breath coming in gasps. "Please, don't do this. Please."

"I'm sorry, my dear, but this is just something that has to happen. You are the perfect vessel to receive this gift. Now, just relax and it will be over soon. I promise." Aezriane ran her hand down the young woman's cheek. Maria blushed again as the smell of herself, the scent of her body's betrayal, assaulted her nose.

Maria closed her eyes, tears streaming down her cheeks as she felt the intrusion start. She could feel the round tube snaking its way into depths that had never felt anything before. Even the creature's fingers hadn't reached these depths. She grunted with pain as she felt the end bump against her cervix. "Please," she whispered one more time knowing the creature above her didn't care one bit how this was affecting the young woman.

The creature watched the tube work its way into the girl as she had done to nineteen others this night. This one was the last of the vessels she would use with the seed she had collected from the Were. When she was sure that the tube was where it should be, she attached a syringe to the end before pushing the plunger until she was satisfied that all of the gift had been delivered.

Slowly, she pulled the tube out looking for any spillage. Seeing none, her eyes lit up anticipating the children she was bringing to Mother Earth and the vengeance they would wreak upon the fairies. "See now that wasn't so bad, was it?" Maria sobbed as the creature stood gazing at her for what seemed like forever. "Oh, come now. There is no need for such hysterics, my dear. There, that should be long enough. Now you can close your legs, my dear."

Maria's legs dropped as she slammed them together. Tears still streamed down her cheeks as she silently cried for her lost innocence. Finally feeling blankets covering her nude body, she opened her eyes to see the creature packing her bag.

Anger flared in the young woman, replacing her fear of the creature. The tears stopped as her eyes narrowed. "If this thing you put in me takes, bitch, I'm going to make sure I get rid of it."

Aezriane gave the young woman a cold smile, freezing her anger. A smile devoid of all humor. A smile that promised pain as great as the pleasure Maria had been given tonight. "You are carrying one of my sisters within you now, human. I promise you this,"—the creature leaned down nose to nose with the young woman— "if you harm her, you will take you years to die. Do you understand me?"

"Y—yes."

"Good." Aezriane stood and pulled together her bag. Joy was back on her face as she patted the young woman on the head like a young puppy that had done a great little trick for its master. "Anyway, all you need to do is carry this child to term and after it is born, I will drop back in and take her off your hands. In fact, the good news is you will have to carry her less time than you would a human child. Six months isn't long at all. Won't that be nice, my dear?"

"What happens to me afterward? After the baby is born?"

"Why, my dear, you will be richly rewarded by my mother for taking care of this special gift. So now you need to sleep. Sleep and remember that no matter what, you must protect the life growing within you. You must never let any harm come to my sister for she is a gift from above. Understand?"

"Yes." Maria's voice faded in the induced slumber as she fought to keep her eyes open. They closed and fluttered open a few times as she saw the delight on the creature's face.

"Good now, sleep," the creature said as she touched a finger to the young woman's head. Instantly Maria's eyes closed as she lost the fight against the creature's magic and she drifted off into a deep sleep.

Aezriane stood looking at the young woman for a few more moments before snapping her fingers. A sheet of old parchment, a bottle of ink, and a quill floated in front of her. She glanced at the sleeping woman for a second before shaking her head and snapping her fingers again. The three items disappeared. "No, I don't think I will put your name on my list, my dear. You, I think, I will keep secret just in case. Sort of my ace in the hole as the humans used to say."

With a wave of her hand, the creature disappeared into the dark shadows. Maria shifted in her sleep; the hand on top of the blanket clutched protectively at her stomach as she felt the first flutter of movement.

4

"There she is, Sin. There's the human." Sebastian yanked on my hair and snuggled closer to my neck. I didn't blame the little guy. The mist hanging in the air earlier had now changed into a cold drizzle that chilled even a dragon's bones.

We were standing in a dark doorway a block from the back of the diner. The young woman I had pegged as bait came limping out the door. The cold wind blowing down the alleyway was kicking up garbage around her legs as she shuffled along the semi-dark tunnel. Her head down lost in her thoughts, she would be easy pickings for any supernatural or human that happened along. "No shit, Sebastian. I see her. I'm not blind."

"You would think someone living in this neighborhood would pay more attention to their surroundings, Sin." My partner was right, the young woman was so wrapped up in her misery, I doubt that our target would have even noticed if he had jumped from my shoulder while banging on a drum.

I took in the beaten attitude and mussed clothes as I moved out of the doorway to follow her. Staying within the drifting shadows of the alleyway, I shadowed her staggering steps. Even from this distance, I could hear the young woman sniffling. "Just what did you tell that damn orc, Sebastian?"

"Uh—I told him to keep her after the shift was over, Sin. Why do … Ooooh—"

Yeah, the imp finally got it as the waitress looked at the night sky just as she walked under one of the dim lights that lined the alleyway. In the flickering flames, he caught the ripped clothes and the bruises on her face. "I think when we're done here, I'm going to go have a talk with that damn orc."

"Sin, she is just a human. Hell, you're using her for bait to lure out a rogue vamp and you're worried that some damn orc took liberties with the girl? How about you keep your mind on the big picture and not worry about the small shit?"

I stopped in another doorway inhaling the night air before blowing it out. I knew my partner was right. Hell, knowing this sector as I did the young woman had probably been sold by her parents to work for the orc to pay off some debts or—

The young woman's scream wrenched me out of my reverie as I searched the dark passageway for her. "Where did she go, Sebastian? Did you see?"

Another scream rent the night air cut off mid-stream. "There. Through that doorway to the left, Sin."

I was already moving toward the sound as Sebastian pointed at an old wooden door that looked like it was banded with iron. One of those barriers that cut off small courtyards or entrances to the backyards of the surrounding buildings. Hitting it with my shoulder, the old wood burst apart sending jagged pieces flying through the air. "Just call her Superman," Sebastian quipped as we stood taking in the scene before us.

"Yeah, Superman my ass," I said as I swung my arm around to get some feeling back into my shoulder. Dragons may be tough and hard to kill, but damn that had been a hard door. I would definitely have a bruise in the morning.

Sebastian directed my attention away from a little bruise to the scene playing out in front of us. "Uh, Sin, you may have a little problem"

I looked at the waitress lying on the ground as the bloody vamp that had attacked her stood. Damn, Sebastian was right. We had a problem. I took in the drawn chalky white face and the blood-red eyes. His fangs were extended and dripped with the blood of the young woman. He wasn't even trying to look human. No, this creature was fucking old. The older the vamp, the harder they are to kill. Oh, we had one hell of a big problem alright.

LUSTFUL SIN   27

The vamp stood over the young woman like a tiger protecting its kill. Looking at the rogue, I decided I would rather have been facing a tiger than him. "Leave here now. This is no business of yours. Leave now and I'll let you live."

Yeah, right. There was no way this vamp was going to let us walk away from seeing him commit a rogue kill. Once he was done with the young woman, he would hunt us down and kill us just for the sport of it. Not that I would walk away even if I wasn't here to collect a bounty on his ugly, dead ass.

I saw his nose quiver as he caught my scent and his eyes widened. "Impossible! A dragon?"

"Well, since you know what I am, bloodsucker, you know I can't leave you here to kill this girl."

"She is mine. You can't have her. I have the right to hunt and feed where and when I want, dragon."

He had balls. I can say that for him. Most supernaturals would have at least ran when they got a scent of me. But no, not this vamp. He decides that whining is the best way to act. I shook my head at the creature before giving him the standard 'you're under arrest' speech that keeps me legal. "I don't want the girl, vamp. You're a rogue. I'm here to take you in dead or alive under the order of the fairy que—"

That's when I got hit from behind by what felt like two of the old human freight trains. We rolled in a tight bundle of snapping teeth and claws as two of the vamp's newly turned women tried to tear me apart.

I had one of them gnawing on the back of my shoulder as the other attached itself to my lower legs. Slamming against a wall, I flipped over in the lower vamp's arms and yanked one leg loose from her grip. A quick kick connected with her jaw, twisting her head back at an odd angle. A loud snap echoed off the courtyard walls as her eyes peered down her back.

Having gotten rid of that nuisance, I reached back and grabbed a handful of vamp hair and flipped her over onto her back. Leather, skin, and some of my hair came with her as she hit the concrete. I pulled a stake from my belt and drove it into her chest. "DIE, BITCH, THAT FUCKING HURT!"

That solved one problem as the newly turned vamp turned to a pile of dust. Bracing myself, I heard the other vamp whose neck I had broken start to move around as she healed. Standing and pulling another stake from my belt, I walked over to her and plunged the wood where it would do the most good.

Her eyes flared open with pain before she too turned to dust like her sister vamp. I looked around for the male that had changed them and the third vamp he had turned. The courtyard was empty except for me and the waitress lying in a pool of her own blood when I heard something scrambling onto the nearest roof.

I looked up just as Sebastian landed back on my shoulder. "Hey, thanks for the help there, partner."

"Don't look at me, Sin. You're the muscle. I set up the jobs, do recon, and gather info. You know—the hard stuff. You do all the easy stuff. You know—like killing them."

Breathing hard, I glanced back at the waitress for a second and flexed my shoulders. I was definitely going to feel tonight's work in the morning. There was a tearing sound as the back of my top ripped open freeing my wings. "Damn, I just bought this shirt too." Three quick flaps put me on the roof where I met the third new vamp.

She came hissing at me, fangs extended, as my feet touched down. Her eyes went wide as the hiss turned to a gurgle of surprise when I whipped out a stake from behind my back. I pinned her to one of the chimneys that lined the top of the building. Leaving another pile of dust for someone to clean up, I took off after the rogue vamp.

He watched as the dragon killed his two new children before fleeing to live another night. He cursed as he scrambled to the other side of the building hoping that his third child would give him enough time to escape. Everything had been going so well. He had three new children. With this fourth one, he had every intention of leaving this area to find another place to hunt.

Hell, with the way things had been going he could have built a small army of vamps that followed his orders in less than six months. An army that would allow his kind to take their first steps toward taking over the rule that the fairies guarded so jealously.

Rogue, she had called him. If only that damn dragon knew the truth. His brothers had sanctioned him. His brothers that, like him, were tired of living off the dregs of humanity. Humans that were sent into the penal system of this new world by the fairies. Tired of feeding off the scraps thrown to them by the fairies. Forbidden by the fairies to reproduce more of his kind without their permission.

If they took him, his brothers would deny any knowledge of him, but what plan wasn't without a risk or two? On the other hand, the rewards if he completed his mission would be unimaginable. The vamp stopped at the edge of the roof and glanced back just as the dragon landed in the middle of the old structure throwing up a puff of dust around her. Well, crap, so much for his third child.

"Hold it right there, rogue. You're not going anywhere. We can do this the easy way or the hard way. It's up to you."

The vamp hissed at me before turning and launching himself off the roof and onto the next lower one. "Guess that means he wants to do it the hard way, Sin."

I threw a quick glance at the imp hanging in the air next to me. "No shit, Sherlock. Don't know what I would do without your help, Sebastian." Flapping my wings, I soared into the night sky.

I passed over the vamp and landed in front of him on the edge of the other roof. It was kind of funny watching him as he came to a skidding halt in the middle of the building. It stopped being funny though when he pulled a small round metal ball out of his pocket. Pulling a pin out of the top, he tossed it on the wood at my feet.

Sebastian wrapped himself around my neck. "SIN, A BOOM BALL! SHIT, A BOOM BALL!" I didn't have time to tell him it was called a grenade by humans. I was too busy folding my wings around us to correct him as that damn illegal went off with a muffled boom.

"Die, bitch." The vamp's hiss turned to laughter as he watched the explosive go off throwing dust, wood, and shrapnel around the dragon. That was one major problem solved, he turned to go back to his newest child.

He had been insulted when one of his newest brothers had offered him the device. He relied on his strength. The strength that alone had been enough to fight his enemies for a thousand years. But after seeing how easily that damn dragon had killed his children, he was glad he had finally accepted the grenade as a last resort.

The vamp reached the edge of the roof where he stood for a second looking at the night sky. He would have to finish off his newest child and get her back to their resting place before daylight, then he heard a voice behind him.

"Going somewhere, rogue? I'm not finished with you yet."

Now, I couldn't help but laugh as the vamp spun around, his eyes narrowing. "You should be dead. My brother said that device would kill anything I threw it at. How?"

I stalked out of the cloud of dust that still hung in the air. I did a quick assessment of the damage. A few holes in the wings and a tiny chunk of meat out of my ankle, but not bad all around. I turned my attention back to the rogue. "Guess your brother never met a dragon before. We're hard to hurt and even harder to kill."

Sebastian disentangled himself from my hair. "Speak for yourself, Sin."

I figured, if my partner was bitching, he would live. I looked at the vamp as an idea pinged at the back of my mind. "Now, I need you to come with me. I think maybe the queen needs to have a talk with you about these brothers of yours and where they got that grenade."

"No. I won't go to that damn creature that calls herself a queen. She is no queen of ours."

Yeah, that pinging at the back of my mind was getting louder as I gazed at the vamp. "You're not a rogue, are you? These women aren't for some harem you're trying to start. You and your brothers are trying to make an army of your kind. Trying to sidestep the limited number of children you're allowed by the queen, aren't you?"

The vamp took two steps toward me, his fists clenched. "SHE HAS NO RIGHT TO TELL US HOW MANY OF OUR KIND WE CAN MAKE! NO RIGHT AT ALL! DO YOU UNDERSTAND ME?"

"That's not for me to say, vamp. I need you to come in with—"

"SHIT," Sebastian said. I leaped forward as the vamp pulled a stake out of his jacket and plunged it into his own chest without warning. The rogue hit the wooden roof of the building, dead before I got to him. I looked down and shook my head at his body. Yeah, even an old vamp wasn't coming back from that, but just the same I pulled out my knife and a special bag from my belt and kneeled to do what needed to be done.

Grabbing the vamp's hair, I sliced through his neck putting my grisly trophy into the bag. "Good thing I made those containers," the imp said as I stood and closed it. The magic contained in it would keep the vamp's head from going to dust just as his body was now doing.

"Yeah, but it would have been nice to take him alive. I have a feeling there is trouble brewing for the fairies, Sebastian. First, Grumble's big talk at the diner. Now this vamp. I don't know? Have you ever seen an older vamp take himself out like that?" I looked at the fading night sky. I had no intention of getting in the middle of whatever was going on, I was only a bounty hunter looking out for number one. After all, that's how I've stayed alive this long.

"What? You mean just because Grumble was in a pissy mood about the queen and we find out the vamps are oh so happy with her majesty. Trouble, Sin? What makes you think there is trouble brewing in paradise?"

"Yeah. Damn shit sounds like it's getting real. Maybe it's time take a long vacation, Sebastian. You know maybe on some deserted island or something like that."

I snapped out of my funk as the imp pulled on a chunk of my hair. "We should get that head over to the fairies, Sin. The magic in the bag will only keep it fresh for so long."

"Okay, Sebastian." My partner was right. I needed to dig myself out of the black funk that tonight's work had thrown me in. "I just want to take a quick check on that waitress. See if she was hurt badly. Afterward, we'll go collect our bounty from the queen."

"Uh, when we collect our bounty, Sin, are you going to mention about what the vamp told you about his brothers or the goblins pissing and moaning?"

"Do I look stupid, Sebastian? The queen is just as likely to kill the messenger as reward them. Besides, I'm not her most favorite person right now," I said as we flew back to the courtyard.

"I agree, Sin. She does seem to have taken a dislike to you lately. Guess that's what you get when you bump uglies with her son. But I just wanted to double check we were on the same page."

The young woman lay in the darkened alleyway. Her eyes were open taking in the stars that painted the night sky. Her mind wandered back through her night as she thought about the green female supernatural that had come into the restaurant tonight. How all her troubles seemed to have started when she walked in the door.

The fight with the goblins. How her boss had kept her over as everyone else had left for the night. She was no virgin. Far from it living where she was. But she was human and had fought hard to keep the supernatural from using her like some women that lived in the neighborhood. After all, she had some semblance of standards.

She had gotten away after a lucky shot with her knee connected with the orc's balls. Guess males of all species hurt when hit there with enough force. After he went down—hard—she had gotten out of that place swearing to herself that she would never go back no matter what her father owed the owner. Still, she should have paid more attention to her surroundings. If only she hadn't been so lost in her misery.

The first she knew the vamp was there in the alleyway was when he grabbed her and pulled her through the doorway of the courtyard. After that everything was a blur of sights and sounds before she succumbed to the darkness.

When she first came out of the dark, she had felt drained, weak. She could feel the blood in her hair. The dried tackiness of it on her neck near twin points of bright pain, but now all she felt was a growing hunger. A hunger that burned deep inside of her. She looked up just as that green creature from the restaurant landed next to her and a low feral growl erupted from her lips.

"Uh, Sin, I think you could say they hurt her. She is turning already. Shit, how is that possible?"

I looked into the red eyes of the young woman. No, the newly-made vamp before I walked over to the nearest pile of dust and seized the stake. "An old vamp like the one that offed himself can sometimes turn their new children this quick. Something in their venom, I guess," I said as I kneeled next to the young woman.

I raised the stake when I caught her eyes. Just for a second, they went from blood-red back to the light blue I remembered from the restaurant. "Uh, Sin—" Sebastian said before the vamp's eyes went back to killer red. She lunged, claws reaching for my throat. Newly created fangs extended.

I plunged the stake into the vamp's heart so hard that the tip went through her back and into the ground. She gasped, her hands still trying to reach me as the light died in her eyes. As she turned to dust, I stood and wiped my hands on my pants before turning and starting down the alleyway back toward the restaurant. "Come on, Sebastian. Let's go collect our bounty."

"Uh, Sin, isn't the gateway to fairy land the other way?"

"Just need to make a quick stop first before we head back to the queen's castle, Sebastian."

"Oh man, Sin. Don't do it. You know that one human woman isn't worth the grief you'll attract if you kill that orc."

"You can leave anytime, partner. I'm not forcing you to go along with this."

"No, I'll stay. Besides, I never liked orcs. Did I ever tell you what one did to my great aunt Tilly?"

I walked toward the restaurant, half listening to my partner's story, loosening my knives in their sheaths as, in my mind, I went over all the delicate spots on and inside an orc's body.

5

Sebastian and I marched down a wooded path toward a tiny door set in the wall of the queen's castle. It had taken three hours to traverse the fairy gates after I had an hour long 'talk' with the orc. "You know, with all the supernaturals we kill for the queen, you would think she would let us in the front door, Sin."

I glanced at my clothes. Or I should say what was left of them. Between the rips from the vamp fight and the grenade, and the splatter of green orc blood I think even if we had been allowed through the front door, the guards would have paused before letting us through tonight. Or more accurately, early morning. I shifted the pack on my back as we marched closer to the end of this job.

"Whatever, Sebastian. Right now, I couldn't care less how we get in there. As long as we get in and complete our business without any of the usual fairy bullshit you deal with here." I know I was in a mood that even the fresh early morning air couldn't seem to sweep away, but dealing with fairies always seemed to bring out the worst in me.

"Ssshhh, Sin. She could hear you and we don't want that kind of trouble. You know how bad the queen's temper can be. So just make sure you keep yours in check while we are here, please."

"Yeah. Yeah, whatever, Sebastian." We walked over to the guards standing on each side of the door. They glared at me from the corners of their eyes, but neither moved nor said a word to let us know they acknowledged our presence. Fairies were such pricks. What little patience I possessed wore thin after a few seconds. "You two going to let us in? Or should I take those spears and shove them up—"

"SIN!"

Exasperated, I stared as both guards stood ramrod straight ignoring the two of us. "Fine. Fine, Sebastian. We're here to drop off a bounty that your queen is anxious to have. So, will one of you please get off your dead ass and ... Ouch, that hurt, Sebastian."

"Damn it, Sin," the imp said as he yanked on my hair again. He turned to the two guards who were now staring at us as they caressed the handles of the short swords that hung at their sides. "We have this paper that gives us permission to see the queen." Neither guard so much as lifted a finger to touch the paper that Sebastian was holding out to them. "Oh, well, see—"

I wasn't sure what the imp was going to say, but I had about enough of these two dipshit's attitudes. My hand dropped to my weapon when the door behind the guards creaked open and a voice floated from the darkness. "Let them enter."

Both fairies snapped to attention at the sound of that low voice. Their backs rigid. Their eyes straight ahead. Eyes filled with fear as a thin, old dragon hobbled out from the shadows hidden behind the door.

I took in the five foot nothing green creature standing there leaning on a wooden cane which was probably as old as him. His wispy silver hair hung around his face and the clothes he wore draped his emaciated body. I wondered, as I always did, how this tiny super could sow such fear in these fairy warriors when they rarely took notice of a dragon like myself. A dragon in her prime and a bounty hunter to boot.

"Hello, Igmun," I said with a quick bow of my head. "I see you're looking as spry as ever."

The queen's right-hand man gave me a quick once over. His red eyes taking in the state of my clothes and the tangled mess of my hair before he sighed and shook his head. "Sin. Sin. Sin. Child, I thought after all these years you would know better than to crash the queen's castle looking like a—a—" He sniffed the air and grimaced. "You smell like an orc, my granddaughter."

Igmun wasn't really my grandfather. Probably more like my great, great, great grandfather or some such somewhere down the line in my family. Maybe that is why the fairy guards were so scared of him. Most dragons die early. Mostly from other dragons. Or because their tempers piss off the wrong creatures. So those that don't die young tend to grow–shall we say–crustier with age.

"More like the inside of an orc, if you ask me," Sebastian said. Igmun's eyes swiveled up to look at my partner cutting off his glee in mid-stride. "Uh, yeah, sorry about that. Didn't say a word, Igmun. Zipping the lip and locking it." The imp zipped his hand across his mouth and made the motion of tossing a key away.

The tiny dragon nodded before turning his focus back to me and the state of my clothes. Or what there were of them. "You know, Sin, when you're summoned to the queen's castle it is a good idea to wear your best clothes and not something that looks like you've been working in a slaughterhouse."

"Summons? What summons, Igmun? I'm here because we fulfilled the bounty on that rogue vamp plaguing the northern zone. You know the one you sent us after. The one turning human women," I said holding up the bag with the vamp's head inside.

"You're telling me you didn't get the summons from the queen? She sent it to your home a few hours ago. In fact, I was just coming to alert these guards they were to let you in without any fuss as soon as you got here."

"Sorry, we haven't been home since yesterday morning. Like I said, we have been hunting that damn rogue." I held up the bag again and gave it a tiny shake. "So, if we can just get our payment. We can go home and get cleaned up and come back. You know, maybe tomorrow to see what kind of job the queen has for us?"

Igmun stood there one foot tapping on the ground as though he was listening to a child explain why she couldn't go to school today. He reminded me of some of the instructors I had growing up. Not that I had been a difficult child or anything. I almost smiled when I caught the two fairy guards holding their breath as though waiting for the small dragon next to them to explode in anger.

Igmun stopped tapping his foot and turned, waddling back into the shadows behind the door. His voice floated out to us as the two guards let out a sigh of relief. "Follow me. We'll find a place for you to get cleaned up and then you can see the queen."

"Yeah, but ... Come on, Igmun. I need a rest day. I just want to collect my bounty and get some sleep." I could hear the whine in my voice, but couldn't stop myself. This had been the fifth bounty in the past month we had been on. If I didn't know any better, I would swear that someone was making damn sure I was being kept very, very busy. With little time for a social life.

Sebastian yanked on my hair again. "Oh hell, for once just do what the old toad tells you without any back talk, Sin. Please? You know how that old guy gets. He is almost worse than the queen sometimes."

The old voice floated from out of the darkness in front of us. "I heard that, imp."

"Shit. Damn," the imp said as I followed Igmun inside the castle walls. The door closed behind us, cutting off what little light filtered through the opening. "Uh, Igmun? Lights would be good about now."

Torches along the surrounding walls flickered to life. "You know there are times I think I overindulge you, granddaughter. In my younger days, we—"

"Must be my sparkling personality. Or maybe that I'm your favorite, Igmun."

He gazed at me for a few seconds before turning and heading down the tunnel. "Yes. I'm sure that must be it, granddaughter. Follow me."

"You know one of these days, Sin, you'll push him too far. You know that, right? And when that happens—" Sebastian brought a finger across his throat as we followed Igmun down the tunnel carved out of the castle walls. I knew in my heart that my partner was right. Most likely one day one of us would have to kill the other. But what the hell, hopefully, it wouldn't be today. Of course, it was still early.

To tell you the truth, I was a little surprised that it hadn't happened yet. Us killing each other, that is. There are so few dragons in the world because we tend to have a low birth rate. It doesn't help that most dragons kill our own if they intrude in each other's territory. For Igmun and I to live in close contact in the same country was a minor miracle. Even if we were related, no matter how distant.

"Here we are, child." Igmun's voice broke through my thoughts as we stopped before another wooden door. The old dragon tapped his staff against the barrier as he muttered under his breath. I felt the heat of magic bloom then die as the wall opened onto a lit corridor.

We followed the old dragon into the light. "We need to learn how to do that, Sin. That little trick could come in handy sometimes. Better than bruising your body against wooden doors."

We turned right into the hallway and went through another thick door. "I don't know. Brute force hasn't let us down so far, Sebastian." It was eerily quiet, and we didn't see another soul. "Where are all the fairies?" I asked noting the absence of moving bodies.

"This is my private quarters, Sin. The queen allows me my privacy here."

We followed Igmun for a while turning down other hallways while going up and down short stairways before we stopped in front of another open doorway. "Here you go, granddaughter. You can clean up in here."

I walked into a small room that had a fireplace at one end of it and a large bed at the other. The fire merrily blazed away in the hearth throwing off a soothing warmth. In the middle of the room was a large metal tub. Steam was rising in waves off the surface of the water. Every ache and bruise from last night was letting itself be known. "Thank you, Igmun," I said dropping my pack on the floor before I turned and gave the old dragon a slight bow. "It's almost as good as a bag full of gold."

Igmun cocked one eyebrow. "If you say so, granddaughter. I will inform the queen you will be ready to appear before her in one—" The old dragon looked me up and down once more while sniffing the air. "Two hours, Sin. By the way, I will take that bag from you and collect the bounty you were so worried about."

I nodded to the old dragon. Handing him the bag with the rogue vamp's head in it. "Thanks again, Igmun."

"Yes. Well, we can't have you going before the queen looking like this." Igmun started to close the door but stopped. "Sebastian, I need you to come with me. We need to have a—a long talk."

I heard the imp gulp once before flying off my shoulder. "Yes, Igmun," he said as he flew out the door and hovered just behind the old dragon. I started to say something when Sebastian shook his head before the door closed and they left me on my own.

I stood for a second warring over going after Igmun and my partner and the hot water in that tub. The tub won since I figured if Sebastian had been in real trouble, he would have said something. Gave me some sign to save him. In seconds, I was stripped. The only thing on my body, the red figure hanging from the gold chain that dangled between my breasts. What was left of my clothes was in an untidy pile as I slowly sank into that tub of pure bliss. Thoughts of my partner, rogue vamps, and goblins were chased from my mind as the heat soaked into my green skin.

Behind Sin, a small part of the wall, at eye level, quietly slid open. Icy blue orbs watched as the dragon stripped off her clothes. Every inch of her lean muscled body exposed to the watcher's gaze. They took in the green and yellow skin marred only by the dark red stone that swayed with each movement of her body.

As the young dragon settled into the tub of water, a low sigh floated across the room before the opening silently closed. After a few minutes, a tiny snick was the only sound as a door in the wall slid open. Those icy eyes looked around the door before the tall lean body moved across the room.

Letting the warmth of the water soak into my body, I could smell a hint of jasmine and vanilla wafting through the steam from the tub. Whatever Igmun had put into the water was numbing the pain I had been blocking since we came through the fairy gateway.

My eyes closed in relief. That's when I heard a tiny noise behind me. Grasping the small knife, I had palmed while I undressed, I took in a deep breath catching a familiar scent. I smiled as I released my hold on my weapon and relaxed in the water. "Hello, Fallon."

I opened my eyes and looked at the tall lean fairy. His long blond hair tied back and slung over one shoulder. His eyes were narrowed, a smirk playing across his lips as he drank in every inch of my body. "Hello, Sin. Need help washing off that grime?"

"I think I may be able to handle it. I have been washing myself ever since I hatched, you know? Besides don't you have a job you should be doing?"

The fairy ignored my question. He kneeled while reaching out to pick up a soft washcloth and soap that lay on a tiny tray attached to the tub. His voice grew huskier as he lathered the rag. "I seem to remember last time you were at my summer place you didn't mind my help."

Sitting up, I splashed water over the side of the tub. I blushed at the memories of that time we had been together. "Yes ... well, I need to get cleaned up so that—"

I gasped as Fallon rubbed that soft cloth across my breasts paying close attention to my hardening nipples. The heat of his lips played up and down my neck. "You were saying, Sin?"

My breath caught in my throat as I felt that cloth slide down my body leaving a soapy trail behind. "I—I—your mother—"

My legs opened of their own accord as the cloth hit my center. "Yes, Sin. What about my mother?" Fallon slowly rubbed the cloth up one side of my lips and then down the other.

All I could do was gasp again, lost in the heat of the moment. I totally forgot what I had been saying. When Fallon replaced the cloth with his fingers, I cried out as I grasped his arm. In the state I was in, I wasn't sure if it was to push his hand away or to keep it right where it was.

Ever so slowly, he moved his hand in a rolling motion that had me breathless as I climbed several small waves of ecstasy until he centered on my hardened nub sending me over the edge. I cried out digging my fingers into Fallon's arm as my legs and hips bucked in the hot water.

Fallon kept concentrating on my center as wave after wave washed over me. Finally, when I couldn't take it anymore, I pushed his arm away as my legs slammed shut sending another wash of water over the side of the tub drenching the fairy.

I lay my head against the side of the tub, panting, as I tried to catch my breath while I heard Fallon's quiet chuckle. "You know, when I get my strength back, I'm going to pay you back for that, you damn fairy."

"I'm looking forward to the payback, my beautiful dragon."

"Damn. It's been so long. I'm not sure that my legs will work any time soon, Fallon. It's lucky that Igmun gave me two hours to get cleaned up before I have to go before the queen."

I felt his lips brush mine. "Well, about that, Sin. Seems my mother sent me here to tell you she wants to see you right this second."

"WHAT!" I said bolting up off the side of the tub. Grabbing the sides as I stood glaring at the fairy. "And you just decided to tell me this now? What the hell?"

Fallon sat with an innocent look on his face. "I heard you were a little, shall we say 'tense' with the door guards. So, I thought maybe I could help you take away some of that tension, my dragon. I only did it to help you out. Relax you a tad."

I looked at the smirk playing on the fairy's face. I tried to muster some anger, but I guess his fingers had taken some of the tension from my body. But still— "Shit, your mot—the queen will kill me if she ever found out about us, Fallon."

Fallon stood, the washcloth back in his hand as he shook his head. "I'll take care of my mother, Sin. You worry too much about things that haven't happened yet." The smile fell from the fairy's face as those eyes darkened. "I swear I will never let my mother hurt what I love again, my dragon."

I nodded as Fallon rubbed me with the cloth. All thoughts of sex washed from my mind as I let him clean my body. "Yeah, well, that's why I'm still alive, fairy. Because I do worry about the things that could make me very, very dead and the queen is at the top of that list. Especially if she knew I was doing the horizontal bop with her heir apparent."

Fallon crushed his lips against mine before pushing down on my shoulders. "You are so romantic, my dragon. Sit, Sin, and we'll get you rinsed off."

I sat in water that was starting to cool. My mind wandered to all the many ways I had heard the queen had taken care of potential problems. The many, many painful ways she had dealt with those problems.

The feel though of Fallon's hands sliding over my body as he rinsed the soap off sent tingles shooting between my legs again as my nipples hardened. "Oh no you don't, you damn fairy." I pushed his hands away from me. I stood and hopped out of the other side of the tub as I grabbed a towel off a metal table sitting next to it.

Wrapping it around me, I watched as the smile fell from Fallon's face. "Oh, my dragon. We were just starting to have fun. Besides you haven't fulfilled that payback you owe me."

Frustrated, I pointed at the wall Fallon had come through. "Out."

He started around the tub, that damn smirk coming back to his lips until there was a knock on the door. "Granddaughter?"

My eyes opened wide with panic. "Yes, Igmun?"

"I am sorry, but the Queen wishes to see you right this second. Something major has happened in the Were's northern sector, and she is growing impatient.

"Uh, okay, Igmun. I'll be right out."

"Alright, granddaughter. Please hurry though. She is not in a good mood."

I sighed in relief as I saw Fallon frown. He stepped toward the opening he had come in. I turned to dig fresh clothes from my bag when we both froze at Igmun's voice as it floated through the door. "Oh, and Fallon? The queen is anxious to know why you haven't returned from the little job she sent you on. Seems she is a little piqued she had to send me to fetch my granddaughter."

The fairy didn't say a word, but I could see he paled a bit. Yeah, so much for him taking care of his mother if she found out about us. I heard Igmun march down the hall as I dived into my pack, pulling clothes out as the opening in the wall silently closed behind me.

6

I was dressed in more or less presentable clothes. Probably less from the looks Igmun kept shooting at my outfit. Okay, so I was dressed in presentable clothes for me. I figured that if the old dragon had problems with how I dressed, he should have found some suitable crap for me to wear. You know, like the long silk dresses that the fairy women we were passing in the hall wore.

Being a bounty hunter, my taste in clothes usually ran to leather or armor. Usually in red or black. I mean I may be hard to kill, being a dragon and all, but that doesn't mean I can't get scraped or bruised from some of the creatures I pursue.

I shot a stink eye at a group of female fairies standing in the hallway. They all wore silks in bright summer colors. "Bitches." It was fun to see the snide looks disappear off of their stupid faces as they took in my dark red leather vest, matching pants, and thigh-high leather boots.

My mind turned away from the fairies as I noticed that Sebastian hadn't reacted at all to my comment. At the worst, I should have gotten a laugh from my tiny partner. Best case, he should have been whispering his own nicknames for the group of skinny, fairy skanks in my ear.

"You alright, Sebastian?"

"What? Oh yes, of course, Sin. Nothing could be better."

Yeah right. The imp had been abnormally quiet ever since he came back from whatever little chore Igmun had given him. I hadn't paid much attention to him since I had been in such a rush getting dressed for the queen. Of course, there was also the afterglow of that little treat Fallon had given me in the tub.

I shook my head to rid myself of those thoughts as I felt my face flush with heat along with a few tremors in my center. Yeah, it had been way too long between visits with the queen's son and heir apparent. Way, way too long. Something the two of us would have to fix. Igmun's gruff voice brought back to the here and now. "You know, granddaughter, I would think your mind would be better focused on the meeting with the queen than on, say 'other activities'."

I glared at the old dragon's back, sticking my tongue out at him as we walked down the hall. It wasn't any of his damn business who I did or what we did. The old crank was just jealous because he couldn't get it up anymore. I snickered at the idea as we neared the throne room doors.

"I heard that, granddaughter."

"Who me?" Stopping in front of two golden doors, the old dragon ignored my whining. I let out a low whistle looking at four of the biggest female fairies I had ever seen. I took in these Amazons with all their golden armor and muscles as my mind calculated the recent price of gold. Then I noticed that each of them had old human weapons slung across their backs in addition to the swords that hung at their sides. Like I said before, I wasn't the only one exempt from the ban on that type of weapon.

Hey, what can I say though? Humans got one thing right about dragons. We love our gold. In fact, when dealing with dragons there is no other payment we accept. Speaking of payment— "By the way, Igmun, did you get my bounty for that rogue?"

"The queen will talk to you about that when we see her, granddaughter."

I was going to protest when Igmun turned, ignoring me again, and walked through the doors being opened by two of the guards. For a quick second, I considered staying in the hallway when Sebastian pulled a few strands of my hair. "Sin, whatever you do, be on your best behavior today and please watch your mouth if you want to leave this place in one piece."

My partner had a good point there. We walked into the throne room, following the old dragon across the long open area as the doors hissed closed. I threw one quick glance behind me and saw that two of the golden-clad guards remained inside the room. Their weapons were now off their backs and held across their chests. Oh, that was so not good. Guess maybe Sebastian knew more than I did after all.

Looking around, I was a little surprised at how empty the large room was. Every time I had been here there were all manner of creatures milling about. Currying favors from the queen or one of her inner circle. Today, the only people around were gathered at the throne at the far end of the room.

When Igmun reached the other side of the room, he marched up three steps and bowed low. "I have brought her, my queen."

I stopped at the bottom of the steps and dropped to my knees, my head bent low. See, I know how to behave myself.

"Come now, Igmun, after last night it's Velocity to you, my dragon." My eyes darted to Igmun, seeing the old dragon blush as 'YECH!' flashed through my mind. Guess the ancient dragon wasn't that old after all.

"Velocity." The old dragon rubbed a finger down her arm. Oh, double 'YECH!'

The queen giggled, and a laugh caught in my throat just in time. I covered it with a low cough. This bitch was not known for her sense of humor. Especially if she thought you were making fun of her royal person. Her haughty voice echoed through the empty throne room. "Rise, dragon." Uh, maybe I hadn't covered that laugh as well as I thought.

I rose as my partner leaned in close to my ear. "Remember, Sin, take care. It is so not good to piss her off. Especially with all the shit coming down today." Just great. Maybe I should have had that talk with Sebastian since he seemed to be in the know about why we were summoned before the high bitch herself.

I hesitated for just a fraction of a second before I looked at the fairy sitting on the throne. Where Fallon was tall and built of lean muscle, his mother, the queen, was tiny. Almost childlike in her appearance. That is until you looked in her dark eyes. That's where the childlike appearance ended. Those eyes seemed to look right through you as though you were there only for her entertainment, and not the kind of entertainment you, yourself would enjoy. "Your majesty," I said as I gave another little bow. What the hell, it never hurts to suck up a little. Right?

She sat there staring at me as though I was something she had found on the bottom of her dainty shoes after visiting the horse barns. Not that this sick bitch would have ever stooped so low. She would never go to the barns for any reason. But, hey, you catch my drift.

My eyes flicked to the right where Fallon stood. His own eyes locked on the distant golden doors of the throne room. I swear I could see the faintest trace of a handprint on his cheek. Okay, so no help there. That was so not a good sign. My eyes went back to the queen's face.

Her eyes narrowed as they flicked sideways to the right and back to me. Shit, so much for her not knowing I was screwing her son. I was contemplating ways I could escape from this room before I became a plaything to the queen's infamous temper when she cleared her throat. "I hear from Igmun that you have brought in the rogue vampire, dragon. Or I should say his head at least."

"Yes, ma'am."

"And you had no other troubles in taking him in. Nothing I or my people should know about, dragon?"

I hesitated for the briefest of seconds when I felt a slight tug on my hair and heard my partner. "Remember what we talked about, Sin."

The imp was right. There was no good reason for the two of us to get mixed up in supernatural politics. "No. No problems, ma'am. No problems at all."

The queen sat gazing at me for a few seconds before she gave a tiny nod. "Alright. I have another tricky situation I need you to look—"

"Um, excuse me, ma'am, about the rogue vamp. We haven't been paid for his bounty yet."

"Shit, Sin." Once more the queen's eyes narrowed at my interruption. Hey, what the hell. A girl's got to be paid for a job done before walking into another one. Right? After all, gold is gold. I mean if you let the customers neglect paying bounties it sets a bad precedent. No matter who the customer is. Even queens.

"I see. Yes, I see," the queen said as the tips of her fingers tapped on the arms of her throne.

Igmun stepped forward from his spot next to the queen. "This is my fault, my queen. I should have—"

The queen held up a delicate hand and the old dragon snapped his mouth closed as he stepped backward to his spot. Yeah, heel like a good lapdog, Igmun. I thought once more how nice it is that I'm no one's bitch. Guess last night wasn't all that hot for the queen after all. I felt a tiny bead of sweat trickle down my back though as those eyes now staring at me seemed to grow darker with a promise of unbelievable pain before she smirked and snapped her fingers.

A small side door opened in the wall and another one of those golden-clad Amazons came marching out. As she came to the steps of the throne, she tossed to me a bag that clinked with the sound of golden coins.

"There now, dragon. Now we have gotten that nasty business out of the way. As I—" I had been weighing the bag in my hands as the queen talked. I shook my head.

"This is short." I looked into those dark eyes. "The bounty is short."

"Oh, double shit." I heard the imp swear as the queen stopped talking. She sat up straighter in her chair. Hey, what can I say? Dragons know their gold. I was just wondering from the look in her eyes if now was the time to prove it. But a bounty is a bounty.

"Bring me my paymaster," the queen said.

The golden Amazon disappeared through the door as though the queen's words had set her ass on fire. In the quiet that followed, I started to rethink even revealing that my bounty was low. Maybe the better option would have been to wait until I was alone with Igmun before mentioning it.

After a few minutes, two Amazons came marching back through the door dragging a weeping human between them. Yeah, definitely rethinking opening my big mouth about a little gold piece or two. The queen looked at the man as the two Amazons dropped him at the bottom step by my feet. "The dragon here says she has been shorted of her bounty, paymaster. Would you know anything about that?"

The human lay weeping as he looked at the fairy queen. "Please have mercy, my queen ... My daughter, she is sick and—"

Stepping forward, I tucked the bag into my pocket and looked at the human before turning and bowing before the queen. "I think I made a mistake, ma'am. I'm sure that the payment is ri—"

The queen raised one finger as anger flooded her face. Her eyes darted from me to the human at my feet and back again. "Oh no, a dragon is never mistaken when it comes to gold, are they, Sin?" This time I kept my mouth shut, not wanting to make matters worse. The queen glared at the human. "How much did you take, paymaster? How much gold did you pilfer to soil my reputation, paymaster?"

"Please, please ... My little one ... I—"

"I—asked—how—much. Do—not—make—me—ask—again—paymaster."

The two guards dragged the human to his feet. His head hung as his tears dripped to the throne room floor. "Two coins, my queen. I took two gold coins from the dragon's bounty, but only to buy medicine for my little one. I didn't think anyone would miss two coins, my queen."

"Yes, well, seems you were wrong, paymaster. Search him."

It didn't take long for the guard to find the two coins on the human. She flipped the coins to me before looking at the fairy queen. "And what of him, my queen?"

The queen gazed at the human for a second as a tiny smile flittered across her lips. "It will take too long to train a new paymaster. So, I guess I can't kill him." I was glad I wouldn't be the cause of this human's death. "Just take him back to his room and keep a better eye on him from now on."

The guards nodded as they dragged the human back toward the door and I tucked those two damned coins in my pocket. "Wait a second." The guards stopped as they turned back toward the queen. The look of relief on the human's face died. "He will live, but you will kill the distraction that caused him to steal in the first place."

"NOOOOOOOOOOOOOOOO! PLEASSSSSSE NOOOOOOOOOO!" The human's cries faded as the guards dragged him through the door and it slammed shut behind them.

"There now that is done, maybe we can get down to the reason I summoned you here in the first place, dragon. Unless, of course, there is something more important than what I brought you here for?"

I heard my partner's voice in my ear. "Sin, Wake up." I tore my eyes away from the door they dragged the human through and focused on the figure sitting on the throne glaring at me.

I bowed. "No, ma'am, I have no other things to discuss."

"Good. Good, dragon. Now as I was saying before, we have a problem."

"A problem? What kind of problem, ma'am?"

"It seems that someone killed a Werewolf, an alpha, last night."

I stood trying to think why this would be the queen's problem. Or even my problem for that matter. Werewolves weren't known for their even temperament and sunny outlook on life. In fact, the only way for a Were to move up in his pack was for him to kill those above him. I stared at the queen. "How is this a problem? Just look to see who the new alpha is and you have the one that killed him. Seems like problem solved to me, ma'am."

The queen's eyes narrowed, and I reminded myself that it wasn't smart to be flippant with this bitch. Not if you wanted to keep your head attached to your body. "Yes, well, the wolf didn't die in combat but died in a locked bedroom by himself from a silver knife. A silver knife that no one can seem to find. I would say that is strange enough to be a problem, dragon."

"Maybe it was Colonial Mustard with a silver knife that killed him." I saw the quickest of smiles flicker across Fallon's face at the mention of the old human game we had found and played one cold rainy night. Played that is between some intense bouts of sex. The winner of the game, of course, picking what the other had to submit to. I blushed at the recollection of the few rounds I threw when Fallon came up with some of his more interesting ideas. Damn fairy always did have a good imagination.

Igmun cleared his throat dragging me from thoughts that set tingles from nipples, that had stiffened, to the V between my legs as I felt a rush of wetness there. I cleared my throat. "Uh, sorry, ma'am. You were saying a closed off room and missing weapon?"

She shot a quick look at her son. "Yes. I was, dragon. What I want you to do is investigate the alpha's death and execute whoever caused it."

I glanced over at Fallon then Igmun before turning back to the queen. "Me? I'm a bounty hunter, ma'am. I hunt rogues, runners, or creatures that are causing trouble in the outer sectors. You surely have things—well, you know fairies or other creatures that can do this job, don't you?"

"I do, dragon, indeed I do have someone that does this kind of work, but he feels that you would be a help in this investigation."

"Who would think that?" I asked sweetly as the queen's eyes flickered toward Fallon again. "Oh, yeah." A tiny smile hit my lips before I could stop it.

I made my face as neutral as possible as I watched the anger flash across the queen's face. "I am against this idea, dragon, but Igmun here,"—she laid a hand on the old dragon's arm—"agrees with my oldest. So, you are now working for us in finding what could kill an alpha Were in the manner in which he died. And more importantly, why they killed him. Do you understand, dragon?"

I tried to ignore the thought of working day and night—especially the nights—with Fallon until we found whatever had done in the Were. I squirmed thinking of the tub incident when the queen's voice brought me back to the here and now. "Of course, I think it would be better for all concerned if you used this castle as your base of operations for this assignment, dragon. You know, having Fallon and you return here each night to report to me personally."

Fallon stiffened. He started to open his mouth then snapped it shut. Well, there goes my idea of sex with that damn fairy, I groused to myself. There was no way the queen would let us within spitting distance of each other when not working on the death of the Were alpha. Not in her castle.

"My queen. I mean, Velocity," Igmun said as he leaned over toward the queen. "I think you would hamper them in this search by making them set this place as their home base. You never know where this investigation will take them."

The queen sat on her throne staring at me as her teeth worried her bottom lip. After a few seconds, she let out an annoyed breath as she shook her head. "Fine, Igmun, as usual, you're right. The important thing is to find out what kind of creature killed this damn Were before it kills again."

Fallon gave me a quick glance. A smile played across his lips as he winked at me. I tried not to smile at my fairy lover before I took my eyes off of him and looked back at the queen. "So, ma'am, about the pay?"

Igmun straightened giving me a quick shake of his head as Fallon's smile disappeared and his eyes locked back onto those two golden doors across the room. "Your pay? And what pay would that be, dragon?"

I should have shut my mouth right then and there. I mean when this bitch went quiet like this, it usually wasn't a good sign for whoever was in her sights. But gold is gold and dragons don't give out freebies. So, I nodded as I felt Sebastian yanking on my hair, hysterically. "No, Sin. Just no. Don't say it."

I shrugged causing the imp to let go of my hair and grab the collar of my vest. "Yes, ma'am, I was thinking since this isn't a normal bounty maybe twice the price I usually charge seems fair."

"So, you think forty pieces of gold would be fair do you, dragon?"

My good sense kicked in for just a second, as I hesitated before it went bye-bye and left me on my own. "Well, yeah, that does sound fair, ma'am. I mean I am doing the job your own people should do, right?"

The queen sat for a few seconds gazing at me. "So you think that would be fair, dragon, do you? Well, what I think is fair is that I pay you ten pieces of gold and let you keep your head on your shoulders. How does that sound to you, dragon?"

I opened and closed my mouth a few times before common sense slapped me across the face. I bowed low to the queen. "Your offer seems more than fair, ma'am."

"Yes, I thought it would, dragon. Now get out of my sight before I change my mind about taking that beautiful head of yours off your shoulders."

I looked at the fairy queen thinking that if she tried to have my head removed, I would not go down without a fight and I sure as hell was going to try to take this bitch with me.

I felt another tug on my hair. "Please, Sin, let's walk out of here with all our limbs attached." Sebastian was right. There was no way I would win a fight here. I gave a quick bow to the queen and turning marched back toward those two golden doors.

As I reached them, I heard the queen's voice float across the room. "Fallon, remember what happened to that human. Sarah, wasn't it?"

"Yes, mother, I remember and she was half human."

The fairy queen's voice followed me out of the throne room. "Good. Whatever she was, do remember her fate while you're working with that—that thing."

7

Six hours later, Fallon and I were standing in a room looking at a dead Were. He lay on his bed naked. Even though there were no restraints evident in the room, the alpha's arms and legs were spread as though they had been tied to the bedposts. Burn marks around his wrists and ankles stood out in painful contrast to his now pale skin. Burns caused by silver from the look. From the expression on his dead face and the trail of dried semen along his lower belly, it looked as if he came and went as they say. I kept that to myself as Fallon seemed in no mood for my humor right now.

In fact, ever since we had left the castle the fairy hadn't said more than one or two words to me. Hard to believe since we had been by ourselves, except for one imp, traversing the fairy gates most of the afternoon. As most everyone knows, these gates are the quickest way for supernaturals to move from one end of the country to the other. Otherwise, it's good old-fashioned footwork since they banned old human transportation.

I watched as Fallon quietly checked over the Were's body for a few minutes. I glanced around the room taking in the mess. Clothes strewn around. A shattered mirror above the cluttered dresser before I looked at the imp that fluttered around the ceiling light. "Sebastian, how about you check all the outside locks? And see if there is evidence of tampering with the security system or the power stone."

"Aww, Sin, do I have to? It's almost dark out there and the fairies already did that and—" He stopped whining as he threw a quick glance at the quiet fairy by the bed. "Fine. I'll go double check their work, Sin. Never can trust those fairies when it comes to security systems like the Were had."

I watched the imp zip out the bedroom door before I closed it and turned back to Fallon. "Okay, what seems to be the problem?"

He looked up from the body, studying me for a second. "Problem? The problem is that we have a dead Were and no clue as to how he came to be in this condition."

"No, not that problem, Fallon. Someone stabbed the Were with silver. See? No problem. Well, except for the dead Were, I guess. The problem I'm talking about is why you are so damn quiet?"

He nodded at the bed. "The problem we have to deal with is a dead Were here. That is the problem we should be focused on. Not how either of us feels right now."

I marched over to the bed. Getting right up into his personal space. "Screw the dead Were."

A ghost of a smile crossed Fallon's lips. "Seems someone already did from the look of the body."

"No, I don't mean—" Irritated, I saw another ghost of a smile flit across his lips. "Come on, Fallon. What's your problem? Why have you been so quiet since we left the castle? This isn't like you. At least it isn't like you when you're away from your damn mother."

Fallon's eyes dropped to the body of the Were. "I can't see you hurt, Sin. My mother can hurt you. She can do awful things to hurt you."

I laughed. I couldn't help it. His head snapped up in anger. "Please, I'm a dragon, Fallon. You of all people should know that I can take hits that would kill most other creatures, even you fairies. Besides, do you think I would stand still and let your mother do anything to me without putting up a fight?"

The anger died, replaced by a look of sorrow that clouded those icy blue eyes of his. "You don't know my mother like I do, Sin. She—"

"Is this about—Sarah, wasn't that the name I heard the bitch say?"

Fallon flinched as that ghost of a smile returned before disappearing again. "You should be careful how you talk about my mother. She has ears everywhere." The sorrow returned to his eyes. "But yes, it is about Sarah or more about what my mother did to her. Sarah was tough too. She thought she could handle whatever my mother could dish out too, Sin."

"Who was she? This Sarah? I heard your mother say she was human."

"She was half human – half fairy and you know how some of the more elite fairies like my mother and her cronies treat their kind."

I had learned the hard way growing up that if you weren't a pure-blood, you weren't shit. Or I guess I should say pure-blood fairy. I noted Fallon had used 'their kind' as well. My lover wasn't as progressive as he thought. "Okay, so what does she have to do with you and me? What happened to her?"

"Sarah was about five years older than me and she was one of the most excellent human weapons instructors in this country. Even if she was a half-blood. When I was eighteen, my mother contracted for Sarah to teach me how to handle human weapons. One thing led to another and—"

"And the two of you did the horizontal bop," I said knowing that since Fallon was eleven years older than me, I wasn't his first. Or even his second or third. Not with him being of royal blood and raised in his mother's court. "Okay, then what? I mean I could see where your mother wouldn't be thrilled with you screwing a half-blood. I figure from today's appearance, she hates us being together and I'm not even half fairy, but—" I figured there wasn't much that she could do about it since Fallon had been a full-grown fairy at the time.

"You don't understand just how truly petty and vindictive my mother can be."

"Oh? From some of the rumors I've heard about her, I would believe it. What did she do anyway?"

Fallon looked at the body of the Were again before meeting my eyes. The sorrow in them was tinged with horror. "She had Sarah chained to the wall of the throne room and skinned alive."

"Shit."

"That was bad, but then she used her magic to keep Sarah alive for a month like that. Until—"

"Until what, Fallon?" I wasn't sure if I wanted to know the answer to my question, but I figured that he needed to get this all out in the open.

The sorrow left his eyes, replaced by anger. "My mother promised that she would keep her like that for years. She promised that there was only one way that my lover could die. I just couldn't. I just couldn't leave her like that. Seeing her like that each day. Hear her begging for death. Begging me to put her out of her misery. One night, I snuck into the throne room and—"

"You killed her? You killed your lover? That was the only way she could die? At your hands?"

The anger was gone as Fallon's eyes pleaded with me to understand. I stepped forward, wrapping my arms around the fairy as he buried his head on my shoulder. "I had no choice, Sin. I couldn't let her suffer like that. My mother wasn't happy. I had not killed her in front of the full fairy court, so I suffered my own punishment later. But, of course, it was nothing like Sarah's."

A single fairy tear stained my shoulder. "If it had been me, Fallon. If I had been Sarah, I would have wanted you to do the same thing."

We came apart as the bedroom door slammed open and Sebastian came buzzing into the room. "HEY, SIN, I DIDN'T FIND—" The imp fluttered around the light hanging from the ceiling, looking between the two of us. "Oh hey, guys, was I interrupting anything, like maybe a little kissy-face or something like that? I mean I can always come back later you know."

"No, you're fine, Sebastian. What were you saying when you came into the room?"

"Uh, well, oh yeah. This place is locked tight. Even a ghost would have trouble getting in here. I mean he had wards against most supernatural creatures around every entrance."

"So, whoever came in and killed the Were, locked it up afterward."

"No, no, no, Sin. I checked the Were's security and power stone systems. (Like I said before, the fairies outlawed human tech except for certain supers.) It's top of the line and shows it was activated at nine last night and it wasn't shut off until seven this morning when they found the body."

I looked at the Were's body splayed out on the bed trying to figure out why a Were this big ... No, not just a Were. An alpha, which fell into a whole other level of badass, this big would lay there and let someone stick a silver knife into his heart. Especially one that had his home so well warded and guarded. Even in the throes of sex, he should have kept some sense of self-preservation. Hell, looking at the size of him, it should have taken a dozen vamps just to tie him down.

"How sure are we that this isn't some internal pack feud or takeover, Fallon? Maybe his mate tired of him and helped his beta or another wolf to kill him and take over the pack. I just don't see him letting a creature he didn't know tie him down. An alpha would never give up control like that. Even for sex. They're more of the restrainers than the restrained."

A grim smile played across Fallon's lips. "My mother had her guards 'question' his mate and the beta of this pack. Both of them swore they had nothing to do with this. Besides, I checked and each of them had a good alibi for when the alpha was killed."

"Maybe I should talk to them and just double check—"

"They didn't survive their questioning, Sin. Seems my mother's guards were a little over-enthusiastic in their methods."

Geez, there was a big surprise. "Well, that's just damn convenient. Any chance that your mother or one of her people had something to do with this and she is just trying to cover it by sending us on a wild goose chase?"

My partner landed on my shoulder. "Sin, that is not a good path to go down with—uh, well, you know," he said as he nodded toward Fallon.

"Don't sweat it, imp. I had the same idea and have already checked into that possibility. In this case, my mother and her people are innocent. As innocent as the high fae ever are."

"If it isn't the Weres in the pack and it isn't your mother—" I stopped talking as a faint odor drifted from the Were's body. I couldn't place it. The smell I mean. It seemed to be a mixture of sex and something else. Something almost obscene. "Do you smell that?"

Both the fairy and imp echoed, "Smell what?"

I bent down toward the Were's crotch and sniffed. Liquid shimmered on his body. Sebastian fluttered off my shoulder and hung just above me as he shot Fallon a look. "Uh, Sin, I don't think … Well, you know, sex with—"

I glared at the imp for a second before turning back to the body. "I'm not planning on whatever your perv mind thinks I'm going to do, Sebastian. Just can't place this smell is all." Baffled by the smell, I sniffed closer to the Were's body.

Fallon stooped over alongside me and sniffed the air just above the dead Were's crotch too. I didn't even want to think about how the two of us looked. Sebastian shot a look at the open door probably thinking the same thing. "I hope no one walks in here and sees what you two are doing. Because if they do. I'm out of here and you two are all on your own to explain."

I waved a hand at the imp as I took another sniff of the strange odor just as Fallon bumped the body. Whatever the smell was, I got a nose full of it and gasped as my nipples hardened and I felt a gush of wetness.

A growl of want from Fallon drew my eyes to his. His icy blue eyes, dark in lust, were now wide as his nostrils flared. "I can smell you, my dragon. I can smell your want, your heat."

This hardened my nipples to the point of pain as they rubbed against the leather of my vest. My eyes flicked downward, and I saw that I wasn't the only one affected by the odor. Fallon's pants were straining as though they were ready to burst apart at the seams.

I swallowed as I clutched my hands into fists to keep myself from reaching over and tearing his pants open. My mouth watered thinking of my lips wrapping around—. I shook the image from my mind as I stood. "I—I—think—maybe—we—"

Fallon grabbed me by the upper arms and turning, slammed me into the wall next to the bed. His body smashed me against the brick as his lips crushed mine. The back of my vest rode up and I could feel the rough texture ripping into my back. I just didn't give a damn right that second. "I smell you, my dragon. You are mine." His hips ground into me. His hardness rubbing deliciously against my crotch.

I never got a chance to answer as his lips crashed back onto mine and his tongue forced itself inside. The fairy's body grinding against me made me orgasm. Gasping for air, I could feel his hardness rubbing against me as I climbed toward another fast crest. I opened my legs and wrapped them around his waist.

Frustrated with the clothes between us, I wished Fallon would let go of my arms just long enough for me to rip off the material separating me from that big beautiful monster of his. It ground into my crotch as I rode closer and closer to a second orgasm.

"Uh, guys? I don't think this is the time or the place. Oh hell—" I heard Sebastian's voice but nothing of what he was saying registered. All I wanted to do was get naked with this gorgeous fairy. Feel him inside me. Pumping me full of—

One second Fallon was humping the hell out of me on the wall, the next the two of us were lying on the floor about three feet apart shivering as though we had been hit by an iceberg. "What the hell, Sebastian?" I gasped and panted as I tried to catch my breath.

"I'm sorry, but I had no choice. You two wouldn't listen to reason."

I shivered as I looked over at Fallon laying soaking wet on the floor and back at the imp. Guess he hit us with ice water like two dogs in heat. "Shit, no problem, Sebastian. Thanks, I think? Oh, damn that's cold."

"What happened? Why did I … Why did we—" Fallon said as he looked over at me with glazed eyes. The lust was still there just below the surface but tempered to a point where his voice was at least even. Or as even as it was going to get after that little tryst.

"I think whatever that odor was caused you two to go crazy with—well, you know."

"Yeah, we got it, partner. Again thanks," I said as I slowly stood, my legs wobbly as I looked over at the dead Were. "Now, I think we know why he didn't put up much of a fight when he was stabbed. Something used some kind of magical aphrodisiac on him."

"Yes, my dragon, as much as I loved that little tussle, it would seem that some kind of magic had a hand in it."

Fallon stood looking at my rumpled clothes and bruised mouth. "Are you alright, Sin?" He paused to compose himself before walking over to me. He pulled up the back of my vest and stared at the scrapes for a second before letting the leather material fall. He turned and eyed Sebastian. "And what the hell did you hit us with?"

"An ice water spell."

"Ice? I thought imps were strictly fire magic creatures?"

Sebastian glanced over at me. "When your partner is a dragon with a temper like Sin's, I figured it wouldn't hurt to learn some protective spells. You know, just in case."

"Yes, I see your point, imp. I must have you show me this spell."

I glared at the two of them for a second. "Any time you two are done discussing my temper. Which, by the way, is considered mild in some circles,"—I heard Fallon snort but ignored him—"we should collect a sample of what seemed to have caused that reaction between the two of us."

"You're right, but how do we collect a sample without being affected again?"

I fidgeted as the scrapes from the brick wall started to let themselves be known. Hell, it wouldn't be the first time I was bruised or scraped from a fight or from sex.

"By the way, sorry about your back," Fallon said.

"No problem. Not your fault anyway."

"Still—"

I turned back to the imp fluttering around watching our interplay. "Sebastian? Do you think you can get a sample of whatever is on the dead Were's body without being affected by whatever magic it is?"

"Sure, why not? We imps have no interest in sex. Remember?"

I tossed him a tiny corked tube from my belt. "Good. Scrap along where the odor is and put it in this tube."

The imp caught the glass tube in midair and swooped over to the body to get his sample. Fallon leaned into me. "If they don't have any interest in sex then how do they—you know, reproduce?"

"He misspoke. Only the males have no interest in sex. There wasn't much left of the last male I saw after a dozen female imps got their hands on him."

Fallon whistled. "Rough."

"Yeah, that's why it's a good thing imps only mate every four years. Otherwise, there wouldn't be a male imp anywhere."

"What do we do now, my dragon?"

"First, I would say we burn that body so no one else gets affected like we did."

"Okay and then?"

"I say we go to my house and see if we can't find what kind of magic affected us like that."

I felt a finger trace along my spine as Fallon leaned into me. "And then what?"

I struggled to keep my face straight. "I think we should hit the rack since we may have a long day ahead of us tomorrow."

That hand slid down my back, copping a quick squeeze. "Yes, bed would be good. Though I'm not sure how much sleep we will get after having a taste of that magic."

Feeling my lust growing, I saw it mirrored in his eyes. I slid a hand behind Fallon's back, reached down, and copped a feel of my own. "I never said anything about sleep now, did I?"

8

The consortium of orcs stood around the kitchen looking everywhere except at the body of one of their own. Someone had tied him to the large wooden table in the center of the room. The back door banged open drawing all eyes toward the three goblins that barged into the restaurant.

One of the bigger gray orcs stepped forward from the crowd. "What are you going to do about this, Grumble? We pay good protection money to your gang and look what we get for it, dead bodies."

Grumble looked at the orcs and threw a quick glance over at the body. "Hey, I told you, Orb, that fights between orcs aren't covered by your protection money. You little gray bastards want to knock each other off, that isn't my problem."

The rest of the orcs muttered among themselves as Orb, their spokesperson, puffed out his chest. "This is your problem, Grumble, since none of us did this to poor Scum."

Grumble eyed the orcs before stepping over to the body. The orc's blue innards lay exposed while the goblin noticed that he was also a missing certain—uh, lower body parts. He turned to the other goblins. "They cut off his cock and balls."

The two goblins snickered as Orb slammed his hand on a nearby counter. "They stuffed them in his mouth, Grumble. Whoever did this had no respect for Scum or for us. We demand that you do something about this."

Grumble stared at the orc that challenged him until the orc took a step back and dropped his eyes to the floor. "I would say it was less about showing respect, maybe more like they were sending a message. Who did Scum piss off?"

Orb turned, pointing toward a female elf, dressed for her nightly customers in a tight skirt and halter which left little to the imagination. "The whore saw who did it. Ask her."

Grumble gave the elf a quick once over. He had been wondering what she had to do with this business. He walked over to her eyeing the haggard face with colorless, hard eyes that spoke of sordid things she had seen. Wicked things she had seen done to others and things that had been done to her in her long life. "So, elf, is it true you know what happened here?" Grumble pointed over his shoulder toward the body of Scum. "What happened to the good orc over there?"

The elf flicked a butt at Grumble. It bounced off his chest. Her eyes went dark as her lip quirked upward. "Say I did, goblin? What's it worth to you?"

Grumble looked at the smoldering butt lying at his feet for a second before his hand shot out and grabbed the elf around the throat, slamming her against the wall. Her hands grappled with his as her feet kicked in the air and she tried to breathe through her constricted airway.

The goblin leaned into the elf as her face started to turn blue. "Do not fuck with me, whore. Tell me what I want and you may walk out of this building alive. If not, there won't be enough left of you to make a mouthful. Do you understand me?" The elf's eyes went wide as Grumble opened his fist and let her slide down the wall.

He turned as the elf sputtered, eyeing the group. "Get her some water." One of the orcs hurried over to the sink and grabbed a glass filling it full of scummy water before walking over and handing the glass to her.

She sipped the water as Grumble kneeled and stroked a finger across her cheek. The hardened eyes were filled with fear and wariness. "Now, I'm going to ask a few questions and you, my dear, are going to answer them without any of your bullshit, right?"

The elf nodded as she set the empty glass down and tried to adjust her clothes. Grumble heard a few chortles from behind him and spun his head around looking for the source. All eyes were now locked on the restaurant's grimy floor.

He turned back to the elf. "Good. Excellent. Now did you see who killed Scum here?"

"I—" The elf started then stopped as she eyed the goblin.

"Just tell me what you know and I'll see if maybe you get a little something for your trouble, elf. Okay?"

"I didn't see what happened in here like I told the orcs, but I saw a red-headed woman walk out of here just before dawn."

Grumble frowned as he eyed the elf. "Did this woman you saw have green skin and an imp that rode on her shoulder?" The elf nodded. "That damn dragon," Grumble said.

"The dragon, boss?" One of the other goblins asked as the orcs muttered behind Grumble's back.

The goblin stood, his eyes going a deep red. "Yeah, that damn dragon lied. She said she was after a rogue vamp, but—"

"There was vamp remains in a courtyard just down the block," the elf said.

Grumble spun around, his eyes glowering at the elf. She cowered into herself as though he had struck her. "Are you sure about this? Very sure?"

She gulped before answering, "I've seen them. She, the dragon, left two stakes in dust piles. They were vamps." What the elf didn't say was that she had pilfered what she could from the dead vamps' clothes. Not that she found much, but no sense losing what little she had taken off the dead.

Grumble looked at the elf wondering why, if the dragon had been after vamps, would she come back here to kill Scum? Thinking back on the few times he had eaten in this place, he could see why someone wouldn't be happy with the food. Or the service. Or with Scum himself, but to kill him?

His thoughts were interrupted as Orb stepped forward. "What are you going to do about this, Grumble? We pay good money for protection. Are you going to just let some dragon come walking into your territory and kill one of us?"

Grumble backhanded the orc into the crowd. "I know what you pay me, Orb. I'll take care of the dragon. Now get out of here."

The rest of the orcs pulled their leader to his feet and scrambled for the back door. A tiny whimper from the elf caught Grumble's notice. Turning he held out his meaty hand to her.

She hesitated for a second before she grabbed it and the goblin hauled her from the ground. Brushing off the few clothes she wore, Grumble turned to one of his warriors. "Pay her two silver coins, Brute."

"Me, boss? But—" the goblin stopped complaining as his leader's eyes zeroed in on him. "Right, boss, two silver coins. Got it right here, boss," he said as he reached into his pocket and pulled out the money. Flipping them toward the whore, she caught them out of the air with a deft flick of her wrist.

The elf jingled the two coins in her hand. This was more than she made in two days. She caught Grumble's eyes as he nodded at the back door. "Get out of here, elf, before I change my mind." She was halfway across the room before the goblin had finished his command.

Brute watched the elf disappear out the door thinking that when all this business was done with the dead orc, he would find that old elf whore and recover his money whether or not Grumble liked it.

"What are we going to do now, boss?" the other goblin said as he watched the elf disappear through the door. Thoughts of what she was like in bed tramped through his mind.

"We need to take care of the bounty hunter. We need to pay back that damn dragon."

"Is that such a good idea? I mean we may lose some warriors over this. Dragons are mean and tough, boss."

Brute sneered at his companion. "What's the matter? You scared of one little girl?"

The other goblin pulled his knife from his belt. "That isn't some little girl, you ass. She's a damn dragon. Hard to kill and meaner than a she-goblin giving birth."

Grumble watched the two warriors argue back and forth for a few seconds before he coughed. Both goblins stared at each other with bloodshot eyes but shut their mouths. "I think what we need is to put a bounty on the bounty hunter." Brute laughed as the other goblin frowned at his leader. "You have a problem with my plan?" Grumble said.

The goblin shook his head at his leader. "No, Grumble, no problem. Just I remember the gang I came from had trouble with a dragon when I was younger. The leader put a price on the dragon's head."

"And? So what? Didn't you have anyone brave enough to collect on the dragon's head?" Brute said.

The other goblin shook his head. "The dragon found out about the bounty and came into camp that night and killed every warrior of age with no effort. I was lucky because I was a child at the time."

"Oh," Brute muttered.

"Yeah, oh, dickweed."

"Yeah, I remember that. But I think I have a good idea that won't fail. Someone that even the dragon won't be able to get away from."

"Who's that, boss?"

Grumble looked over at Brute. "We send the twins after the bounty hunter. They've never failed us before on a bounty."

"Oh, shit, boss. No. Come on."

"The twins?" the other goblin said.

Shaking his head, Brute went pale. "Trolls," Grumble said.

"Please, boss, don't say it. Please?" Brute pleaded.

"I don't get it?"

Grumble eyed Brute, the humor leaving his face. "You know what I want. Now go talk to your girlfriend and get her to go after the bounty hunter."

"Shit, boss, she's not my girlfriend. I was drunk that one time and we—"

Grumble and the other goblin roared with laughter. As the sounds of their amusement settled, Grumble walked over to Brute and slapped him on the back. "Do whatever you have to do, but don't come back until the twins take on the bounty for the dragon. Tell them I'll give them ten pieces of silver for her head. Understand me?"

"But, boss, there is no way they will take on a dragon for such little money."

"I suggest you figure out a way to sweeten the bounty, Brute."

"SHIT! Yes, boss," Brute said as he walked out the back door, his feet dragging and his head hanging low on his chest.

The two watched him disappear out the door. "Just how bad are these twins, boss?"

"I've never been drunk enough in my life to screw something like that and never hope to be." The goblins both laughed as they followed Brute out the door.

9

The vampire, Spartacus, was old. So old that he distantly remembered marching in the Roman legion. So old that he had stood guard duty as the son of the Christian God was nailed to his cross. So old that he had died his first death while fighting the barbarians on the Roman frontiers.

He dimly remembered the last time he walked this world with a pulse. He hadn't recalled that night in ages. It amused him that his mind now wandered back to the night of his rebirth.

Their centurion had sent him and two others of his company out to scout a small section of woods that lay in the path of tomorrow's march. The three, armed only with their swords and knives, slithered into the foliage looking for any sign of barbarians or traps that may have been set that day. Halfway through the grove of trees, he caught sight of a tiny flickering fire. Signaling his two companions, they crept forward until they were gazing into a clearing. Gazing at a sight the three old war-weary soldiers had never beheld before.

The soldiers stood transfixed as they watched a tiny nude female dancing around the fire as though listening to music that only she could hear. The girl whirled around the flames. Her hair, the color of golden sunlight, danced around her face and shoulders. Her laughter tinkled in the cool night air with a certain brittleness that set the three soldier's teeth on edge as she spun around and around. She danced as though no one was around to see her. The flames of the fire flickered across her sweat-slicked body.

They stared at the strange sight, half filled with curiosity – half want. The young girl stopped across the fire from the three men and raised her arms outward, her voice floating across the flames on the light breeze. "Come my friends, dance with me. I'm so hungry and so alone."

Spartacus' two companions stepped out of the tree line, looks of lust painting their faces. They could see the tiny hardened nipples of the girl perched high on well-formed breasts almost too big for her petite frame. The dark V between her legs, darker than the night, called them forward. He had stepped forward also, but a sudden urge to run caused him to stop in his tracks as he whispered his companion's names.

The girl's laughter rang in the dark night like tiny bells as she glided around the fire. Her dainty feet looked as though they never touched the ground. That's when Spartacus noticed the girl's eyes. Eyes that were as dark as the pits of Hell and just as deep. "They are mine, soldier. They are my dinner. You on the other hand—"

The soldier couldn't break eye contact if he wanted to. And by all that was holy he really, really wanted to. His feet felt rooted to the ground like the trees behind him. All he could muster though was a whisper. "What are you? Who are you?"

The girl leered, fangs barely showing as she drew his face toward hers. "As for what I am, I am what you are about to become. As for who I am, I am the living dead. I go by no human name." As he drowned in those eyes, those ice-cold lips caressed his. The tips of her fangs nipping at his skin, drawing blood.

His ears twitched as the first screams from camp echoed through the night. The girl released him from her grasp. "Don't worry about your friends. They are only cattle. Cattle for the slaughter. Cattle that others of my coven will feed upon. You, on the other hand, are so handsome. I am looking for a new plaything. You will be my new friend, my new lover." That's when Spartacus felt the sharp pain at his neck and fell into the dark depths of a long living night. Never to see the sun again.

Three days later he awoke as a vampire. His maker had kept him around for a century before they parted ways. Now, he was in the new world. Leader of the vampires that called this place home. Leader of a group of supernaturals that were chafing at being ruled by the fairies. Treated like dirt and trash by those that thought themselves the vamp's betters.

Spartacus retired for the day knowing that the one they had sent out on the mission of turning more vampires had failed. He had watched through the creature's eyes, being his maker, as that damn dragon had caused him to cross over to his second death as those such as he called it. The dragon was a nuisance they needed to be rid of.

Hours later, green eyes looked at the nude vamp as he lay on his four-poster bed. Green eyes filled with lust as she took in the scarred muscular body of the former Roman soldier. Aezriane ran a red-painted fingernail across the center of his chest stopping just above the triangle of pubic hair. "Very nice. Very nice indeed. Yes, you will do splendidly. You have much more to offer than that damn Were."

She lingered for a few minutes, her gaze taking in the vamp's erect shaft before running her fingernail from the bottom to the tip. Aezriane sighed as she felt her nipples stiffen and the wetness gather between her legs. "This will definitely be a more enjoyable night for me."

With only an hour before full dark, Aezriane leaned down and laid a kiss on the tip of the vamp's shaft before she reached to the floor and picked up the bag that lay at her feet. The clink of metal on metal caused the vamp's eyelids to twitch. She stiffened in alarm. After a few seconds, when he didn't wake, she prepared the vamp for his rising.

Spartacus woke blind. His face a mask of pain as he felt blood drip down his cheeks. He tried to move. To bring his arms to his face, but he could feel, by the burning, that they and his legs were tied outward by silver. His mind flittered briefly to his pet, hoping she was not suffering as he was.

Damn, how had the fairies found out so fast about their plans? That he was the one that—

A throaty female voice interrupted his musing. "Hello, bloodsucker. I see that you're awake."

"What have you done, fairy? Are you here on your damn queen's orders to send me to my second death?"

"What have I done to you? I figured I would be safer if you didn't have your eyes in case you can spell me. Sooooo, let's just say I decided to remove them for you."

Spartacus rattled the chains in anger. His fangs showed through his lips. "You know that a vampire can't spell a fair—" The vamp stopped his tirade then sniffed the air for a second as a coy smell tickled his nose. "You're a fae, but not a fairy, are you?"

"Very good. No, I'm not a fairy. Not even close."

Something puzzled the vamp as he sniffed the air again. There was that faint aroma. Remembered from long ago. In a different age. A different time. "You—I have smelled you, or one like you. A long time ago. When I was younger."

Aezriane reached out and caressed the vamp's face. "Yes, you probably have come across one of my sisters before. A long time ago there were many of us. Well, not many, but we were like you. A group of supers that ruled our little part of this world. That is until that damn fairy queen killed us all off."

"Then we have a common enemy. Let me go and we will—"

She tapped the vamp on the face. "Oh yes. Just let you go. After I've taken your eyes? Oh, I'm sure you'll just forgive me for that little indiscretion won't you, bloodsucker?"

The vamp shook his chains. With the pain it caused, he stopped moving. "A mistake is all. My eyes will grow back. I give you my word that if we work together, I will not harm you."

Another tap – tap on the face. "You know, bloodsucker, I would like to believe you, but—"

Spartacus forced as much command into his voice as he could. "But what? But nothing. I demand that you let me go right this second, creature."

"Nice try. That voice thing doesn't work on my kind. The eyes could spell me, but not the voice. Now, I think we need to get down to business before those blue orbs of yours make a reappearance."

"What are you talking about, creature? What business do you have with me?"

A hand grazed the vamp's cheek before gliding down his body until it reached his hard shaft. Spartacus could feel the softness wrap around him as it tantalizingly moved up and down his length. "I just need you to give me a little something. Just a little something to make more of my sisters so we can take out the fairies."

"Creature, you are crazy. A vamp's seed is as dead as the rest of us. You can't conceive a baby by a vampire. That is why we need to make more of our children through our bite."

The vamp could feel the creature crawl onto his bed. She settled on his stomach. A knee on each side of his hips as she said, "Oh, but you see there you are wrong. Once my mother blesses your seed, you will be the father of a whole new race of children."

"You are truly crazy. Untie me now and I promise that I will forgive you for this transgression."

Spartacus stopped talking as the creature above him went up on her knees and slid backward taking in his full length. Her pelvis came down hard. Her voice hissed out half in pain – half in pleasure. "Oh yes, bloodsucker, it has been so long since I have felt anything like this—sooooo damn long." The creature moaned as she rocked her hips back and forth.

Aezriane moved slowly at first. Pushing down as she rocked forward on the vamp's pubic bone. Her hardened nub rubbing the stiffness each time she moved forward. As the motion brought her closer to her climax, she increased her pace. She rode the vamp's shaft hard. Somewhere in her mind, she registered his moans and curses as she climbed closer to her peak.

She felt wave after wave of pleasure from her climax wash over her as she came once – twice – three times before she stopped. Her breath coming in ragged gasps as she leaned down over the vamp, her damp hair riding over the vamp's hardened nipples.

A low moan below her caused her eyes to open to slits as she looked down at the vamp. His sightless eyes were closed in concentration as he tried to pump his trapped hips into her. Sighing deeply, she climbed off the vamp causing him to let out a low moan.

"Don't worry, bloodsucker. I won't leave you high and dry," she said as she placed her golden bowl between the vamp's outward spread legs. Pulling out a wooden stake that had engraved symbols carved over every inch, Aezriane leaned close to his ear. "Do you want release? I need you to beg me for release." She gripped the bottom of the vamp's shaft and slowly moved her hand up and down.

The vamp was lost in his lust. The loss of the tightness. The wetness of this creature that had ridden him like no other had in a long time. Even his pet. His Sadie had never felt like this. Had never sent him to these heights of passion. "Please. Yes, please. More—"

"Oh, I think not, bloodsucker. I wouldn't want to get carried away and lose any of this special seed, but I think I can figure out something just as good." The vamp felt her hot lips kiss their way down his body.

He hissed as his back arched in pleasure. Those hot lips engulfed him to the base of his shaft in one smooth motion. The blistering wetness that held him trapped slid up and down, while her tongue flicked along every inch of him. Faster and faster his hips bucked upward to meet that hot wetness. He was going almost mad from not being able to grab the creature's head. To tangle his hands within the hair that was tickling his stomach on each downward stroke.

Aezriane could feel the vamp climb closer to his climax with each stroke of her head. Her eyes went wide as she felt the vamp's body stiffen and the first spurt of his seed hit the back of her throat.

She ripped her mouth off of the vamp's shaft and pointed the tip at the receptacle. Her hand milked it as shot after shot hit the inside of the bowl. Soon there was only a tiny dribble of seed hanging at the tip. "Oops, looks like I missed a drop." She leaned over and with the tip of her tongue swiped up the last of the seed hanging there.

The vamp hissed as his hips bucked in pleasure. That's when Aezriane shoved the wooden stake below his ribs and into the vamp's heart. His sightless eyes opened as the wood tore its way through skin and muscle reaching for the one part of him that was still alive. The last vision the sightless vamp had was of the son of the Christen God looking down on him from his cross. He saw his lips move as the man, nailed to the cross, whispered, "Forgive him, father, for his life and take his soul."

Aezriane stood over the vamp, his face peaceful in his second death as a tiny smile played across his lips before he dissolved into a pile of dust. She grabbed the bowl and set it aside to pack the rest of her stuff away. She wasn't interested in how the vamp died, just that he died giving her his seed to appease her mother. "Well, at least he died with a smile on his face."

Magic wavered in the air as the vamp's room disappeared. Carefully, she picked up the golden bowl and glided over to the altar. The mist in the black bowl behind her faded. Setting the bowl on the altar, she threw back her arms and prayed. "Mother, Lilith, I have brought you another gift to bless. Take this offering and change it so I may avenge my sisters, your daughters."

A dark cloud roiled over the altar before it solidified into a shadow. Red eyes peered at Aezriane, kneeling before the altar, as she dropped to the ground. "Daughter, you dare bring the seed of the undead before me?"

The room grew as cold as death. Aezriane trembled, not daring to look at the figure floating above the altar. "Forgive me, Mother. I have brought you the seed of an old warrior. A warrior that lived at a time when you were revered. I thought this gift to you would make strong children. Forgive me if I have failed you."

A ghostly hand reached out to touch the seed that floated in the golden bowl. It rose, touching where dark lips would be. "Yes. Yes, I can feel that you speak the truth, daughter. Very good. Very good, indeed. I shall bless this seed so you may plant it in vessels and I shall have my revenge."

The bowl glowed an ugly green as the contents inside boiled before settling back into a black sludge as the shadow dissolved. "Thank you, Mother."

10

Leaving behind the charred ruins of the Were's house and his body, it was full dark by the time we hit the fairy gate nearest my home. In this case, nearest meant we still had an hour's worth of walking to go. Hey, what can I say? I liked my privacy.

Once we had gotten away from the Were's sector, the trip to this point hadn't been so bad. The sexual magic that hit us earlier and the idea of having Fallon all on my own put us both in a pretty frisky mood. Much to the annoyance of one imp. "Hey, guys, mind if we get home before you play any more kissy face?"

Fallon pushed me against another tree and crushed his hot lips against mine. I tangled one hand into the fairy's long blonde hair and waved the other at the imp. I couldn't believe how much in love I was. My life couldn't be any more perfect.

I felt Fallon grow harder as he pressed his body against me. My nipples hardened, rubbing against the leather of my vest in such a delicious, wanton way that sent tremors to the center of my belly until a certain odor hit my nose.

My brain screamed, 'oh shit' as I tightened my grip on Fallon's hair and yanked his lips off mine. "Sin, we have big trouble coming," Sebastian said.

Give the fairy credit, he went from humping my bod one second to full-on alert the next. His sword was already halfway out of its sheath. "What is it, my dragon? Who—or what is coming?" A tremor rocked the ground around us.

I looked down the road curving around a tiny grove of trees and sniffed the air. Oh yeah, we were in major trouble. Hearing metal on leather, I grabbed Fallon's hand. Shaking my head, I pushed his sword back into its home. "It isn't so much a who or a what, Fallon. Whatever you do, don't pull your weapon. Understand me?"

"I don't get why I shouldn't have a weapon ready if there is danger around, my dragon."

"Listen, fairy, if it is who I think it is coming down the road and you attack it with your sword all you will do is piss her off. And pissing her off is an awful, awful idea." Fallon looked down the road and back at me, disbelief written across his face as the sound of heavy footsteps echoed through the night.

"What are we going to do, my dragon? What is your plan?"

"Just let me do the talking. Okay?"

The fairy nodded just as a huge two-headed troll came stalking around the curve in the road. The twins. Damn. There was probably only one reason they were in my neck of the woods tonight. We were in trouble with a capital 'T'. I heard Fallon inhale sharply at the sight before us.

The eight-foot monster stopped about ten feet away. Two female heads sat on top of a solid body that looked like it was made of granite. Long arms with hands the size of boulders hung almost to the ground. Two sets of beady dark eyes gazed out at us from under heavy brows.

Dragons are scarce and hard to kill, but trolls, especially eight-foot trolls, could put a good dent in our hide. "Hey, Marigold. Hey, Petunia. What are you doing here in my neck of the woods? I don't remember having an appointment with you."

Both sets of eyes stared at me for a second then at each other before one of the heads—I could never tell them apart since they were identical twins, and could never remember which side of the body was who. "We have a bounty on you, Sin."

Damn, I hate it when I'm right. This was what I was afraid of when I smelled the troll. We didn't need this right now. Whoever had put a price on my head was serious if they could afford the twins, they were almost as expensive as I was. "Listen, girlfriends, there must be some mistake. Who would put a bounty on my head?"

"It was a goblin that came and gave us the contract, Sin. So, we would think it was his boss, Grumble, that is paying out the money."

"Damn goblins."

The imp landed on my shoulder and flicked my ear. "See, I told you not to piss him off, Sin. I told you this would come back and bite you in the ass. Didn't I tell you that at the diner, Sin?"

"Yeah, thanks, Sebastian," I said before looking back at the twins and held out my arms. "Now, listen girls, aren't we friends? Didn't we just have a makeover last month? I mean who was it that gave you that pink ribbon, Marigold?"

"I'm Petunia."

"Sorry. Sorry. Okay, who gave both of you those beauty tips. I mean here I thought we were best friends and you take a bounty out on me for what—"

"Ten—"

"Really? Ten gold pieces is all you're getting for my bounty."

The trolls shook their head. "No, Sin. Ten silver pieces," Petunia said.

"WHAT! Why that cheap son of a bitch. I'll—"

"Sin, focus on what's important here. Remember? Trolls wanting to kill you," Sebastian said.

"Oh yeah." The imp was right, now was not the time to worry about how much the bounty was. I needed to do some fast talking to get out of this situation. "Look, girls, ten pieces of silver is an insult to both of you. I mean, I wouldn't have taken out a bounty on me for less than forty – maybe fifty pieces of gold."

"Well, we got the use of the goblin that brought us the bounty, Sin. So. You know, there was that," Petunia said.

"Well, just give the goblin back, girls. I mean what good is a goblin, after all?"

Petunia hung her head. "We sort of can't give him back, Sin," Marigold added.

"Yeah, we sort of broke him."

"Yeah, broke him bad." Our eyes darted from head to head, as they confessed.

"Yeah, broke him dead bad."

We watched as the two heads giggled like little girls and wiped tears off their faces. "You know, I almost feel sorry for the goblin," Sebastian said.

Knowing the twins as I did, I was pretty sure that whatever they had done to the goblin had been neither pleasant nor quick. But, I wasn't as generous. Well, good. Screw him.

The trolls stopped laughing and looked at Fallon and Sebastian. "Well, we need to get this over with so these two can just go on their way since we have no bounty on them."

Fallon puffed out his chest as he laid his hand on his sword. "Creature, I stand with my dragon. If you want to collect a bounty on her head, you'll have to go through me first."

The two heads glanced at each other before looking back at Fallon. "As you wish, fairy. It is of no concern of ours if you die at our hands."

"WAIT!" I grabbed the fairy's hand once more and pushed his sword back into its sheath. "Listen, girls, putting our friendship aside for one second, do you think ten pieces of silver is worth what is going to happen?"

The two heads looked at each other for a full minute before turning back me. "We're listening, Sin."

Relieved, I nodded at them. "You both know that I'm a dragon. Right?"

"Well, of course," Marigold said looking slightly annoyed that I thought she was slow.

Petunia looked even more annoyed than her sister. "Yeah, Sin, we may be big, but we're not stupid."

"I could argue that one."

"Not a good time, Sebastian," I said out of the side of my mouth as I kept an eye on the trolls. "Listen. The point I'm trying to make is that if we fight, I guarantee you I will not be going down easy. I will take one or both of you with me. Now, is that kind of trouble worth ten pieces of silver?"

I watched as they considered my position. Trolls take a long while to think over problems. Even longer than goblins for the most part, but I figured that they would come to the right conclusion. Or I hoped they would. They both knew how tough I was and, that out of all the supers, I would probably be the only one that could give them a run for their money in a straight up brawl.

Petunia nodded at her sister before Marigold turned to me. "That may be true, Sin, but we did take the bounty on you. So, we need to carry it out or we could lose our reputation and business. You understand, right?"

"Hey, I'm a working girl too, guys, but we should be able to figure something out. I mean did this goblin you broke, did he ever go back to his boss and say you accepted his bounty?"

Both heads glanced at each other, tiny smiles playing across their lips. "Well, no, we sort of played with him as soon as he came to give us the bounty and, of course, broke him dead. Why?"

"So, Grumble doesn't know that you took the bounty, right?" Both heads nodded. "Okay. So, just tell him that the bounty is an insult and refuse to take it. Simple as that."

"And what of the goblin that we broke, Sin?" Marigold said.

"Yeah, what of the goblin? We can't return him since—uh, we had him for lunch after we broke him."

"Just tell his boss he was compensation for having to listen to an asinine deal."

"Yes, that may work," Marigold said to her sister.

"So, are we good now, girls? Back to being besties and all? What do you say, girlfriends?"

"What if Grumble offer us more money, Sin? You know, he puts a bigger bounty on your head. Then what? I mean we need to make a living too, Sin, no matter how we feel about you," Petunia said.

Gazing at the two, I walked over and patted her arm. "I'll tell you, right now, I would never, ever take a bounty on the two of you. No matter how much gold they promised me. You're my friends, one of my best friends."

"Then we will do the same, Sin. For you are our only friend," Marigold said as she wiped a tear from her eyes.

Petunia leaned down and patted me on top of my head. "My sister is right, Sin. You are our only friend. By the way, the fairy has a cute ass. It would have been a shame to kill him."

I laughed as I patted her arm again. "Thanks, girlfriend. You should see it when he's out of his pants."

The trolls laughed as they straightened. "I think we would break a fairy way quicker than a goblin, Sin."

Yeah, they probably would at that. The trolls walked past us giving the eye to Fallon. It amused me to see him move a few feet away from them when Marigold winked at him. Fallon was pretty smart for a fairy. We stood there watching until the troll disappeared around the corner.

Sebastian took flight again, laughing. "That was close."

"Yeah, too close." I looked back at Fallon. "I think we should hurry and get into my house without any more grab ass, fairy."

Fallon looked down the road and back at me. "But, you said that each of you would never sell out the other for gold."

"Oh fairy, you need to get out of that castle more and into the real world. What makes you think a dragon or a troll would ever give up a bounty of gold?"

"Yeah, but ... That means you both lied, Sin."

"Fallon, it is only your kind that cannot tell a lie. We lowly supers living in the gutter don't have that luxury. Besides, you may not lie, but I know for damn sure you fairies know how to twist the truth so it comes out to your favor. So, don't get all high and mighty with me."

The fairy's eyes narrowed as he stared at me for a few seconds. "You don't like fairies much do you, my dragon?"

Stepping to him, I wrapped my arms around his waist. I looked into those icy blue eyes. "I love you, Fallon, with all my heart. But as a general rule, yes, I do dislike fairies."

He looked at me. His eyes darkened with anger for a few seconds before they lightened to their usual color. His lips brushed mine. "And I love you, my dragon. Whether or not you like the rest of my people."

"That's all well and fine, folks, but I seem to remember someone mentioning that it would be a good idea to head straight home now. I mean I would hate to have to use that ice water spell on the two of you again."

I looked at my partner. "You ever use that spell on me again, imp, and I'll make sure I cut off the equipment that those female imps are always after."

"If you think that was a threat, Sin, you need to try harder. You should have seen what those female savages did to my cousin, Mell." We listened to the imp's story as we walked toward my house.

11

"I don't get why you have all these books, my dragon," Fallon said as he walked around the room his fingers playing along the spines that lined the shelves.

I glanced up a touch annoyed as he picked out two human paperback novels from the shelf. His eyes roamed over the faded covers before he stuffed them back into their resting places. I fought the urge to stalk over and arrange them into their proper order.

"And why so many old human books, my dragon? What could you possibly expect to learn from them? They are just one step up from the animals they tend in the fields."

I closed the thick volume I had been pouring through and slipped it back into its place on the shelf. Walking over to Fallon, I reached out and placed the two books he had handled into their proper places. "The humans may have been stupid about how they treated Mother Earth, but when the supernaturals destroyed their civilization, they destroyed a lot of good to go along with the bad. Medicine, art, books. Hell, the humans went out to the stars before we destroyed them."

"Yes, and they made terrible things like that weapon you so lovingly carry with you, my dragon. Give me a good blade any day. Besides, humans were destroying Mother Earth and probably would have destroyed any world they had settled on. They needed to be taken out," Fallon said with maybe just a touch of jealousy tainting his voice.

"The Supernatural Council gave me permission to use my nine-mil as a bounty hunter. Besides, your mother's guards have heavier weapons than I do. Do you begrudge them their use for her protection?"

The fairy was quiet for a few seconds as his eyes roamed over my small library. "If it was my choice, everything human would have been killed or destroyed when we took over our world. Or if nothing else, sent out to those stars they were so interested in."

"You're hard on humans, Fallon."

"They bring nothing to this world, my dragon. Nothing worth saving them for," the fairy said as he glanced at the books surrounding us.

I stared at the fairy. I wanted to argue with him but knew that was a fight I wouldn't win. His face was set as though made of rock. "What would the vamps feed off of if there were no humans to—"

"Vamps. Another inferior species along with the Were's that the world would be better off without, my dragon."

"I see, Fallon. Then who else should be eliminated from Mother Earth? Goblins, orcs, elves, maybe even dragons? Would it be only a perfect world if all there was left were fairies to tend to Mother Earth? Is that what your mother is shooting for, Fallon? Is that what you want?"

His eyes narrowed as he stared at the anger that flushed my face. Slowly his face relaxed as he stepped to me and tried to take me in his arms. Holding a hand against his chest, I pushed away from him and turned my back. I felt his hand on my shoulder. "It's not like that, my dragon. You're not like those other lowly creatures or humans. Dragons are almost as—

Spinning around, my eyes flared wide. "Be careful that you do not finish that sentence, fairy. Remember you are in my home and I am well armed."

I could see a flush creep up the fairy's face. His eyes shifted from side to side to take in the room. "Yes, well, home—"

Whatever he started to say was cut off as Sebastian flew into the room. His wings were buzzing almost as loud as his voice, a long sheet of paper hanging from his hands. "Hey, Sin, I think I know what killed the Were and …"—he stopped just inside the room—"Am I interrupting something between you two again?"

I glanced over at Fallon. His face was closed off as only a fairy could do. I turned back to the imp. "No, Sebastian. You're not interrupting anything important. What were you saying? You think you know what killed the Were?"

The imp glanced between the two of us before he looked at the paper he held. "Yeah, well, I got some interesting readouts from that sample that sent you two into a sexual frenzy. Truly fascinating readouts, indeed.

I tapped my foot, in no mood for the imp's dramatics. "And?"

"Well, I won't go into all the gory details of what that shit was made of, but I would say what you two are dealing with is a succubus."

"That cannot be, imp. My mother had them all killed when we fairies took over the world from the humans."

"What? Another inferior species that wasn't good enough to live in the same world as fairies?"

Fallon threw me a dark look. Sebastian saved the fairy from retorting as he landed on my shoulder. "No, Sin, they were all killed because they were trying to push their foul beliefs on others. Pushing their creator."

"So, what was the problem? So, they had different beliefs. I mean I pray to Brigit, Goddess of Fire. So—"

The imp went pale. "They believed in the goddess, Lilith, the mother of all demons."

"Okay? Hate to ask, Sebastian, but aren't you a demon?"

"They sacrificed babies to their goddess in their rituals," Fallon said, distaste washing across his face.

Sebastian angrily buzzed off my shoulder, waving the paper in front of my face. "And their magic required the use of virgins. Dead virgins. And I resent the implication I'm on the same line as these creatures. I'm more in line with you dragons than scum like that."

"Okay, chill there, partner, I got it. So, if all the succubi are dead how was the Were killed by one?"

"I would say fairy boy's mother missed one, Sin."

Fallon appeared lost in thought for a moment then looked at my partner. "I hate to admit it, but I think the imp may be right."

Shock washed across Sebastian's face and disbelief dripped from his voice. "Uh, thanks for that vote of confidence, fairy boy, I think."

"So how does a succubus get into a locked room? Didn't you say, partner, the Were had his house warded with a top-notch security system? That even a ghost would have a hard time getting through it."

"According to what I know of them, these succubi appear in the dreams of the ones they want to—uh, collect from."

"Collect? Collect what, Sebastian?"

"Uh, collect—well, you know—baby batter."

Fallon's eyes darted between the two of us. I couldn't help the tiny smile that painted my lips at the imp's discomfort and the puzzled look on the fairy's face as I answered his unasked question. "The Were's sperm."

"Yeah, seems they use it to make other little succubi."

"She screwed the Were so she would get pregnant?" I said.

Sebastian tapped the paper. "No, they collect the sperm then find a host to put it in to make a little succubus baby. A virgin host."

"So, you're telling me there could be little babies in the making out there?"

"Yeah, no telling how many she could make out of what she collected from just the Were, Sin. I bet he won't be the last one she collects from either. Not if she is planning on making a lot of little succubi," Sebastian said.

"Damn. This could lead to a lot of trouble for my people."

I agreed with him. Of course, the succubus wouldn't be the only problem for the fairies after listening to the goblins and the vamps. "Okay, Sebastian, can you find out how long the baby takes to bake in their host? And how do we kill this creature before it collects any more samples?"

"Right. Got you, Sin," my partner said as he flew out the door.

Out of the corner of my eye, I saw Fallon exhale deeply. "Listen, my dragon. I'm sorry about before … What I was saying about other creatures. I—"

I stood, my arms crossed, as I eyed the fairy, watching him stumbling over his apology. I wasn't angry with him anymore. His outlook on supers other than fairies was due to his upbringing, but that didn't mean I was going to make it easy for him either.

I saw a tiny flash of irritation in his eyes. "You can be headstrong, my dragon. Did you know that?"

I moved closer to the fairy. "Sorry, Fallon, I figured that was one of the reasons you loved me."

He reached out, taking me in his arms. "Oh yes, my dragon. Your stubbornness is so adorable. It's just one of the many qualities of yours that turn me on so."

I ignored the sarcasm that spilled from his mouth as I buried my face into his chest. "Well, good. Then I don't have to worry about changing. Not that I was going to for you anyway. Besides, I think you enjoy slumming in the gutter with us non-fairies."

"I would never ask you to change, my dragon." He tipped my head up with one hand and his lips pressed against mine. The heat from his lips ignited a spark deep within my belly. I heard a low growl that could have come from either of us or both, as he clutched me closer. Our bodies ground into each other as his tongue split my lips and found my own.

This went on like what seemed like hours until I could catch my breath. Pulling away from him, I looked into those icy blue eyes. My face flushed from the heat we were both throwing off. "I—I think we may still have some of that magic crap from the succubus in our system."

Fallon grinned at me as I felt his hands running up and down my back. One hand reached to cup my ass while the other ran itself under my shirt. His fingers sliding along my spine sent chills up and down my body. "I think you may be right, my dragon. Whatever shall we do about it?" He stopped talking as his lips crushed mine again.

As his lips slid off my mouth and found their way down my neck, I felt both of his hands grab me around my bottom and lift me off the floor. I wrapped my legs around his slim waist as he kissed and laid tiny bites along my neck and collarbone. "Fallon! Fallon, we shouldn't give in to—" I stopped as my body rubbing against his carried me up and over the crest. A small one, but big enough to take my breath away for a second.

My body shook as the fairy's low growl seemed to intensify the feelings rippling through my body. As it receded, I could feel him moving forward until he stopped and gently laid me on the couch.

I lay panting, my back against the cushions. My legs spread out on either side of him as he kneeled on the floor. His eyes drank in every inch of me as his hands worked their way under my shirt. Leaning forward, he rolled the material up and over my breasts.

The cool air hitting my nipples hardened them even further as his hands cupped and explored each mound. I closed my eyes and a tiny whimper escaped. Fallon leaned forward, his mouth finding first one then the other hard nub.

Fallon released the second nipple. "I want to taste you, my dragon." I felt his mouth go back to work on my breasts as his hands worked to undo my pants.

I felt the material loosen, I lifted my hips so he could slide the cloth down my legs. Soon his lips disappeared from my breast as they worked their way over my belly toward my center. I could feel my legs opening of their own accord. "Yes, my dragon, that is what I want."

Through the heat, I felt his cool breath wash over my wetness. Crying out, I reached out and grabbed a handful of his hair and pulled his face into me.

As his mouth and tongue performed their magic on me, I was lost in the waves of pleasure. I rode from one orgasm to another screaming out each one as he wrapped his arms around me, refusing to let me escape from the crests that racked my body.

"Please, please, no more. I can't—oh godddddddddd—" The largest wave washed over me and I could feel my body go limp as Fallon's arms finally released me from their grasp.

Through half-lidded eyes, I saw Fallon lean over me. Seeing but not caring when he had rid himself of his clothes. Feeling his shaft rubbing against my wetness sent me up another crest. Just as another aftershock racked my body, I felt him split me open and slide deep within me. A half sob – half hiss escaped my lips and I arched my back as he filled every inch of my being.

Fallon paused fully within me as he looked down with concern. "Are you alright, my dragon?"

I panted as my body adjusted to his size. "Yes, it's just been awhile"—he twisted his hips causing me to gasp—"awhile since we have done this—" He smiled as he slowly moved in and out of me. "Ooooooooooh shitttt—"

I was lost as I wrapped my legs around his waist. He increased the pace. Soon I was riding another wave of pleasure, cresting higher than ever before. I went over the top as Fallon growled out his own orgasm, filling me with a molten heat that spilled out of me and dripped down my thighs. My world went black.

"My dragon? Sin? Are you alright?"

Sluggishly, I came back to reality hearing Fallon's whispered voice. My eyes fluttered open as I saw the concern in his face. "I'm fine, Fallon. I just think we need to get together more often. Your size takes getting used to."

The concern was still there, but I could see a ghost of approval and pride cross his face. "You may be right, my dragon."

After the job the fairy had done on me, he should feel some satisfaction for a job well done. Now the only problem was my legs weren't working, and I didn't want to sleep on the couch.

Fallon must have read my mind as he reached out and scooped me into his arms. "Where is your bedroom, my dragon?"

"Through there," I said pointing out a red door in one wall, "but I can walk, Fallon."

"If you can walk, my dragon, then I must not have done as well as I thought."

I snuggled against his chest like a contented kitten full of cream. Fallon headed toward my bedroom door. "Oh, believe me, fairy, you did one hell of a job on this dragon."

12

Aezriane stood at the crypt door. Her eyes locked into the distance. Her mind wandering in and out of her dream state. It was a cool crisp late night. The dew gathered on the tombstones surrounding the old stone building. It was four o'clock in the morning. The time just before the day world woke and the night world went back to hiding in their holes. Only the sound of dripping water from the building's eaves broke the stillness of the tombs.

For another half hour, the succubus stood like this, still as the dead that lay around her. Silently calling the chosen ones. Finally, the rustle of bare feet echoed through the quiet. Her eyes lost their distant look as ten women moved through the early morning mist.

They threaded their way through the markers and trees that dotted the graveyard. Some fully clothed in work grab. Others in their nightclothes. One young woman fully nude. All of them wearing a lost, faraway look in their eyes as though they wandered through a dream that only they were privy to.

Aezriane rejoiced as all ten came to a stop before her. This was the first time she had ever used the powers her mother had granted her to enter this many dream states. A small part of her had doubted she could call so many at once, but another part admonished her for not believing in the powers her mother had granted her.

She looked over the ten women as the night lost itself to the day not far off. A tiny spark of regret flickered through her consciousness. These hosts wouldn't share the pleasure that the ones who carried the Were's blessed seed had.

No, these hosts had a different fate in store for them–not a blessing but a curse. Still, it was something that needed to be done if she was to complete the mission her mother had given her. She put her conscience aside as she gazed at the women. "Come my lovelies. We need to finish this before the sun rises." She turned and entered the crypt. She knew what she must do to avenge her sisters. The women compliantly followed her into the dim building.

Aezriane closed and locked the door behind the women as they gathered in the middle of the tiny room. She wasn't taking any chances that one of the hosts would come out of their dream state and try to escape from their breeding place.

Torch flames flickered along two walls that held a long stone shelf. Along the back wall, a makeshift altar holding the succubus' golden bowl sat – along with her black bag.

"Alright, my dears, I need you all to strip off all your clothes and pile them in the middle of the room." Nine of the women disrobed as the tenth stood, her gaze locked into the far distance.

Within minutes all the women were as naked as the day they were born. The succubus walked past them to the altar giving a quick glance at each body she passed.

"Yes, you will all do nicely, my lovelies. Now I need all of you to lie on the shelves on your backs." Once more, without a word, the women shuffled to one side of the room or the other and climbed on the cold stone slabs.

Aezriane watched as the last woman settled in place before turning back to the altar. "Mother, I have brought you these women so they will be able to host this blessed gift. Please see they are given a place at your side after they have served their purpose." She kept her head bowed as though listening to a voice only she could hear for a few minutes. "Yes, Mother. Lilith. Your will be done."

Turning, Aezriane saw a few of the woman start to rouse from their stupor. "Sleep. All of you sleep. When you wake, you will all be at the right hand of my mother. Songs will be sang of the new children you will bring into the world."

The women's eyes drooped closed as Aezriane gathered her bag and the golden bowl and moved to the first one. Leaning over her, the succubus gazed at the serene face. She brushed away a tangle of red curls that fell across her brow. "Open for me, my child."

The woman moaned and thrashed as though having a nightmare before going silent. Her legs spread out and up, exposing herself to the succubus. Aezriane's mind flashed to thoughts of a wasp she had heard about when she was growing up. The insect would find a spider and stun it before taking it to her nest to lay her eggs within the still living creature. These women would share the same fate as those spiders.

Pulling the syringe out of her bag, she hesitated for just a second as she once more gazed at the face lying before her. In the flickering light of the torches, she heard a harsh voice from the altar. "They are only humans, my daughter. They are nothing compared to us. Compared to the unborn sisters that wait to avenge themselves on the fairies. Do not fail me now that we are so close."

The succubus' heart hardened. "You are right, my mother. Forgive me. What must be done, will be done in your name." With that Aezriane put the tip of the syringe within the golden bowl and sucked up a portion of the demon seed that lay within.

Attaching the tube to the syringe. She worked the tube into the woman, none too gently, feeling guilt at faltering at her duties. When the device was where she wanted it, she gave a quick shove to the plunger and the dark substance disappeared within its host.

Pulling out the tube and laying it aside, she commanded the woman to close her legs as she reached within the bag and pulled out a golden knife that carried symbols of an ancient evil along its blade and hilt.

"Do it, my daughter. Complete the spell that will bring forth the children of the undead warrior. For these will be the strongest of all your sisters and will lead the others in my quest."

"Yes, Mother." Aezriane laid one hand on the woman's forehead and with the knife in the other carved shallow patterns into the woman's belly.

The woman arched her back in pain as a gasp left her lips before the succubus poured more magic into her. "Sleep. Sleep deeply, my dear." Once she finished, she looked at the symbols she had carved into the woman. Satisfied, she moved over to the next to repeat the procedure. Each one easier than the one before.

Two hours later the sun was rising over the trees, promising a bright morning, but not necessarily a happy one for those that looked on its face. Inside the crypt, Aezriane had finished with the last of the woman. With a sigh of relief and blood covering her hands to her elbow, the succubus moved toward the altar to say one last prayer to her mother.

As she passed the first woman she had impregnated, she stopped as a slight movement caught her eyes. Aezriane stared at the woman before she caught the tiny movement of the woman's belly. "Mother, what—"

Throaty laughter came from the altar. "My child, you did well. Even better than I knew. For already the children of the night are growing inside these hosts."

Aezriane caught another movement as the woman's belly seemed to extend by an inch or two. "How long, Mother, how long until these creatures—I mean my sisters—are born?"

"Two days, my daughter."

"That quick?"

"Yes, my daughter, two days and the first shall be born. A week later they will be big enough to unleash hell on the fairies."

"So where will I keep them for a week, Mother?"

That laugh again as Aezriane caught more movement from the other women. "You will not have to worry about that, daughter. These children are not your concern. They will have enough food here to meet their needs. You need to gather the seed from others to make more of my children."

Aezriane bowed her head. "It is as you say, Mother." She gathered her belongings together and started out the door. By the time she reached the entrance of the crypt, every woman's belly was moving from the hellish babes within them.

The succubus quickly shut the door of the birthing place and locked it. She drew protection wards on and around the heavy metal slab with blood she had taken from those inside. Wiping her arms with an old rag, she threw it to the side without another thought of what lay within. She faded into the early morning, as the warding faded from sight.

13

Sebastian's strident, faraway voice dragged me from my sleep. Ignoring the imp's chatter, I tried to snuggle back against the warm pillow that was Fallon's muscled chest. Sleep, sleep, and more sleep was what I needed after the long night of passion the fairy and I had shared. By the time we fell into an exhausted slumber, it had been about five thirty in the morning.

My body flushed recalling all we had done after Fallon had carried me into my bedroom after our loving session in my library. Gods above it had been worth every lost second of sleep. Every inch of my body felt relaxed. I stretched, bringing forth a low murmur from the sleeping form next to me as I tried to recapture the dreamless state I had been in.

The bedroom door slamming open along with the imp's shouting had me rolling off my bed and grabbing the weapon I had strapped to the bed frame. "I TOLD HER, SIN! I TOLD HER SHE COULDN'T COME IN HERE WITHOUT YOUR PERMISSION! I COULDN'T KEEP HER OUT OF—"

I came off the floor my feet planted with a two-handed grip on the forty-five as my eyes focused on the figure standing in the doorway. There stood a female fairy clad in golden armor from head to foot. A set of icy blue eyes peered from behind her open helm taking in my body before she let out a low sniff I took as disapproval. Whatever, she wasn't exactly my type either. Screw her.

The imp went silent as I cocked the pistol. "It's alright, Sebastian," I said before turning my attention back to the fairy. "Just so I know who I'm about to kill, who the hell are you? What are you doing bursting into my bedroom at—" I glanced at an old Mickey Mouse wind up clock on my dresser. "Fuck. Please tell me it isn't seven in the morning."

The fairy's eyes roamed my body from top to bottom before she leaned against the doorjamb. Arms crossed, she appeared unconcerned with the weapon pointed at her. She must not think I would shoot her. After being woken this early in the morning, all bets were off. "I have come for my betrothed. The Queen requires his presence at another killing and, yes, it is seven in the morning."

"Uh, awkward. I think I'll just go and make coffee. Yeah, that's what I think I will do, Sin," the imp said before he disappeared from the doorway.

I stared at the fairy trying to process her words through my sleep-addled mind. "I think maybe you have the wrong house, honey. There is only me and—" I stopped talking as I turned and gazed at the fairy who was lying quietly on my bed, basking in the afterglow of our all-night sex session. "And Fallon."

"My betrothed."

Fallon's blue sleep-filled eyes gazed back at me, a tiny smirk playing at the corners of his mouth. "I was going to tell you, my dragon, but this thing with the Were came up, and well, you know, we were busy last night."

I lowered the pistol to my side as I held a hand up to silence him. I turned back to the female fairy standing at the door of my bedroom. "Uh, do you think you can give us a little time here? I think maybe Fallon and I need to clear the air."

She glanced between the two of us. I could see the stubborn set to her jaw as Fallon sat on the edge of the bed. "Please, Rose, give us some time. We will be out after we have had a talk, me and my dragon."

The female fairy's face flushed. "Your mother—" Falling silent, she turned and marched out of the room and down the hallway. I walked over to the door, the pistol still in my hand wondering what would happen if I used it on the fairy still sitting in my bed. Just what would Queen Velocity do if I killed her only heir? Whatever it was, right now, I was thinking it would be worth it.

I closed the door, locking it. I turned and leaned against the cold hard wood taking in the body that had satisfied me so thoroughly last night. "So, Fallon, your betrothed, huh? Seems like a nice girl from what I can see."

The fairy eyed me. Eyed the pistol still in my hand. "Are you going to shoot me, my dragon?"

I stood thinking over my choices for a few seconds. "I just might, fairy." I was fighting the urge to shoot that insolent smile off his face and believe me it was a real struggle. Making what I hoped was the right decision, I eased the hammer back in place but didn't click the safety on. "I just might. It all depends on what you say next. Start talking."

Fallon patted the side of the bed next to him. "Come here, my dragon, I—"

"Oh, hell no, Fallon. I think I'll stay right here and you'll stay where you are until you tell me what the hell is going on. Got me?"

"As you say, my dragon," Fallon said as the smile faded.

"Good. So how about we start with exactly who this bitch is and why she thinks you two are going to be married. Yeah, I think that would be a great place to start this conversation."

"I was going to tell you about her, like I said, but—"

I stomped my foot, my anger flaring. I know childish, but damn the fairy's wife to be just burst into my room catching us in the afterglow of sex. And Fallon was acting as if it was no big deal. "AND YOU WERE GOING TO DO THIS WHEN? AFTER SCREWING MY BRAINS OUT AGAIN THIS MORNING? OR MAYBE AFTER YOU WERE MARRIED, FALLON? JUST TELL ME! WHEN EXACTLY WERE YOU GOING TO TELL ME?" Pissed, I flung my pistol at his head.

Lucky for the fairy he had quick reflexes. He caught the weapon in his hand and clicked the safety on before gingerly putting it on the bedside table next to him. "Feel better, my drag—"

"Don't you call me that, Fallon."

"But you are my drag—"

"I SAID DON'T CALL ME THAT, FAIRY ... I'm still not sure if I'm going to shoot you or not."

Fallon arched one eyebrow, the smirk returning to his lips as he glanced at the weapon sitting beside him. "Alright, Sin."

If that damn fairy thought for one second that was the only pistol I had hidden, he was sorely mistaken. Despite the fairy's indifference to my anger, I tried to calm myself and act mature about this whole situation. Or as mature as I was capable of right now. "So, what is going on here? Who the hell is she?"

The sheets barely covered the fairy. His chest was bare, and I stared at those muscles as he moved back to lean against the bed's headboard. I felt a flush of want creep through me. Oh shit. What the hell was wrong with me? I closed my eyes for a second. Damn fairy knew how to get to me.

Fallon looked amused as he got comfortable knowing the effect he was having on me. "My mother arranged for Rose and me to marry to unite our two families, my drag—Sin. Her family rules the largest house in Europe."

"How long have you known about this, Fallon? That you were going to marry this bit—this woman."

"Two weeks, Sin. We made the deal two weeks ago."

"So, last night—last night was what? A goodbye screw? Get in your last jollies with an inferior creature before you go off and marry some royal fairy and have little pointy-eared children with her? Is that what last night was, Fallon?"

"No, of course not, Sin. I would have told you before, but—"

"But what, Fallon? What kept you from telling me you were going to marry someone else, fairy?"

"I haven't seen you in the last three weeks, Sin. Besides, my marriage to Rose doesn't affect how I feel about you and our relationship."

"Oh really? And just how do you figure that, fairy? How did you figure I would be okay with this?"

Fallon grinned like the cat that just lapped up all the cream. "Yes, I have to marry Rose. Yes, we will have children together. I mean the whole idea of this marriage is to make my mother happy. She wants heirs, but that doesn't mean that you and I can't—"

"You're an ass!" The humor in the fairy's eyes died. "Oh, I have news for you, Fallon. You marrying that female makes all the difference in the world. What kind of a woman do you think I am?"

"Listen, my mother and my father were married, but that doesn't mean that she didn't have her advisor to—"

"Oh, so you think I'm going to be like Igmun? Is that it, Fallon? Stand by your side, next to your throne and be at your beck and call? Am I going to have my own private quarters? Some place we can screw whenever you feel like it?"

"It wouldn't be like that, Sin. Not like my mother and that old dragon."

"So, how would it be? Tell me how it would be? What are you going to do, Fallon? Leave a gold piece every time you leave my room?"

"Listen, Sin, it wouldn't be like that. I would never treat you like a whore. I don't love Rose. I love you, my dragon. Only you." I let the endearment pass. "Yes, you would have your own chambers. Chambers we would share."

"Yeah, right, share when you weren't with the wifey and the kids, you mean. Oh, be still my beating heart, I should be ever so grateful at the crumbs you would throw me."

The fairy hung his head. "I see that you are angry and not willing to listen. I figured you would jump at this chance to stop being a bounty hunter, to live in luxury. You could stop living in the gutter with the rest of these creatures. I thought you would want to rise above all this. I see that maybe I was wrong."

I stared at the fairy not quite believing what I was hearing. It was a good thing I had thrown my pistol at Fallon before. My hands opened and closed on empty air. "You think I would give up my life? My life as a bounty hunter so I could go to court to be—to be your whore? Because, no matter how you pretty it up, that's all I would be."

"Sin, I—I told you already it wouldn't be like that with you."

I straightened up from the door and moved across the room to my dresser. I leaned against the scarred wood as my life came crashing down around me. "Get out of here, Fallon. Get out of my room so I can get dressed and we can go see about this latest killing."

Fallon's mouth went slack. I almost would have laughed at the shock in his eyes if I hadn't been fuming. "I don't understand, Sin. I—we—"

"That's the problem, Fallon. I'm beginning to think you never understood who I was and I think I am finally seeing who you really are. Please get out of my room so I can get dressed. We have a job to do for your mother."

"Fine, if that is how you want it," the fairy said standing up. The sheet fell to the floor. A little part of me died when the sight of his body didn't bring about the feeling of want I had felt only what—was it just minutes ago?

"That is what I want, Fallon."

He grabbed his scattered clothes from where they lay. I stood quietly, my heart breaking little by little with each piece he picked up. Finally, he had all his stuff, and he stomped to the door.

I heard the click of the lock and glanced over at him. His face was like I had never before seen directed toward me. His nostrils flared as those icy eyes drilled into me. "If the gutter is where you want to be, Sin, then that is where you shall be. Just don't come crawling back to me when you find out what you gave up."

"Dragons never come crawling, fairy. You, more than anyone, should know all about dragon pride. And besides, I think I like the gutter. It has a better class of people in it."

Fallon's face shut down. He threw the door open and marched out of my bedroom. As the door slammed behind him, a single tear slid down my cheek and hit the floor. Maybe the imp had been right. Pride would be my death, eventually, but right now it was a source of pain I never expected to feel.

14

Sebastian put the kettle of water on the stove as Rose stalked into the kitchen. She stood in the middle of the room fuming, one hand grasping the hilt of her sword. The imp stood on the edge of the counter keeping an eye on the water for a few minutes before he cleared his throat. "So, you and Fallon, huh? When is the happy day? Are we invited? To the wedding, I mean."

The fairy scowled at him before she moved to another counter and leaned against it, her arms crossed over her chest. Sebastian waited for a response. "Okay, so we're the strong silent type. I'll take that as a big 'No' on the wedding invitation."

The water started to boil in the kettle. He reached up and grabbed a small jar of instant coffee from a shelf. He waved it in her direction. "Want a cup?" The fairy stared at him, her face a blank mask. "I'll take that as a 'No' also."

Sebastian poured himself a cup of coffee and was reaching over for the sugar when the fairy straightened up. "I don't see what she has that I don't. I mean I'm a full-blood fairy. And she is only some, some dragon. I mean why go slumming when he could have someone like me?"

The imp dumped a couple spoons of sugar into the cup and stirred as he gave the fairy a once over. "Guess sometimes men want a little something different, you know, exotic."

The fairy sniffed. "I saw nothing exotic about that creature. Why I could have torn her in half without trying. I am one of the finest warriors in our kingdom."

"Yeah, well, I wouldn't take Sin too lightly, fairy. She may be small, but she is a full-blooded dragon."

The fairy wrinkled her nose as though something bad had passed under it. "Dragon or no, I see no reason Fallon should wish to lie with such a creature as her. Why my breasts are—"

Sebastian held up a hand and waved it in the air. "Whoa, whoa. I have no desire to hear about your anatomy. Damn. Male imps don't like to talk about sex much less have it. What part of that do you other fae not understand? Let it alone, will you?"

"Male imps don't like sex?"

"No, fairy, we don't. As I said, we not only don't like sex, we hate talking about it, we hate hearing about it, we hate everything about it. Now can we talk about something else? Besides, Sin is my friend."

"You are right. It was not right for me to burden you with my problems, imp. You are an inferior creature and wouldn't understand the problems of your betters."

Sebastian stared at the fairy before shaking his head. "Yes, I can't see why Fallon wouldn't love such a warm-hearted girl like you." The fairy stared at the imp not sure just what he meant when Fallon came storming into the kitchen naked with his clothes in his hands.

"That dragon is going to drive me crazy. I—" He stopped in mid-sentence as he noticed the imp and the other fairy. Stalking over to the kitchen table, he threw his clothes on it before he started to get dressed.

It was quiet for a few seconds. Sebastian sipped his coffee. "So, is Sin coming? I have some information about how to kill the succubus."

Sitting on a bench, Fallon finished pulling his pants on and looked at the imp. "She will be out in a few minutes. She is getting dressed."

"I see no reason why we need that creature with us. We can handle this job all on our own."

Fallon stared at the cause of his current discomfort. "Are you the queen in this land, Rose? Do you make the rules?"

"Well no, but—"

The imp looked the female fairy up and down. "Rose? Really? Someone named you that? For reals?"

Ignoring the imp, she turned back to Fallon. "I'm not the queen yet, but when we marry and you become the king—"

"Yes, well, when that happens you can make the decisions about who works on these killings and who doesn't. Right now, my mother is the ruler of this land and she wants the dragon to work with us." Fallon stood and stomped his feet into his boots before he marched over to Rose. "So we will do exactly what my mother wants. Do—you—understand—me—my—betrothed?"

Rose's eyes dropped from Fallon's as she gritted her teeth. "Yes, my husband to be, I understand you perfectly. Whatever you and your mother say. That is what I will do."

I finished dressing making sure I had all my weapons, plus a few extras. I wasn't sure if I had added them because of the second killing, the feeling I might need them for Fallon's wife to be, or maybe I still might shoot that damn fairy. But no matter the reason. I would make sure I had all the firepower I needed from now on.

Stopping at the doorway of my bedroom, I looked back at the messy bed. Sheets and blankets were strewn all over the floor and, looking up, I could see yesterday's panties hanging from the ceiling light. A tiny sigh escaped my lips as I closed the door on that chapter of my life. There were more important things to take care of right now. My love life would have to wait.

Walking into the kitchen, I caught Fallon and Rose inches from each other. Anger was written all over his face and, as impossible as it seemed, she looked like she was about to cry. Now, what the hell was going on?

Sebastian waved an empty cup in the air. "So uh, Sin, you want some coffee?" Fallon backed away from Rose and went to sit at my kitchen table while grabbing his shirt and putting it on.

"Yeah, that would be great, Sebastian."

My partner poured some crystals from the cache of jars we had found months ago. I walked over to the stove and poured the boiling water into the cup he handed me. "Sugar, Sin?"

"No, I'll take it like this." I stirred the mixture in the cup eyeing the two fairies before sipping the dark liquid. Fallon was glaring at Rose. Her eyes were still locked on the floor. I took another sip, feeling the caffeine streaming through my blood. "So, who got killed, Rose?"

The fairy looked at me, anger set in her eyes and jaw. I didn't think she was going to answer me. Fallon slapped the table, the sound echoing off the walls. She threw him a quick look, her shoulders hunched. "Someone killed the leader of the vampires last night."

Shit. This was getting better and better. "Do they know if he had sex before he was killed?" Fallon said.

Sebastian snorted. "There wouldn't be enough left of him to tell, fairy."

Fallon ignored my partner and looked at me. "Yeah, what he said. Remember, when a vamp is killed, they turn to dust."

"Right. I thought maybe if a succubus killed the vamp like the Were—well, maybe the magic would work differently on him. I guess there was small hope of that though."

I had to give Fallon credit for that one. We all looked over at Rose. "From what I could tell, the vampire turned to dust as soon as he died his second death."

"Well, there could still be some residue from the succubus at the scene. We should check it out."

Rose's gaze went distant. "Uh, why would you think it is a succubus doing these killings? I thought they were all killed when we took over this world."

I finished the last of my coffee. "We found sex magic at the Were killing."

My partner fluttered into the air, a mischievous look in his eyes. "Boy, did they ever find sex magic. Why I had to—to—never mind."

Rose glared at me but dropped her eyes to the floor again as Fallon stood. Oh, I could see that would get old quick. I put my empty cup in the sink before turning back to Fallon. "Listen, I think we need to get a few things out in the open here."

"NO! All we need to do is find out who is doing these killings and stop them," Rose said before she turned and marched out of the kitchen.

My eyes followed the fairy out the door. Well, that went over just peachy. "Rose is right. Our main duty is to find the killer and take care of her. Your imp seems to think that he knows a way to kill it."

My eyes wandered over to Fallon. Seeing his face set as if in stone, I turned to look at Sebastian. "Okay, so how do we kill this succubus?"

"Basically, she is a demon. So, you trap her in a mirror and break it. Easy-peasy."

I thought back to the wolf's house. "Damn. The Were's mirror was broken."

Fallon rubbed his hand across his chin. "Yes, my dra—Sin, so it was. Your imp may be on to something." Now it was Sebastian's turn to glare at Fallon.

I figured I'd better step in before this pissing contest escalated. "Is there a spell, Sebastian, that we need to do or do we just get her to stand in front of a mirror?".

Sebastian turned to me anger still burning in his eyes. "You wish it was that easy, Sin. Yeah, you need a spell to get her inside the mirror. Then there's the whole warding the sides of the mirror bit but, of course, me being me, I found all that you need to trap this creature."

"Cool, let's find this bitch and shatter her into a million pieces."

"There is just one little problem, Sin."

"Isn't there always? So, what is it now, Sebastian?"

"It seems that the succubus can impregnate between ten and twenty women with the baby batter she takes out of each of her kills."

"Shit."

"And, of course, the children coming out won't be quite like their parents."

"Damn, is that all? What do you mean not quite like them? Not like them how?"

"From what I got from my reading, the creatures will be more mutated than their parents in strength and temper. Killing machines right from the womb. Oh, and they don't take nine months to bake in the oven. Such as it is."

I glared at my partner. I hated when he fed me bad news piece by piece. It was almost like he thought I would blow a fuse or something if he gave it to me in one huge chunk. "Oh great. How long?"

"For the Were, I would say maybe four to six months. For the vamps, a couple of days."

"You have to be shitting me. That means—"

"Yeah, if the succubus implanted them last night, right after she got the goods, the babies will show up tomorrow or the next day at the latest. Depending when she put the dough in the ovens, so to speak."

Fallon couldn't help but put his two cents in. "Are you always full of such good news?"

"Hey, lay off my partner, fairy. He didn't make the rules. He is just letting us know what the books say. It's not his fault you and your kind killed off these creatures and now they are coming back to look for revenge."

"Thank, Sin."

"No problem, Sebastian. Now are you going to sit there and grumble, fairy, or are we going to go out and find this thing and kill it before she uses her magic on someone else to make more little monsters?"

Fallon glared at me for a second then, without a word, he marched out of my kitchen. Sebastian seemed to enjoy watching him leave. "My, my, making friends left and right aren't you, Sin?"

"Bite me, imp." I followed Fallon out the door, Sebastian's laughter chasing after me.

15

Aezriane's eyes slid open as the last of the light fled the world. The smell of mildew, old urine, and ripened bodies filled her nose as she rose from the sagging mattress and crossed the room to look on the graveyard below. By all rights, she should be out tonight. Out looking for other donors, getting more of the seed she needed to create her sisters. But some inner sense of curiosity had kept her in the old human city. Almost a sense of pride. The need to see what she had created in that dark, dank crypt.

The graveyard and the house where she stood overlooked the city. From her windows, she could watch the night envelope those below. Lights from cooking fires and candles popped up here and there, marking the rundown buildings housing the humans who lived in the squalor of the once mighty city.

After a while, restlessness seeped into the succubus' body as she lost sight of the crypt below her to the dark. A restlessness that gnawed at her belly. Drove her to a wild madness to leave the room she had used for her day of sleep.

Below her, toward the water, a square was lit by a huge bonfire. Barely seen figures were dancing around the flames to an unheard melody. Her eyes wandered to the huge island that lay out in the bay. A smile slipped along her lips, before her eyes were drawn once more to those flames in the square.

A longing lit in her center, heating her core. The vamp last night had not quenched her fires as much as she had hoped. Maybe there would be some supernatural creature by that bonfire who could help her fulfill the itch she felt. And if not, who knew, maybe a human or two would. Maybe that would be for the best, she had been feeling her age of late. She could take energy from humans, and fix that little problem. Yes, that would be wonderful. Her tongue flicked across her lips at the thought.

The succubus' smile grew as she glanced down where the crypt stood before turning and walking toward the door of the bedroom. Yes, she deserved time to satisfy her needs what with all the work she had been doing for her mother the last couple of days. No sense in denying her own needs in this holy quest. She waved her hand over her naked body and a silver and red dress appeared, barely covering her lushness.

Darren and his four brothers sat at the outdoor table of the makeshift inn. Drinking the place's home-brewed crap from broken cups. The fire in the middle of the square lit the night. A night of celebration for him and his gang. He watched as his warriors drank, danced, and screwed the woman of his rivals, the Sharks, that they had defeated just this afternoon.

It had been a bloody battle, but the fight had gained them another five blocks of territory and would increase his fighting force by another eighty men. Of course, they had killed all the top men in the rival gang out of hand. As his would have been if he had lost today. That was just expected in the world they lived in.

Darren watched as four of his men pulled a naked, screaming woman from inside the inn and dragged her to stand in front of the table where he sat. His eyes danced over the young woman. A smile played across his lips, a smile that never reached his eyes. Taking in the rival gang's tats along her body, he locked his eyes on the group's leader. "Is that who I think it is? Where did you find her, Gene?"

"Yeah, it's the leader's whore, boss. We found her and five other sluts trying to cross over to Rats' territory just like you said they would."

Darren nodded as he contemplated the Rats. Another gang that had territory adjacent to his own. The Rats were the second biggest gang in the city next to his own. They had been trying to make a truce with the Sharks, a truce that would have spelled trouble for his gang. Just one of the reasons that Darren had taken over Shark territory. "Where are the other whores, Gene?"

"We gave them over to the commanders like you told us to, sir."

"Good. Good. You men did well finding them. This will earn all of you extra rations," Darren said as he stood from the table and drained the cup of piss that this place called liquor before slapping it back on the table.

"And her, sir?"

Darren's youngest brother stood as he drained his own cup and grabbed at his crotch. "We'll take care of this bitch ourselves, boys, won't we, Darren? That is before we give what's left of her to the vamps."

The rest of his brothers gathered around the table roared and pounded on the wood as the woman's head shook from side to side as fresh tears rolled down her face.

A voice floated from the dark corner of the inn. "Now that seems to be such a shame, boys. Having a piece of trash like that when you can have something a whole lot better."

All eyes swiveled toward the shadow. Darren's hand fell to the crude knife at his side. "Who are you? Come into the light."

A blonde woman slinked into the light cast by the fire. Her mesmerizing eyes capturing them all. The silver and red dress she wore shined and shimmered in the dancing flames. It pulsed to a rhythm that seemed to have a life all its own. "No problem, my good boys. I just thought you five might like something that could satisfy you better than the leavings from your defeated foe."

Their souls were lost in the blond hair and green eyes that promised wicked pleasures. Pleasures that not even these downtrodden men had ever seen. The night itself seemed to hold its breath as the men drank her in. Darren fought through the cloud covering his mind. "Who—who are you?"

The woman in red slithered over to the gang leader and rubbed a soft hand across his face, tracing it down his chest and below. "Does it matter who I am? What matters is: do you think you and your brothers are man enough to take me on, Darren?"

All of Darren's brothers were standing now, their glazed eyes locked on the woman. "I—We … You're a super, aren't you?"

She brought her hand to the gang leader's face and gave him two quick, sharp taps. "My, aren't you the bright one? Now, why don't you have your men take this woman away and we'll go find a place for us to play. What do you say, Darren?"

The leader stared at the woman, fighting to listen to the voice in his head that was screaming. Screaming a loud warning that going with this creature would be fatal. The succubus saw this and trailed one sharp fingernail down Darren's chest. A thin trail of blood followed her finger. She leaned into him, rubbing her body against his. "You know what they say, Darren. Once you been with a super, you'll never go back to a human."

The voice stopped screaming, now it whispered. 'Yes, you never go back because most of the time you die.' But the scent of the woman overrode that voice, pushing him past any reasoning. Inhaling the aroma of her heat filling the air, he waved a hand at Gene and his men. "You can have the Shark's whore. Do what you want with her."

His men dragged the woman away. Laughter filling the night as the blonde woman beckoned Darren and his brothers. "Very good. Now let us go find a place we six can have some fun." The four brothers followed Darren and the woman in silver and red as though in a trance as they headed toward the water.

Three blocks later, the group stopped before an old two-story warehouse. "Yes, this will do nicely, boys, don't you think?" The brothers stood in the middle of the rubbish strewn streets, their gaze locked on only one thing: The blonde in silver and red before them. Aezriane laughed at the lost look each man wore before grabbing the front of Darren's shirt and leading him inside the building.

The others followed like obedient sheep. Inside the door and up the stairs. Into a room that had numerous mattresses spread around the concrete floor. The succubus whirled around taking in the building's shell. "Yes, this will do nicely indeed."

She let go of Darren's shirt and waved his brothers toward her. As they formed a circle around the woman, she waved her hand at four of the men. "Sleep."

They folded as though they had no bones inside their bodies. Each man was out before he hit the floor. Aezriane slinked over to Darren and snapped her fingers under his nose, rousing the gang leader from his stupor. His eyes took in the empty dark space and his brothers lying on the ground. "Where the hell are we? What did you do to my brothers, bitch?"

"My, my, aren't we a touchy one, Darren?"

"If you know what is good for you, whore, you'll answer my questions. Where—" Darren's voice cut out as the woman swiped one finger across his lips. Panic filled the leader's eyes as he struggled to talk.

His face turning red, Darren took a step toward her, his huge hands raised as though to wrap them around the woman's throat. "Oh, I don't think so, Darren." She waved her hand at the man. His legs and arms snapped to his side before he fell backward to the floor.

The succubus walked over to him and looked at the helpless human. Fear, panic, and a touch of anger warred within his eyes. "Oh, don't be such a spoilsport, Darren. You're going to enjoy this—well, at least until the end. Then, well, you'll have served your purpose." Aezriane glanced at the others lying on the ground. "Maybe you can find comfort in knowing your brothers will join you very soon."

She kneeled at the man's side and ran her hand up and down his body as his whimpers fought through sealed lips. Her hands sought the zipper of Darren's pants. "Hush now, my boy. It will be over soon."

Pulling his shaft from his pants, she giggled at his limp state. "Now, now, this won't do at all, Darren. No. Not at all. You should be embarrassed, this is no way a big badass like you should be."

The gang leader sucked in what breath he could as the creature lowered her head. Her hair brushed his thighs as her mouth worked him over. His eyes closed, she soon had him moaning, his head reared back.

Lust overrode his fear as his hips bucked, his mind lost in the pleasure that her mouth and tongue were giving him. Aezriane lifted her head. Darren sobbed in frustration despite the danger his mind told him he was in. She slowly moved her hand up and down his shaft. "Oh, don't worry, Darren. I plan to give you the best sex you'll ever have in your life."

The gang leader's eyes went wide as the creature hiked up her dress and straddled his hips. Her hot, bare, wetness swallowing him as her hips slammed onto his. A low hiss escaped her as she looked into his eyes.

"Now, my dear boy, let us waste no more time and get to the main event, shall we?" Slowly she pulled the top of her dress down so that it pooled at her waist. Darren gazed at the hardened nipples as Aezriane moved her hips back and forth and leisurely up and down his rock-hard shaft.

As she rode him, she could feel the life force seeping out of the human and into her own body. Between that and the friction of her movements, she could feel the crest of her orgasm building.

She looked into the human's eyes just as she hit her peak and she fell over the crest as he filled her with his seed and the last of his life force. He threw his head back as the light died in his eyes. She finished riding him bringing herself to another orgasm.

After a few more seconds, she stopped her movement. "You humans. You just don't last long." Glancing around the room selecting her next victim, she climbed off the dead human husk. "Good thing I brought some spares with me."

Hours later, Aezriane woke from a quick nap and stretched as she walked to the window looking out over the bay. Stopping, she stared, in a broken mirror, at her nude body. She looked ten years younger. Around her, the five dried out husks of the brothers lay.

At least humans were better than supers for one thing. A little gift that her mother had given her that only worked on the non-super: The ability to drain the life force of humans to add years to her life.

She watched as the night moved on. The stars and a partial moon lighting the dockside below. The feeling of being sated made her smile as her body glowed in the few flickering candles that lit the darkened room.

Movement below caught her eyes, and she shifted to the corner of the window as three people came down the road that lined the water. She took in the two fairies and—and was that a dragon? Her anger flared mixed with fear at the sight of the creature below her.

"Damn." She saw the dragon's head swivel around. Her heart seemed to skip a beat as her breath came in shallow gasps at the sight of the creature.

She looked behind her at the bodies and back to the three waiting at the edge of the water. Getting her breathing back under control, she slipped out of the room. She must get back to the crypt and keep an eye on it, especially if those damn fairies had brought in a dragon to try to hunt her down.

16

We took most of the day and half the night to travel through the fairy gates to reach our destination. Well, not quite our final one, but close enough. We stood on an old pier in what was left of the human city of San Francisco. Sebastian perched on my shoulder, Rose and Fallon standing side by side as we looked out over the dark bay at an island barely seen in the distance. "So just how in the hell are we going to get all the way out there? You do know imps don't swim, right, fairy? In fact, if no one told you we are actually allergic to water. I mean we don't even use water to bathe."

Fallon sniffed the air. "I was wondering what that smell was."

The night hid my smile from the imp. "Someone will come across soon. They were told we were coming," Rose said.

The murky city was at our back. After the years of neglect by the humans who called it home, it looked like the picked over bones of a massive beast lying among the surrounding hills. Sounds of things scurrying in the alleyways along with the cries of the humans packed within the desolate buildings made the hairs on my neck stand up. This was not the best place for four supernaturals to be waiting on their own, no matter how well armed and armored they were.

Sniffing the air, I caught a trace of a cloying scent. It seemed to play on the light night breeze. I searched the windows around us but saw nothing as the scent vanished. I turned, ignoring the city behind us as I stared out at the island. "So, this 'king' of the vamps had his home out there?"

"Yes. He thought it best if he had his main headquarters at the old human prison. Plus—" Rose glanced back at the outline of the broken city behind us, "it is safer for the vamps than on the mainland."

"Plus, they're closer to their food right, fairy?"

Rose and Fallon stiffened at the imp's voice. "The only humans sent out to the prison are those who commit capital crimes against supernaturals, imp. You know that as well as anyone here."

Yeah, right, and I'm an elf. They only allowed the vamps to feed on humans accused of capital crimes alright. It was just that the fairies decided what was a capital crime. The fairies sent the accused to 'The Rock' as the old island used to be called as punishment. To keep the vamps in check, the fairies had to supply a steady stream of humans or the vamps would find their food elsewhere. I found it hard to believe that many humans were committing those kinds of crimes.

The creak of oars roused me from my musings as a shadowy shape emerged from the night. Rose stepped toward the edge of the pier as the shadow took the shape of a long boat. "Ho. Edge, is that you?"

A voice floated across the water from the dark as the long boat bumped the side of the pier. "Who the hell do you think it is, my lady? Keep your voice down unless you want half the city brought down on us."

The large fairy standing in the bow reached out and grabbed one of the old worm-eaten posts and hung on as another fairy at the aft did the same. "Come on. Get aboard so we can shove off," he said as he eyed the shadows behind us. As though to emphasize his words, a bottle came flying from one of the dark alleyways and landed at our feet and smashed into a thousand pieces.

As soon as the four of us were onboard the ship, Edge grunted as he pushed off from the pier. "You're late, cousin," Fallon said not intimidated by the fairy despite the size difference. Edge stood over him by a good three inches and probably outweighed him by a hundred pounds or more, none of it fat. I had always wondered if somewhere down his line, Edge might have a touch of goblin blood in him. Not that anyone would be stupid enough to say that to his face. Not if they wanted to live, that is.

He glanced over at me, ignoring Fallon and gave me a quick smile and a wink. "Glad to see the queen took Igmun's advice and brought you in on this, dragon. This is a nasty one." Another reason I liked Edge. He didn't walk around like he had a stick up his ass, like most of his kind did.

I watched as Fallon flushed with anger. "I said, cousin. You—"

Edge spun around and stared at Fallon with cold blue eyes. The fairy's mouth snapped shut, and it was quiet on the boat, except for the sound of the oars as the boat pulled away from the shore. "I know I'm late, cousin. We had a few things to iron out with those damn bloodsuckers before we came to pick you up."

I stepped between the two fairies, trying to defuse the situation. We had enough problems without these two males getting into a measuring contest. "Put down the rulers and put 'em back in your pants, boys. So what's the problem, Edge?"

Edge's eyes warmed as he turned to me. "Nothing I couldn't handle, Sin. It just seemed that the bloodsuckers didn't want us on their island."

"Think they are hiding something, Edge?"

"Could be, Sin. I finally got it through their thick undead skulls that we were only on their island to investigate their leader's death and nothing more. Still, they were pretty pissy about it. Even for stuck up bloodsuckers."

"Why would they think we cared about anything, but their leader's death? Once the humans are sent to that island, your queen could not care less what happens to them, right?" Rose said.

I thought back to the conversation with the rogue vamp before he offed himself. "Yeah, unless they are turning humans." Sebastian yanked the lock of my hair he held bringing me back to the situation at hand.

Edge's eyes bored into my own. "What was that, Sin? What do you know that we don't?"

"Nothing, Edge, it was just a thought."

"Yeah, well, that is one nasty thought, dragon. If the vamps are turning humans on that island, we could have a big problem on our hands."

"Impossible, cousin. You know that my mother has fairies check how many humans are sent out to the prison. They are allotted just enough humans to feed on and no more."

I glanced back at the darkened city fading behind us. "And what if the vamps are coming off their island and taking humans from the city?"

Fallon was indignant. "They wouldn't dar—" Cutting off his own protest, he looked back at the city. It was quiet the rest of the way across the water.

As the city faded behind us, I could see the island in the middle of the bay seemingly grow out of the sea. The oars stroking the water was soothing and steady as we slid toward a single light that dangled at the edge of the old stone pier. Rose and Fallon were at the aft end of the boat having a heated discussion while my partner was flittering around somewhere. Probably causing mischief knowing him. I was enjoying the quiet, my mind wandering over how fast things could change in life. I heard a footstep behind me, rousing me from my thoughts. "So Sin, about Rose and my cousin?"

"Yeah, I know about them, Edge. In fact, I found out about them when she came busting into my room this morning."

The huge fairy scratched the back of his head. "I take it Fallon was there in bed with you?"

"What do you think?"

"Yeah, figured that. Sorry."

"Why should you be sorry, Edge? It wasn't you that took me to bed without telling me you were to be married. Besides, I'm a big girl. I knew this thing would never last between us. Either his mother would interfere"—I threw a quick glance toward the back of the boat—"or he would tire of slumming and settle down with one of his own kind."

"Well, be that as it may, my cousin was never tactful. And as for slumming. You are not like some of these creatures living in the cesspool of this world, Sin."

Even Edge. Though he was one of the better fairies, he too had a bit of that higher than thou attitude. "You may be right, Edge, but at the end of the day, I'm just a dragon. Not a fairy. So, I guess I stay in this shithole where I belong. Right?"

"I—"

The sound of angry footsteps echoed over the water. "This is none of your concern, cousin."

We both turned seeing the fairy standing a few feet away, his face white in anger as those icy blue eyes bore into Edge's. Edge gave him a little bow. "As you say, cousin. It is none of my business. We will be docking in a few minutes. I need to go and see that my warriors are ready," he said as he brushed past Fallon.

Fallon watched him stroll toward the middle of the long boat, before turning his gaze to me. "I don't appreciate you talking about our troubles to others, my dragon."

I stepped up to the fairy, my hand on my knife. "First off, if you call me 'my dragon' again I'll cut off something you'll need to bed your wife. Second, 'we' have no troubles because there is no 'we'. Third, you can kiss my ass." I brushed past him. His jaw dropped as I followed Edge toward the middle of the ship.

Sebastian landed on my shoulder. "I bet that wasn't the first time you told that fairy to kiss your ass, Sin. Of course, the other times I bet you meant it differently, huh?"

I shrugged my shoulders, knocking the imp back into the air as I heard Edge chuckle. "Screw the both of you."

The fairy had a hurt look on his face as he put his hand to his chest. "Who me, Sin? I'm just an innocent." Even I couldn't stay mad at the two of them as a small grin tugged at the corner of my mouth.

"Yeah, innocent, my ass," I said as the side of the long boat touched the dock. Two of Edge's warriors hopped out of the ship and tied off the ends. A shadow detached itself from the darkness and glided toward us.

A tall, skinny vamp clothed all in black came to a stop under the only light on the pier. "It is about time you have arrived. The dawn will come soon and I wish you off my island by then."

"And you are who?" Fallon snarled as he hopped to the stone pier turning to reach a hand down to help me from the ship. Catching a quick glance at Rose and the flash of anger in her eyes, I ignored the offering and jumped to the pier.

Fallon shot a look of annoyance my way before turning to Rose with the offered hand. I had to give the female fairy credit, she knocked the hand aside and hopped up on the pier much to the amusement of Edge and his warriors. Even the vamp's lips seemed to twitch up for a second.

The vamp straightened as he brushed some imaged dirt from his jacket and the sound of his teeth grinding sounded in the quiet night. "I am the king of the vamps and in charge of—"

Edge leaped from the long boat and landed on the pier next to me. "There is no king here. The only ruler of this land is our queen, bloodsucker."

The vamp gazed at Edge for a few seconds before turning his attention to Fallon. "Be that as it may, I am in charge on this island and demand that you be gone from our home before the sun rises. Besides, we have the one that killed our king."

Fallon took a step forward, poking the vamp in the chest. "You are in no position to demand—"

I saw more shadows detach themselves from the dark. Great, more vamps. I needed to diffuse this situation before it turned into a blood bath. I stepped between the vamp and the fairy. "Whoa. Whoa, boys. What is it with you males? Let's stop the pissing contest and get down to the job we're all here for. We're supposed to be finding out what is killing supernaturals." I turned my attention back to the vamp. "And for your information, whoever you're holding is probably innocent. We think a succubus is doing the killing."

The vamp held up a hand stopping his advancing undead. He gazed at me for a second before taking a step backward. "The dragon is right. As long as you are truly here for your stated purposes and leave before the sun is up, there will be no trouble."

"Okay, see how well we can all get along? So, just to start off on a better foot—what is your name?"

The vamp gave me a slight bow. "I am called Dark One."

My partner snickered as he buried his head in my hair next to my ear. "Did your mother name you that?"

I guess the vamp's hearing was excellent, much better than Sebastian thought. He glared at my partner as I jostled the imp. "Not helping, Sebastian." I tried to distract the vamp so we wouldn't have another killing. "So, how about we get to the house of your 'king' and check out where the murder happened?"

The vamp gazed at Sebastian and me for a few seconds. I thought for sure he would try to kick us off the island. Then he turned and started up the pathway to the old prison as he called back to us, "Follow me."

"I guess we follow him," I said.

17

As we drew nearer to the prison, the cries of humans cut through the dark night. Vamps and fairies alike seemed to be immune to the sounds of anguish that hung on the night breezes.

My head kept swiveling to the huge dark structure that dominated the island. My partner leaned in so only I could hear him. "Leave it be, Sin. We aren't here for the humans. Remember?"

I knew he was right, but— "So, Dark One. Seems the natives are a little restless."

The vamp leading us up the path gazed at me for a second totally ignoring the sounds coming from the prison. "It is none of your business, dragon. You are only here for the death of Spartacus and nothing more. These prisoners are ours to do with as we wish. "

"Yeah, I know. I was just saying—"

"We are here. The house that our king lived in," the vamp said as he came to a stop in front of what looked like a recently built little ranch house.

Fallon took in the human-like house. "Spartacus lived here?"

"Yes, our king was old. The oldest of us in this country. He wanted a place where he could retire to meditate on his own. Away from—" the vamp glanced at the prison and the noise of human misery coming from it.

"Yeah, I can understand that," I said as I tried to shut out the sounds from my mind.

The vamp sniffed before turning to Fallon. "I have business to attend to. Justin will see to anything you need." He nodded at an emaciated human standing at the side of the house. "Remember you are to be gone before the sun rises."

Fallon looked like he was going to protest. I stepped in front of him giving the vamp a little bow and my sincerest smile. "Thank you, Dark One. I'm sure we won't need much time to finish our investigation."

"Yes, see that you don't," he said before disappearing into the night.

Fallon looked like he was going to burst a blood vessel. "Listen, Sin, I don't like—"

I turned and slammed a hand into his chest. "No, you listen to me. We need to get into that house. We need to find any evidence that shows the succubus is our killer. That is if the creature left anything for us to find. Then we need to get our asses off this rock in one piece."

"I agree with the dragon, cousin."

Fallon's face was a mask of confusion. "Why? What?"

I frowned at the fairy then glanced at the prison. "I don't have any concrete reasons. Just a gut feeling, okay?"

Fallon's eyes followed mine as a loud scream echoed from the concrete building. "Well, tell me what your gut is telling you, Sin."

I glanced at the human standing at the door of the house and shook my head. "Now is not the time, Fallon."

The fairy gave the human a quick once over, taking in the glazed expression and slack-jawed look on his face. "It is only a human, not much of one at that."

"You need to get out of that damn castle you live in, Fallon. You need to get into the gutter. You'll learn things. Like how some older vamps can enthrall their human servants so they can see through their eyes and talk through their mouths."

Three sets of fairy eyes darted to the human giving him a wary look. "Fine. Let's get this over with. Rose, you and my cousin stay out here and keep an eye out for trouble while Sin, her imp, and I will go inside and check things out."

The female fairy's face set in a stubborn look. "Why should I stay out here while these creatures get to go inside?"

"Because you have already been inside and, most importantly, because I told you to stay out here, bitch. Now if there are no more arguments from anyone, I suggest we get inside and check out the scene of the killing before the sun comes up."

I watched as Fallon stood, fists clenched, as he glared at Rose. Edge's mouth stood open large enough I think even Sebastian could fly inside it. Hearing those hateful words from Fallon something inside of me truly died. I swore to myself that no matter what happened between the two fairies, Fallon and I were over for good. I had never seen this side of him, but now that I had I would never let him talk to me that way.

Fallon glanced around, our silence speaking volumes. Even the misery from the prison seemed to be quieter after his outburst. He stiffened before turning and stalked over to the human. "Unlock the house so we may enter."

The human didn't say a word as he turned and unlocked the door before resuming his earlier position. "Are you coming in, dragon?" Fallon threw open the door and stomped into the house without waiting to see if I would follow.

"Come on, Sin. Let's get this over with and off this island," Sebastian said as he tugged on the lock of hair he had in one hand. I followed the fairy inside without another word to the others.

Stopping just inside the door, I saw an alarm panel beside it. "Sebastian? Think you can check out the vamp's security network without getting in trouble?"

The imp flew off my shoulder casting me a hurt look. "Please, dragon, just who do you think you're talking to? Me? Get in trouble? Pleassse."

"Just watch yourself, partner. I don't trust these vamps after the one offed himself like he did."

That stopped the imp as his face went serious. "Good point, Sin." He flew within inches of my face and glanced over his shoulder. "And you keep an eye on that fairy, Sin. I think he is losing it. I mean you and him—"

I waved one hand cutting off the imp. "After that little scene outside, it will be a cold day in Hell before there ever is a him and me again, Sebastian."

The imp studied my face for a few seconds before giving me a quick nod and flying off toward one of the side rooms. From the back of the house, I could hear Fallon's low voice and headed off toward it.

Following a short hallway, I saw two doors to either side and one at the end. The first door led to a full bathroom. I looked around, seeing a huge garden tub, big enough to fit five people. The next room was an office, its walls lined with books ranging from old human paperbacks to honest-to-goodness scrolls.

Staring at the shelves, all on their own my feet started to enter the room when I heard Fallon's voice and another softer one from the back of the house. I took one last wistful look at the books before sighing. I headed to the last room.

The first thing I noticed when I came into the room was the king-size bed with the large pile of ash lying in the middle. It was vamp size with four smaller piles leading toward each of the bedposts. Definitely a dead vamp and by the looks of it he died chained just like the Were. Then there was that underlying scent. That scent I had smelled at the Were's and—somewhere else. I sniffed the air in frustration trying to pick it up again, but it was gone.

I was snapped out of my daydreams—or maybe at this point nightmares—by Fallon's high-pitched voice. "There you are, dragon. Took you long enough to find your way back here."

I turned and looked over at the annoyed fairy. One eyebrow cocked. "I'm not Rose. Never take that tone with me again, fairy, or you'll regret it. Understand?" I know I was taking out my frustration at not identifying that smell, but what the hell. No fairy uses that tone with me.

I could see the annoyance turn to anger before Fallon huffed and turned to a petite human female sitting in an old rocking chair. She was so small, for a second, I took her for a child. Until her eyes met mine. Her face was young, but those eyes told a story of pain, misery, and something more. Something someone that young should never have lived through.

Her voice was soft, tiny like her as her pained eyes seemed to look into my soul. "You're a dragon, aren't you?"

I took in hair so blonde it was almost white and light blue eyes. She definitely had some fairy blood in her down the line. "Yes, I'm a dragon. Who are you?"

"I'm Sadie. I was …"—her eyes darted to the bed—"that was my master."

"I was just questioning the girl here trying to find out what she knew. So far, she has been less than forthcoming, dragon."

I watched as Fallon's harsh voice washed over Sadie. Her eyes dropped to the ground and her head hunched between her shoulders as though the fairy had delivered a blow.

"Here's an idea. How about you quit being a dick and go see how Sebastian is doing with the alarm system? Sadie and I'll talk, girl-to-girl."

Fallon stood; his face flushed. I could see a tiny smile flit across the girl's face. It disappeared as the fairy glanced at her before he strutted out of the room without a word to either of us.

"You shouldn't make fairies mad at you, dragon. They can do horrible things to you. Things that—" Sadie's eyes lost focus and peered into the past as her body shuddered.

I crossed the room and kneeled before the girl, looking deep into those eyes. They were like looking into the darkest parts of her soul. "Why are you here, Sadie?"

A sad smile played across her lips as she came back to the present. "How I got here is of no importance, dragon."

"My name is Sin."

The waif's smile brightened as she nodded. "Thank you for giving me your name, Sin."

"It's my name. No big deal."

Her eyes went wide as that mouth formed a tiny 'O'. She slowly shook her head from side to side. "You should never think that, Sin. Knowing a person's name can be very important. In the olden days, some used it to perform dark acts against others."

"You mean those silly stories of human witches and the spells they cast on the supers? Those are just old tales meant to scare creatures like us and gave the fairies a reason to kill off humans with any taint of magic."

"Think what you will, Sin, but the stories were true."

That was all well and fine, but right now, there were more important things to talk about than some old bogeyman stories. I glanced over at the bed then back at Sadie. "Can you tell me about what happened here?"

"I—I was here, but I was working in the office. I fell asleep. They woke me later in the night and told me I had killed my master, but I don't remember anything."

"Don't worry. I know you didn't kill him."

"Thank you, Sin. I'm not used to being believed. You've been so kind."

"Yeah, I can see that. So, you know nothing except you fell asleep? Right?"

"Well, yes, and—" The girl hesitated as she looked at the floor.

"And what? Any little thing can help us, Sadie. Just tell me."

The girl frowned then gave me a small nod. "Well, when I was woken by the other masters before they brought me here to await your arrival, I noticed that someone had broken the mirror in our bathroom."

"You don't think it was the vamps"—the girl winced at the slang—"that broke the mirror when they came in here, do you?"

"No. Spartacus bought that mirror especially for me. Most masters have this thing about mirrors, they avoid them. In fact, most masters will go out of their way to never be in the same room as one. I guess maybe it has to do with not being able to see their reflection. It is another reminder they don't have a soul anymore. Or at least that is what I think."

"Right, so the Were and the vamp had broken mirrors in the house. Interesting. I guess the imp's research may be spot on."

"What Were and what imp are you talking about, Sin?"

"Nothing for you to worry about. I was just talking to myself. So, I'll just let the Dark One know that you aren't responsible for your master's death and all will be alright, okay?"

The girl's voice was so soft, I could barely hear it. "If you say so, Sin."

I gently raised the girl's head. "Sadie, tell me what will happen to you after we're gone? You didn't kill your 'master'. So, you should be just fine, right?"

The girl's soulful eyes stared into mine for seconds that seemed to stretch into an eternity. "I think that—" Her eyes went wide and turned a deep dark red. Her arms gripped mine with a strength that belied her tiny size. "You must look to the graveyard on the hill. The undead children are born in the unholy crypt—"

'HOLY CRAP!' my brain screamed as I twisted my arms out of those hands. The violence of that act landed me on my ass as Sadie moaned and her eyes shifted back to their original color.

Confusion was writ all over the girl's face as she looked at me. "Sin, what are you doing down there? I—I—" The confusion cleared as terror and tears filled her eyes. "I did it again, didn't I? I went away and said something—that's why you're down there, aren't you? That's why you're frightened of me."

"What are you, Sadie?"

The girl hitched in a quiet sob. "My mother was a witch. My father was a high court fairy."

"What did you do to end up here?"

"My mother was a witch. My father was a high court fairy."

I wasn't surprised since I knew a bit about fairy politics, hanging around with Fallon. "Okay, who sent you here?"

"Queen Velocity sent me here when I was a little girl. I think maybe forty years ago or so. It's so hard to keep track of time on the island."

I stared at Sadie, refining my perception of her age. "Why would she do that though?" Then I thought of the queen and Fallon's tale of what she had done to Sarah, Fallon's lover, and figured that was a stupid question. Sadie's eyes mirrored my thoughts, and I barked out a laugh. "Okay, stupid question. Who was your father, Sadie?"

"My father was the queen's younger brother." That explained a lot right there alright and put a new light on just how far that fairy bitch would go to keep her family blood 'pure'.

I sat there thinking for a few minutes before I got up off my ass and kneeled next to Sadie. "Does Fallon know about you? I mean that you're family? That you're related?"

She looked at me puzzled. "No, I don't think so. I mean why would it matter? Related how?"

"Fallon is the queen's son, Sadie."

Her eyes darted to the door, then back to me. "You won't tell him … I mean he wasn't even born when I was sent here. He could make my life here a living hell if his mother found out about me. I mean found out I was still alive."

I rubbed her hands that were twisting in her lap. "I won't say anything to him, Sadie. Besides, you're not staying here. You're coming with me."

Her eyes lit up as her hands stopped their dance. "I am?"

"Yes, you are."

The light dimmed as she gazed at me. Suspicion playing across her face. "Why? I mean why would you take me with you?"

"I won't leave you here with the vamps. Besides you may have helped us find some monsters."

Sadie stared hard into my face for a few seconds, before she leaped from her chair. "Can we leave now, Sin?"

"Sure." I stood and brushed off the back of my pants. The two of us headed toward the door. I figured now all I had to do was convince the fairies we needed Sadie to catch the creature and the vamps she needed to be with us. What could be easier than that?

18

Fallon stood red-faced, arms across his chest. Edge, Sadie, and Rose had been quietly standing around for the last five minutes as the fairy and I had a heated 'discussion' about taking Sadie with us. "No, dragon, we aren't taking this creature with us. I don't care what you think she knows. She is here for a reason."

"Listen, fairy, she has powers I think we can use. She has already told me where we can find the babies that came from the vamp. Now, are we going to stand around here arguing and wasting time? Or are we going to go kill these monsters, before they kill some of your kin? This is an argument you know you are going to lose in the end."

Fallon's eyes darted between Sadie and me as he bared his teeth, but it was Edge that I was keeping an eye on. He was gazing at Sadie, his eyes narrowed as he rubbed his chin. I knew that he was about ten or twelve years older than Fallon and I hoped that he hadn't recognized her.

Finally, Fallon blew out a breath as he threw his arms in the air. "Fine, if you're so fired up to have her along, just fine. You'll need to get the vamps to agree to let us take her off the island and—" He glanced at the horizon that had just the hint of pink along its edge. "They are probably ready to bed down for the day and we have to leave before daylight. Remember, dragon?"

One hurdle down. Ignoring Fallon, I turned to the human who had never once moved from his spot after he had locked the house back up. "Dark One, we need this one to find the killer of your king."

The human's eyes focused as the body straightened. "I hear you, dragon, but this one is ours. They sent her here as punishment."

"What? Is her punishment more important to you than finding the one that killed your king, Dark One?"

It was quiet for a few seconds as the light went out of the human's eyes. "They'll never let her go, Sin. Give it up. We need to go now so we are gone before first light," Edge said.

"She will be released to you, dragon, but you will return her once her usefulness is done, that is our condition. Understand?"

I looked at the three fairies as their eyes darted between the human and me. "Yeah, sure, no problem, Dark One," I felt a slight tug on my hair from the imp perched on my shoulder. Flicking a finger at my partner, I had already made up my mind; Sadie was not coming back. But, hey, what old Dark One didn't know wouldn't hurt him, right?

"Dragon, you will give me your word that this one will be brought back to us."

Shit looks like things were getting serious. "Yeah. Yeah, sure, Dark One. You have my word, I will return Sadie as soon as I have no use for her."

"Very good, dragon. Just remember one does not live long if a promise to the undead is broken."

My hand instinctively dropped to my weapon. "Is that a threat, Dark One?"

There was a hint of dark amusement in the voice issuing from the human. "No, dragon. No threat. A promise. Now be gone from our island." The human's eyes went blank as his body sagged within itself. He turned and plodded up the path toward the prison.

Fallon watched the human disappear before glancing over at Sadie and then me. "I hope you know what the hell you're doing, dragon. The vamps are not known to take kindly to a double cross."

"Yeah, whatever, let's get out of here, guys," I said as I took hold of Sadie's hand and led her down the path to the boat.

I took in Sadie's strained eyes and clenched jaws from the corner of my eye and gave her hand a little squeeze. "Don't sweat it, girl. Everything will be alright."

My partner leaned in close so only I could hear. "You have no intention of bringing her back here, do you, Sin?"

"Sure, I do, Sebastian. Just as soon as I have no use for her. Just like I promised. I just didn't say when that will be."

"Why do you do this, Sin? Why not just adopt a tiger or a three-headed ogre? Why can't we have a simple life, without all the complications and the attitude?"

"Hell, life would be boring without a few complications. Besides, attitude is everything. You know that, partner."

Sadie glanced at the imp before looking at the ground. "The creature is right, Sin. You should not lie to the masters. They will not take kindly to being tricked."

"You let me worry about the vamps, Sadie. Now, we need to find this hill with the graveyard—" I stopped talking as the fairies leaped onto the boat and I stared at the land across the bay.

Edge helped Sadie into the boat and turned to me. "What is it, Sin? Come on. Let's get off the bloodsuckers' island before they change their mind."

I glanced back at the prison before hopping into the long boat. "It can't be that easy."

Fallon scanned the horizon. "What can't be easy? What is it, dragon? What is your problem now?"

"Hey, Edge, can I see that spyglass you own?"

The fairy gingerly opened a fur-lined pouch and handed me a gold tube with glass at each end. "Just be careful with it, Sin. My father gave it to me before he died."

I tuned out the fairy as I opened the tube and looked through the smaller end. It took a second for me to find what I was searching for, but there it was. An old broken-down church on a hill. With a two-story house next to it. A rusted fence ran along the back of the buildings and inside I could see several crosses and smaller buildings. "There is our graveyard on the hill," I said handing the spyglass back to Edge.

It was almost noon by the time we got back to the mainland, through the city, and up the hill to the graveyard I had spied. Edge had left ten of his warriors back on the long boat to guard it against any humans who got it in their mind that it was easy pickings.

That left us with twenty warriors to accompany us on our quest. For the most part, we didn't have any trouble with the locals. For some reason, they seemed leery of so many supers marching through their territory.

Fallon was in a foul mood throughout our travels as once again he had lost an argument with me before we had set out on the march. He had wanted to leave Sadie back on the boat and there was no way I was going to leave her out of my sight. I won when I reminded him that if it wasn't for her, we wouldn't even know where the possible baby incubator was. That seemed to shut him up. Though it didn't keep him from throwing dirty looks my way.

We all stood outside the fence around the old graveyard. Fallon sneered at Sadie standing beside me. "Well, where are the monsters, girl?"

Sadie's head dropped as she leaned against me so hard, I thought we would become one. "Leave her alone, fairy. There could be another graveyard on a different hill."

"So, what are we supposed to do? Check out every one of them?"

Rose had been quiet the whole march through the city, until now. "It's our best option, my husband to be." She walked up to the rusty gate and swung it open. The old hinges screamed in protest sounding like the ghosts were warning us away.

Edge struggled to hide his amusement bringing Fallon's icy dark eyes his way. Nonchalant, the huge fairy nodded after Rose. "What? She has a point, cousin." He turned and, ignoring Fallon, issued directions to the warriors standing around. "Well, don't just stand there with your thumbs up your asses. Get in there and find that crypt."

His men jumped at the roar of his voice and they followed Rose into the graveyard. He turned and gave me a quick wink as he followed them through the gate. I turned to Fallon. "Well, shall we?" Without waiting for an answer, I took hold of Sadie's hand and started after Edge.

"This is a huge waste of—"

Fallon's cutting remark was cut short as a voice close to the house yelled, "I think I found it. Over here." I threw a grin over at the frowning fairy, without saying a word, before heading toward the broken house.

I didn't quite catch what he muttered as Sebastian tugged on my hair. "You know, Sin. I know you two are over and all, but do you think it is wise to piss off the queen's son at every turn?"

"Screw him, Sebastian. If he'd stop being a dick, I wouldn't have to keep slapping him down."

"I think you have already done enough of that. You know with goblins, orcs, and vamps pissed at you already, you would think it would be prudent to at least be friendly with the fairy. You know, just so you have one type of supernatural that isn't out to kill us."

I stopped as we reached a small gray, crumbling building where the others were standing. I was thinking to myself that it looked like nothing special when Sadie shuddered, and her hand gripped mine more tightly. "This is where the monsters are. I can feel the evil seeping from it."

Glancing down at her then back at the building, I tried to see whatever she saw. "Are you sure? It looks like any old crypt, Sadie." Then I felt it. It was like a subtle taste of ash in the mouth.

Sebastian's eyes roamed over the front of the building. "I see it too, Sin. Demon wards cover the whole front door."

Edge stared hard at the door. "Can you tell what they say?"

Sebastian squinted at the crypt. "Yeah. Just hold your horses a minute. It says something about my mother protect this blessing ... then something, something. Then those that dare to enter will suffer— mud—no rock—" One of the warriors closest to the door must have tired of listening to Sebastian. He huffed in annoyance, swore, and grabbed the bar across the door. He stood still for a second before he let out a bloody scream as he burst into flames. "Oh yeah, fire. Beware of fire is what it says."

Edge looked at the pile of ash that only seconds before had been one of his warriors. He turned to my partner. "Think you could have translated the marks any slower, imp?"

"Hey, I didn't tell him to touch anything. Besides, if you think you can see, let alone translate, demon runes better than me you should just go ahead and do it. I'll sit over here on one of the tombstones and mind my own business."

I gazed at the pile of ash. "Enough, you two. The question is, can you get us past these marks, Sebastian?"

The imp reached down to the front of his stomach and rummaged in his pouch. "I think so, Sin. Just need to find that damn book somewhere ... now, where is—" We all watched as his hands moved from side to side.

Edge eyed Sebastian while clinking sounds floated from his belly. "I didn't know imps had that. Sort of looks like a kangaroo."

"Yeah, you'd be surprised how much an imp can carry in their pouch."

"I found it," Sebastian said as he pulled a thick volume from its hidey hole. The look on Edge's face was priceless as he watched the imp page through the book. "Oh yeah, here we go. Demon curses. Demon goods. Demons, how to cook. Demon marks. Ah yes, demon runes."

Edge looked at me. "Cook a demon?"

"Don't ask."

Sebastian's lips were moving as he read down the page. After a few seconds, Fallon's patience wore out. "Well, imp? Can you get us in there or not?"

Sebastian looked up from the book for a second as he glared at the fairy. "I can if you give me some time. Unless you want to end up like your friend over there, that is."

Reaching up, I gave the imp a quick pat on one of his arms. "Easy, Sebastian, we're all a little tense here."

He relaxed his shoulders. "You're right, Sin. Sorry. Can you get me closer to the door? It's a little hard to hold this book and fly at the same time."

I glared over at Fallon before walking over to the door of the crypt. Without realizing it, I stepped into the pile of ash and scattered it into the light breeze blowing on the hill. Gross. "Is that close enough, Sebastian?"

"Yeah, it is. Now, hush up so I can concentrate on what I'm doing. I don't want to end up like that fairy you're standing in, Sin."

I shut up as he read down the page, once again muttering under his breath for about five minutes. I was staring at the door trying to see these marks when Fallon's harsh voice made me jump. "Any day, imp."

I turned and glared at the fairy. He shrugged at me, his face a mask of anger. Sebastian ignored the fairy's outburst. "Okay, Sin, I got it." He reached out and traced his fingers along the door.

"Careful, Sebastian, I don't want you catching fire like that warrior."

The partner stopped and rubbed his hand along the side of my head. "Why, Sin, that's the nicest thing you've said to me in a while."

"Yeah, well, you're sitting on my shoulder. If you go up in flames ... I may be a dragon and all, but these are demon runes. They may hurt me too if I can't get you away from me quick enough."

Sebastian went back to tracing marks on the door. "You're all heart, Sin. Now shut up so I don't get this wrong. Or I swear, we will both go up in flames."

Ten minutes later, Sebastian gasped causing me to jump. "That was not funny, imp. Not funny at all."

"Whatever, Sin," he said tucking the book back into his pouch. "It's safe for you guys to open the door now."

He flew off my shoulder and perched himself on a headstone next to the crypt. Stepping back, I eyed the big brave warriors that surrounded me. Not one of them moved forward to touch the door as several fairy eyes drifted down to the pile of ash that had been their companion. Not that I was all that eager to try that door either.

I glanced around the group one more time. "Really? Fine, I'll do it then."

Rose stepped out of the group and grabbed the bar across the door and flung it to the side. I let out a breath I hadn't realized I had been holding as the female fairy stared back at the others.

Without another word, Edge moved past her and opened the door. From the dark opening, the smell of corruption and blood floated out into the sunlight.

19

Aezriane looked down from the upper windows of the old house. Anger filled her eyes as she watched the fairy standing before her crypt. She wondered how these creatures could have found her incubator so soon. She had made sure that no one from that cursed island had seen her after she had collected her gift from the vamp.

No, it had to be something else. Something that … She stopped as the dragon she had seen last night and a large group of fairies joined the other one by the small building. Yes. The dragon. That could explain how they had found the building so fast.

Flashes of a night long ago filled her mind. Of fairies breaking into the temple her older sisters tended. Of being hidden under blankets in a corner. The screams of her sisters as they fought and died. The last of her kind. Of peeking out and seeing the male dragon that beheaded the oldest of her sisters as she kneeled before him, her hands tied behind her back. Slaughtered like a common farm animal.

It wasn't the same dragon, but a dragon nonetheless. She knew how dangerous they could be. Just like that one on a night long ago. The one she found out later had led the fairies to the succubi's last sanctuary. Now, this one was leading another group of fairies to kill her new sisters. Well, they wouldn't find it so easy to get into the crypt.

She was delighted when one of the fools below grabbed for the bar that sealed the crypt. Her laughter caught in her throat as the fairy went up in flames and a creature below glanced back at the house. The strange light eyes took in the dark windows as Aezriane peeked at the little one from her hiding place.

What sort of creature is that she pondered as it turned back to what was happening around the crypt? Then her attention zeroed in on something even more disturbing. The thing that sat on the dragon's shoulder. Fuck. It was an imp. No wonder the fairies and the dragon found her incubator.

Her eyes went as black as the night while her lips pulled back from her teeth. Imps. Damn traitors to the demon world. Selling themselves to the highest bidder or attaching themselves to whatever creature seemed to be on the rise.

She watched as he pulled a book from his pouch and worked his magic on her wards. She jerked, as if in pain, as each one fell, one after the other. A tiny part of her mind yelled, now was the time to leave the area. Once the fairies and the dragon gained entrance to the incubator, they would destroy her sisters, without mercy, as her older sisters had been on that night long ago.

But another part forced her to stand there as they opened the door. Who knew? Maybe the creatures inside the crypt had hatched from their hosts and these fairies would be the first victims. She could only hope that her new sisters would feed on the intruders as the fairies below her crowded into the darkness.

The smell inside the crypt hung heavy. The light from the outside barely reached past the threshold. Edge turned to the nearest warrior. "Torches."

Great idea, I thought as I cupped my hand and willed a small flame to flare, while with the other I pulled my pistol from its holster. Fallon looked at the tiny flame I had produced as four warriors with lights moved into the room. "Expecting trouble, dragon? That little flame isn't going to do you much good."

"That's fresh blood I smell. Yeah, I'm expecting all kinds of trouble," I said as I turned to follow the fairies. The light threw shadows over the room that held bodies of nude human women along both sides and an altar at the end.

Moving over to the first woman by the door, I looked at the body and saw a large bulging belly on the young blonde woman. I was reaching out to feel for a pulse when something shifted inside her. Pulling back my hand, I glanced over at where Edge was looking at a woman on the other side of the room. "I think these might be the women we were looking for. We might be in time."

"I think you are right. This one is pregnant too, but she looks like she is close to giving birth. I suggest we—"

One of the fairy warriors called out as he stood at the other end of the room closest to the altar. "Edge, we may have a problem here." In the torchlight, we both looked at the fairy's pale face as he gazed in horror at what lay on the shelf below him.

We both moved down the room and looked at the body lying on the shelf. This one was definitely a body. Gore coated the walls to the side and the floor next to her. Whatever monster had been in her had burst out of her belly, leaving a gaping hole in her middle. I took in the sight, glad I had left Sadie outside with three guards while we explored the crypt.

A trembling voice came from the other side of the room. "There's one on this side too." I turned and saw that whatever had come out of this woman had also started to work and worry at the woman's neck like a rabid dog.

Edge gulped as he looked around the room. "How could anyone do this to someone? Even a human doesn't deserve this end. We need to find these creatures." I looked at his face. It was as white as fresh snow except for two bright red spots high on each cheek.

Edge was right. Whatever had come out of these women needed to be destroyed as soon as possible. Maybe Sadie could use her powers to help us find where these creatures had gone. But in the meantime, we needed to get these monsters out of the other humans without killing them.

A low hiss caused me to turn and look at the body lying next to us. Red eyes stared at me as one hand reached out. I heard Edge take a step away from the wall. "What in the hell, Sin? She should be dead."

Without thinking, I reached for a stake and planted it in the middle of the woman's heart. The creature's eyes went wide as her hand gripped my arm then she turned to dust. "Shit, we're in trouble, Edge. These women are infected with the vamp virus from the babies they carry. We need to get out of here now." I didn't wait for a response, I just turned and headed for the door.

I had just about made it when a loud ripping sound echoed off the walls of the crypt. Spinning around, I saw one of the fairy warriors covered from the waist up with blood and gore, bending over the open belly of the woman below him. "No, don't—"

I was too late with my warning as a dark, wet mass leaped from the woman's belly and attached itself to his throat. "EVERYONE OUT. NOW!" Another loud rip sounded from across the room and another bloody mess launched itself onto the back of a fairy warrior.

Everyone rushed for the door. A warrior went down as a small hand reached out from under a shelf and grabbed his leg. He screamed as it yanked him into the darkness where his voice stopped in a wet gurgle.

Another warrior was grabbed by one of the women and taken to the floor. She worried at his neck like a dog with a bone as her belly burst open, covering them both with gore. Both she and the warrior lay still as a wet red body slithered up to the warrior's ruined neck. As one warrior after another went down, I couldn't take my eyes away from this hellish scene as I moved toward the light.

I reached the outside and turned just as Edge reached the door. A dark mass reared up behind him, grabbed the huge fairy, and dragged him back into the darkness of the building. I slammed the door shut behind me and threw the wooden bar across the door. No one else was getting out of there alive. Fallon stood, his eyes wild as he looked around the graveyard. "What the fuck was that? Where did Edge go?"

I looked at the fairy as he bent over, his hands on his knees, gasping. He stared at the closed doors of the crypt. Rose was gentle. "He didn't make it, Fallon."

Fallon stood and marched toward the doors, a determined gleam in his eyes. I turned to one of the nearby warriors. "Stop him now before he opens the door. We can't let those things get out."

Usually, these warriors would ignore any command I gave, but seeing the horrors inside that building they decided that maybe I had a good point. Four of them tackled Fallon. He fought for a few seconds before he grunted and lay still. "Alright, let me up."

The fairy warriors on top of him looked at me, uncertainty in their eyes. "Are you going to open that crypt, Fallon?"

The fairy glared at me for a few seconds before the anger left his face and he seemed to fold inside of himself. "Are you sure that Edge is dead, dragon?"

"I'm sure. Whatever grabbed him was drinking his blood as he dragged him back into the room."

"Shit. That is no way for royalty to die."

I grimaced as I looked at the closed doors thinking of the human women inside. "That is no way for any creature to die, fairy."

We all stopped at the sound of scratching at the crypt's door as a low voice moaned. "Cousin, let me out. Fallon, help me. Pleasssse—"

The fairy threw a quick look at me before he squirmed out of the warriors' hold. Leaping to his feet, he headed to the door. "You were wrong. Edge is still alive and needs help."

I did the only thing I could as the fairy started to lift the lock from the door. I hit him with the butt of my weapon. When it connected, Fallon dropped as though a switch had been turned off.

Looking at the fairy, I almost felt sorry for him. I knew what it was like to lose someone you cared for. Someone that was family. Rose broke through my thoughts as she came and stood next to me gazing at the fairy laying at our feet. "You know, dragon, he will not thank you for this, right?"

There was more scratching at the crypt door, drawing all eyes toward it. I glanced around at the closed faces and it hit me. In all the confusion of escaping the dangers of the crypt, I hadn't seen Sadie, Sebastian, or the three fairy guards that were supposed to have been watching out for them.

"Uh, where's Sadie?"

Aezriane watched as the group of fairies and the dragon went into the crypt. Briefly, she thought of trying to protect the precious assets inside but knew that she would not be a match against this many fairies and a dragon to boot.

A smile lit across her face as she watched the imp land on the young girl's shoulder. Well, she may not be able to kill them all and save her sisters, but maybe, just maybe, she could take a few down before she left.

Picking out one of the fairy guards standing toward the back of the tiny group, she concentrated on him. Slowly, she entered his weak mind and made her command. She turned and left the room just as the first screams sounded from the crypt.

Sebastian was lost in thought when the first sounds of horror floated out of the small building in front of them. "Oh, now what the hell has that girl done?"

Sadie closed her eyes and bowed her head. "I think some of the undead children are alive, imp."

"Yeah, well, no shit, kid. Even I could have figured that out." Sebastian stopped talking as hot liquid splashed the two of them. "What the fuck," the imp said as he looked at the blood that coated him from head to foot.

The clash of steel caused both of them to turn their heads toward the warriors behind them. They could see that a fairy was down on the ground, headless, as the other two fought.

"Well, just don't stand there, kid. RUN!" Between the sounds from the crypt and the dueling warriors, Sadie figured the imp's suggestion had some merit and ran toward a large statue of an angel.

The imp flew off Sadie's shoulder as they reached the back of the statue and crouched down. "Stay right here, girl. I'll go— " There was a loud yell and the clash of weapons stopped.

Sadie looked at the imp. "What happened?"

Sebastian watched as one warrior killed the other. The surviving fairy gave the body a quick kick before his eyes wandered over the graveyard looking for the girl he had a sudden urge to kill. "Hush, girl, just stay still and maybe we can live through this long enough to ... Oh shit."

The imp watched as the fairy started toward where they were hiding. "What's happening?" Sadie said as she peeked around the corner of the statue. The fairy saw her and cried out in triumph as he stalked toward them.

Sadie got up to run but tripped over some old vines growing along the bottom of the statue. Sprawled out, she turned over onto her back just as the fairy came upon her. He had a vacant smile on his face as he raised his sword above his head when a voice floated from between the angel's wings. "Hey, asshole, forget someone?"

The warrior looked up, confusion on his face as Sebastian took a deep breath and let out a long stream of flame that took the fairy full in the face. His hair and beard went up like a roman candle. He danced around, the flames devouring his head until he fell dead at the feet of the stone angel.

Sadie looked between the fairy and the imp. "How did you do that?"

Sebastian bowed low as he swept his hand in front of him, doffing an imaginary hat. "You're welcome, kid. But you live with a dragon long enough and you learn how to do dragon fire."

"Thank you, imp."

"Don't mention it, girl. In fact, don't tell Sin that I did this. She doesn't know that I can do this little trick, okay?"

Sadie stared at the imp for a few seconds before she gave him a quick little nod and a bow of her own. "You saved my life, imp. So, I owe you. I will keep your secret if that is what you wish."

Just then half the fairies that went in, came pouring out of the crypt as though every demon from hell were on their tails. Sadie and Sebastian hid behind the angel watching as Sin threw the bar across the door. The skirmish with Fallon. Finally seeing the dragon coldcock the fairy from behind. "Ohhhhh. Now that had to hurt. Bet that fairy feels that in the morning. So much for that girl listening to my advice about making friends with the fairy."

The two of them watched Sin look around the graveyard. "Where's Sadie?"

"Here I am, Sin," Sadie said as she stood and waved at the dragon as the imp landed on her shoulder and huffed out his annoyance.

"Yeah, sure. 'Where's Sadie? Where's Sadie?' What am I? Chopped liver? I'm only her partner but does she care where I am?"

I noticed the two dead guards as I hurried over to Sadie and Sebastian. Catching the scent of burned hair and flesh, I glanced at the base of the statue and saw the third guard. Stopping, I eyed the two. "Sebastian, I leave you out here for a little while and you can't seem to stay out of trouble. Remember fairies are our allies. Did you have to kill them?"

"Me? I didn't do this." I stared at the imp; one eyebrow raised. "Fine. So, I may have barbequed this one, but he killed the other two first and was going to kill Sadie here. Just ask her. Go on. She'll tell you I was just trying to protect her. Besides, I wasn't the one who coldcocked Fallon."

My partner finally wound down enough for me to get a word in edgewise. "Chill, Sebastian, I wasn't accusing you of anything, I just want to know what happened out here."

"Well, okay, but sounds like you had your own trouble in the crypt."

"That's an understatement. Seems like some of the creatures were born before we got in there and more were popping out. Then there was the whole deal of dead women coming back to life."

"So, what are you going to do? You know that door won't hold them forever. I mean once it's dark those things are going to come out of there."

"Is there any way for you to put up some runes to keep them inside, Sebastian?"

"Yeah, dream on, girl. I can't do a spell strong enough to fight the demon magic that formed these monsters. You're talking about the mother of all demons creating those things."

"Fine, let's get back over there and see if we can't figure something out, partner."

20

Walking back to the crypt, I got the lowdown about what had been going on out here while the rest of us had been running from the monsters inside the building. There didn't seem to be any reason why one warrior had attacked the others before going after Sadie. "Do you think a succubus could get inside a fairy head and make him go on a killing rampage, Sebastian?"

He looked at me from Sadie's shoulder. "They can come into dreams. So, I don't see why they couldn't control a weak-minded creature. Even though—"

I waited for a few seconds as the imp rubbed one claw along his chin in thought. "Even though what, partner?"

"Oh. Sorry, Sin. I was just thinking she would have to be close to put that kind of whammy on the fairy."

"How close?" I said spying the old church and the house next to it.

The imp followed my gaze. "Yeah. That close, Sin."

By then we were at the crypt. Fallon was still out, lying by the door where I had left him. We could all hear something sniffing at the barred door. All eyes turned to me as we walked up. Rose stepped closer, her voice low. "What do you think we should do, dragon? I don't think these warriors will hold much longer. Especially if whatever is in there breaks out."

I looked around and saw she was right. The warriors were holding on to their courage by a thread. I looked at the gray sky above us. "Since these creatures are half vamp, I would guess that they won't come out into the sun. We should be safe for a few hours at least," I said loud enough for all to hear. My words had the desired effect—the warriors visibly relaxed.

Rose eyed the crypt as something heavy slammed against the door. "And once it gets dark? Then what keeps them inside, dragon?"

"I think by then we had better be far away from here, but right now we have another more pressing problem."

"What other problem could we have that outweighs what is in there?"

"Sebastian thinks someone took over the mind of one of the warriors left out here to guard them and forced him to kill the other two."

Rose glanced at the two dead warriors lying near the gravestone. "I was wondering what had happened."

"He also thinks that to take over the warrior's mind, the succubus has to be close by. Like really close by," I said glancing over at the decrepit church and its accompanying house.

Rose's eyes followed mine to the buildings. "I see. And if the creature is in one of those places, dragon?"

"If she is, maybe she will get rid of the monsters in the crypt since she is the one that created them. Or if we find and kill her, they may die on their own without her magic. Your guess is as good as mine, Rose. You fairies know more about this magic crap than I do."

Rose glanced at Fallon. "It is too bad you had to knock out my husband to be. He should be the one in charge and making these kinds of decisions."

"Time to suck it up, buttercup, and take charge. Because you're all we have for right now and the only one these warriors will listen to."

Rose stared at me for a few seconds before she shook her head. "You have a unique way of talking. I find it irritating, but you are right. If we can find this creature, maybe she can destroy the monsters inside the crypt."

"I don't see any other choice, Rose. Do you?"

She looked back at the crypt before turning to the surrounding warriors, ignoring the scratching and low murmurs still coming from the structure. "Alright, we need to search those buildings from top to bottom for the creature that made these monsters."

One of the biggest warriors stepped forward. "Woman, who gave you the right to—"

Rose stepped forward, her sword flashing from its sheath and swiped it across the fairy's throat. He gasped for air, drowning on his words and blood. His hands were wrapped around the wound as his life drained down his chest.

He fell to his knees, then flat on his face as Rose wiped her sword across the fallen warrior's back. She eyed the remaining fairies. "We don't have time for this shit. Does anyone else have a problem with my orders?" It was silent in the graveyard. Even the scratching and low murmur of voices from the crypt had stopped. "Good. Now, as I was saying, I want you to split into two groups and search that church and house from top to bottom. We prefer the succubus be taken alive but dead if all else fails."

The warriors stood for a few seconds, eyes shifting between Rose and the dead fairy at her feet. For a second, I thought they might attack Rose en masse. She waved her sword. "NOW! MOVE IT!"

You would have thought she had thrown one of those monsters into the middle of them as they scrambled into their groups and ran toward the church and house next to it. "I'll try to remember never to piss you off, Rose."

The fairy grimaced at me; her fist white-knuckled from the hold she had on the hilt of her sword. "Since I found you in my betrothed's bed, I would say it is too late for that, wouldn't you?"

Any humor I had felt at seeing those fairy warriors scramble died as I looked into those cold steely blue eyes. My anger flared at the unfairness. "If you remember right, fairy. It was my bed your husband to be was in. Not the other way around. And I had no idea you were even in the picture."

Rose stared at me for a moment before she turned to follow the warriors to the two buildings. "You know, Sin. I do so admire the winning ways you have with the other creatures in this world," Sebastian said from Sadie's shoulder.

"Bite me, imp."

"What? And take the chance of catching something? No thanks."

I glared at him as my fist clenched the weapon in my hand. "You know one of these days, partner, you will push too far. Just wait and see."

"Yeah, but it won't be today. You need me to figure out a way to kill those things in there." He nodded toward the crypt doors as the scratching and low murmur of voices started up again.

Sebastian was right. I wouldn't kill him today. "Then why are you just standing around? Find something we can use to kill those damn things or come dark we may all be in a world of hurt if ... no, when those things get out." The humor left the imp's eyes as he flew over to a tombstone and perched there while he dug inside his pouch for a book.

Three hours later, Sebastian was still sitting on the tombstone flipping pages as he muttered to himself. My eyes wandered over to Sadie who was standing before the door of the crypt lost in her own world while I knelt over Fallon to check on him for the tenth time.

I caught Rose and the other fairies, out of the corner of my eyes, coming down from the buildings they had been searching. I stood looking at the fairy at my feet thinking maybe I had put a little too much oomph into my swing when I knocked him out.

Rose came up to me as the rest of the warriors spread out around the front of the building. "We didn't find her, but there are signs that someone had been staying in the upper floor of the house."

"She probably took off when she saw her monsters weren't going to kill us all."

"Probably, dragon, probably. But now we are back to the same problem: What do we do when it gets dark and these monsters get loose?"

I looked over to where Sebastian sat. "Let's go ask the expert."

Both of us walked over to the imp who was still lost in his book. Rose stopped short of the tombstone. She stared at the book in his hands for a few seconds. "Is that the Tome of Darkness, imp?"

Sebastian glanced up for a second before burying himself back in the black pages. "It's one copy of it, fairy. What of it?"

Rose glanced over at me then back at the book and shuddered. "I thought there was only one copy out in the world, imp."

"There is one copy out there, but this is my personal copy. Now if you don't mind, I'm a little busy here. Or don't you want me to find a way to kill those things?"

I had never paid much attention to the book in his hands, but now that Rose had named it, I looked at the book a little closer. The cover was dark green with an almost slimy sheen that looked wet to the touch. Peeking over the edge of the cover, I could see that tiny red writing filled the black pages that went from top to bottom and margin to margin.

As I stared at the book, I could almost feel a slimy coating in the back of my throat. I swallowed and looked away from the book. "What's the Tome of Darkness? And is that blood it's written in?"

"It is the ultimate book of evil. Written by the foulest of creatures, from the darkest depths of Hell."

The imp slammed the book shut tossing it to the ground. I watched as the grass underneath it wilted at the touch of its cover. Sebastian stood on the tombstone, his hands on his hips. "For your information, fairy, this book is not evil." I glanced at the dying grass under it and wondered.

"The creature who wrote it—"

"I WROTE THE DAMN BOOK, FAIRY! I AM THE DAMN AUTHOR!"

Rose's mouth slammed shut as her face went crimson. "Oh, well, I—"

"And for your information, fairy, the book itself isn't evil. It is the assholes that use it for evil that has tarnished its reputation."

I glanced between Sebastian and the book that lay at the base of the tombstone. I was having trouble reconciling my perception of just how harmless my partner was with this new knowledge. Especially when a whiff of brimstone assaulted my nose from where the book lay.

I mean he was the one that helped me when I was just a young dragon after I had lost my family. The one that had taught me how to track my bounties and bring them in. The smell of more sulfur wafted up from the ground and I took a step back as the imp flew down and grabbed the book. "It doesn't matter anyway. There is no specific way in these pages about how to kill those things in the crypt."

"There must be something. These are not the first creatures that a succubus has made. Throughout history, there are stories like this."

Sebastian flew back to the top of the tombstone and tucked his book back into his pouch. "Yeah, human history, fairy. This is the first time I have found one of these creatures that has mixed supernatural baby batter with their magic."

Rose scratched her head. "Uh? Baby batter?"

"Super's seed, Rose." She glanced over at me, puzzled. Really? She couldn't be that naïve, could she? "The vamp's sperm, Rose. This is the first time that a succubus has used a vamp's sperm to make her sisters."

"Ooooh," Rose said as the confusion left her face. She turned to Sebastian. "Well, then why didn't you just say that?"

"I did, you stupid—"

I saw the anger flare in Rose's eyes. "Sebastian, now is not the time."

"Fine, Sin, I'll behave. Even though it's hard to believe that any fairy this old could be that naïve."

Rose frowned at the imp and opened her mouth to retort when Sadie's voice drifted over from the crypt. "Dragon fire will cleanse the beasts from this world."

All eyes swiveled toward her. She stood facing the crypt. Her arms spread out to her side as her hair blew wildly around her head in a wind that wasn't there. The fairy warriors stepped back from the building. Several of them signed wards to prevent evil.

I took a tentative step toward the girl. "Uh, Sadie are you alright?"

She turned toward us, her arms still wide as though to embrace us all. Her eyes were wide open with only the whites showing, as she slowly rose about a foot in the air. Two of the warriors had had enough. They turned and ran down the hill.

"Only dragon fire will destroy these creatures. These creatures that were created from the undead." With that pronouncement, Sadie's eyes closed, and she collapsed in a heap.

21

Rushing forward, I kneeled at the girl's side checking for a pulse. Rose stood over us as Sebastian landed on my shoulder. "Is she okay, Sin? I mean she isn't dead, is she?"

I got a strong pulse at her throat. "No, she isn't dead, Sebastian."

"Oh, good. She seems like a nice kid."

"What did she mean that dragon fire would kill these creatures, Sin?"

"I have no idea, fairy. Dragon fire is hotter than most." I glanced over at the stone building and back at Rose. "But, I've never been able to create a fire hot enough to destroy something like that crypt."

"I thought that was part of being a dragon."

"Yeah, well, this dragon's fire doesn't run that hot. So just drop it, Rose."

Sadie's eyes fluttered open. Her expression was puzzled at first then changed to worry. "I did it again, didn't I, Sin? You're not going to send me back to the masters because of this, are you?"

"Yeah, you did, Sadie, and no, I'm not going to send you back to the bloodsuckers." I helped her to sit up as she rubbed her forehead. "Are you alright?"

She scrunched her eyes shut for a few seconds, her forehead wrinkled in pain. "I get a slight headache whenever—whenever I go away like that. I'll be alright in a little bit. What did I say, Sin?"

"You said something about dragon fire destroying the creatures inside the crypt."

"Then you must do what is instinctive to dragons and use your flames to clean out that nest of monsters."

"Listen. I may be able to produce a fire. I mean I am a dragon, after all."

Sadie grabbed my arm in a death grip. "I saw what these creatures will do. You have to get rid of them now or—"

"Or what?"

Sadie looked into the fairy's eyes. A single tear streaked down her cheek. "Or else they will get loose and decimate this world. Everyone will be turned, humans, fairies, even dragons."

As gently as I could, I pried her hand off my arm and helped her to stand. "Sadie, I know I can't make a fire hot enough to burn that building down. I mean it's thick stone, and even if it was wood, I'm just not good enough to create a fire that hot."

"You don't need to destroy the building. You just need to destroy the monsters. So all you have to do is open the door of the crypt and direct your flames inside, Sin."

I stared at the girl thinking about the dimensions of the crypt. It wasn't really that big, but it was big enough for me. Especially if I was to create a flame that would ensure that none of those monsters escaped. From past experience, I knew my limits and this far exceeded what I could do. "Sadie, I just don't think I can. No, I know I can't do what you're asking me to do. Ask Sebastian."

"Oooooh, dragon fire. Yeah, that just might work," Sebastian said from my shoulder as he slapped his hand across his forehead. "Damn, I should have thought of that. How can I be so stupid?"

I was getting angry at this damn fool idea of dragon fire. "Now listen to me, I'm tired of repeating myself. This isn't going to work. You have been around me long enough to know how big a flame I can produce. Remember when my nest was attacked? Remember when my mother, my siblings were all killed? I couldn't do it then. What makes you think I can do it now, Sebastian?"

"So, how long will it take you to get this fire ready, dragon?" Rose said as she glanced at the horizon where darkness was playing along its edges.

I spun toward the fairy, my anger beating against my chest. "WILL ALL OF YOU SHUT THE FUCK UP? I—CAN'T—MAKE—THAT—MUCH—DRAGON—FIRE!"

The three of them stared at me for a few seconds before Sebastian flew off my shoulder and landed on Rose's. "It won't take her long, fairy. We just need to figure out how we will time this. You know getting the lock off and the door open so that someone out here doesn't die, but none of those creatures get out."

"So, we need to factor in the distance she needs to stand from the door? Oh, and the timing, right?" Sadie said.

"Oh, and the wind. Yes, the wind will factor into how the flames hit the crypt," Rose put in as the three walked over to the fairy warriors still on the hill.

I watched them walk away. The anger died, as first annoyance, then confusion flickered through my mind. I looked at Fallon's still unconscious figure. "But I can't make a fire that big. We are so going to die. Why won't they listen?" Damn stupid fairy just lay there and didn't answer me.

Night was folding in on us, embracing us as the first few stars flickered to life. The sounds from inside the crypt became louder as the seconds ticked by. For the last hour, Rose and some of her warriors had been measuring distances around the crypt's door. Others had been gathering buckets of water and sand nearby, so I wouldn't burn down the graveyard and us with it, I guess.

Fat chance of that happening. Once more Sebastian's strident voice pulled me from my dire thoughts. "Come on, Sin. Concentrate. You need to be one with the flame. Be the flame."

"Yeah, I'll show you one with the flame, imp." I flicked my wrist toward the tombstone Sebastian was sitting on. A tiny fireball burst as it hit the stone just below his feet.

"HEY! That's not funny." Sebastian sulked as he looked around at the gathering darkness. "We don't have time for you to get into one of your snits, girl. If you want to get out of this alive, you need to get your head into the right place."

"I don't know. I think it was as funny as you insisting I can make a fire big enough to fry those monsters in that crypt. You of all people should know better." I marched off toward an empty part of the graveyard.

Sebastian stared at Sin shaking his head as Sadie came to stand next to him. "I think we're screwed, kid. She's right, she'll never be able to get her dragon fire big enough to take out those things. If—hell, who am I kidding? When they get out, we're all dead."

Sadie watched the dragon lean against a tombstone and gaze at the approaching night sky. "Maybe, Sebastian. Why don't you let me see if I can talk to her?"

The imp glanced at the girl, then over to his partner. "Go ahead, Sadie. It's not like we have a lot of choices right now. Keep in mind, I've known her since she was a hatchling and stubbornness is her middle name. I don't think even you will change her mind." Ignoring the imp's warning and without another word, she walked over to where the dragon stood.

I heard the tiny footsteps behind me in the dead grass of the graveyard. "Whatever you have to say it doesn't matter, Sadie. I can't make a flame as big as we need to destroy those creatures. This is like when I was younger all over again. Everyone around me is going to die because I can't do what every other dragon can."

"Listen, I know that you can do this. I saw it in my vision when I 'went away'."

I glanced over at her for a second seeing the worry on her face. "Do all your— visions come true?" Her eyes dropped from mine. "Yeah, that's what I thought."

The two of us stood quiet for a few seconds. I was taking in the beauty of what could be my last night in this world. I heard Sadie's quiet voice. "My visions don't always come true because of how they are seen. Or used, I guess, but I know that you can do this."

"Yeah, right. It doesn't matter, I'm not a big believer in that mystic bull anyway."

"I know what I saw." Sadie stopped talking and her arm shot out like a striking snake, her hand wrapping around my wrist in a death grip. I started to jerk away from her when I felt a jolt slam into my body.

The graveyard around us disappeared and I saw myself in a swirling mist standing before the open door of the crypt. The entrance was awash with fire. Inside of the flame, I could see the curling blackened bodies of the monsters.

I blinked and I was back standing next to Sadie, her arms at her side as a mischievous light played in her eyes. "What the hell did you just do me, girl?" I took a few steps back out of her reach. I didn't want her touching me like that ever again.

"I had to show you what I saw, so you would know you could do it. You can make a flame big enough to kill those monsters before they get out to kill us and everyone else in the world."

"You really think I would fall for that kind of trick? Or, whatever the hell that was. Go play your mind games on someone else."

Sadie took a step toward me. Annoyance crossed her face as I stepped backward hiding my hands behind my back. "It wasn't a trick, Sin. It showed what will happen. You will kill those monsters the only way you can."

"Don't touch me, Sadie. Just don't touch me. Let me think here, okay?"

"Alright, if that is what you want." She looked at the encroaching night sky. "But, you better think fast, Sin. Because our world is running out of time."

I watched as Sadie turned to march back toward the crypt. She was right about one thing. We had just about run out of time with the coming of full darkness. Those creatures would come out of that crypt like a storm and wash right over the little group here to stop them.

So, I guess I had to decide. Do nothing and die when the monsters escaped the crypt or try to barbeque them and die when I failed. I looked around as more stars winked in the coming darkness. I turned and started over to the crypt. Yeah, dragons were never known to wait around for death to come looking for them. So, I guess I go look for the bitch and spit in her face.

A few minutes later, I was standing about five feet away from the door of the crypt. Rose had hold of the bar, ready to yank it free. The rest of the warriors were standing behind me in a semicircle, their weapons at the ready for when I screwed up.

I took a deep breath and braced myself when Fallon, who was still laying in front of the door, moaned. I looked over at Rose. "We need to move him." Rose glanced between the two of us with a sour look on her face. "He'll be in the way when you open the door, Rose. I want a clear shot at the inside of the crypt if I'm going to do this right."

Rose heaved a loud, put upon sigh. "Fine. Someone get him out of the way." Two of the fairies grabbed Fallon and none too gently dragged him behind the line of warriors.

Once everyone was back in position, I nodded to the fairy at the door and brought both hands up concentrating on making a ball of flame between them. I could hear Rose count down from three. Catching the bar over the door and throwing it free, she turned and bolted to safety.

Shit, she forgot to open the door my mind snarled, breaking into my concentration just as the door burst open. Inside the crypt entrance stood Edge, or what they left of him. One arm was ripped off at the shoulder and I could see that his throat and chest were torn open. He didn't say a word, just grinned at me when I saw darker shadows moving behind him. I stood frozen at the gruesome sight. "Dragon, no! That's my cousin."

Fallon's voice released something in me as whatever was left of Edge stepped out of the crypt. I stepped forward, the flames in my hands heating to a temperature I never knew I could reach. I wasn't sure if it was fright or anger at what they had done to Edge and the other warriors in the crypt.

The wash of flames I threw toward the crypt engulfed Edge and the shadows behind him. An eerie, keening scream erupted from the tomb as I concentrated on making the inferno bigger. I took another step forward, driving it deeper into the building.

Black greasy smoke escaped along the edges of the doorway as the smell of burned undead flesh wafted across the graveyard. I kept moving forward, making sure I reached every inch of the building. I couldn't let any of those creatures escape.

Behind me, I could hear the sounds of someone arguing and fighting, but I had to concentrate on what I was doing. I had thought I wouldn't be able to make flames big enough to kill these monsters and now I had to concentrate on not losing control of the fire I had created.

I was just inches from the door by now. The dragon fire bathed the whole inside of the crypt when Sebastian landed on my shoulder. "See, I told you. I told you that you could do it, partner."

"Yeah, you did, partner, but I seem to have a small problem."

"Oh? What problem?"

"How do I stop this now that I got it going?"

"Oh yeah. Forgot about that part."

"You think," I said feeling the heat building up inside me as the flames grew.

"Okay, Sin, nothing to panic about. I just need you to calm down and breath." I took in a deep breath as my partner suggested and noticed that the heat inside of me seemed a little less—well, hot.

"Now what?"

"Now I need you to slowly release the heat inside you. Not all at once, but just bit by bit." I concentrated on doing what the imp said. Bit by bit, I released the heat and fire inside me until I had the flames between my hands once again. "That a girl. Now, just let go like you would with a normal dragon fire."

I felt the flames go out between my hands. "I did it, Sebastian. This time I could do it."

My partner patted me on the shoulder. "I never doubted you for a second."

Rose and the rest of the warriors walked up to the crypt. Torches were lit as full dark was upon us. "Good job, dragon. I imagine you got rid of all the monsters or we would be fighting for our lives about now."

I glanced over at the dark smoking void in front of me. The smell of cooked flesh hung in the air. "Yeah, if I had missed anything in there, we would know about it by now.

Looking at the faces around the crypt's door I saw relief written on everyone. "Uh, where's Fallon. I thought I heard his voice."

"My husband-to-be woke as the door opened and you flamed the monsters inside."

"Shit, so he saw what they had done to Edge?"

"Yeah, he did. He tried to get to you as you were using your dragon fire and I figured that wouldn't be such a good idea. So, I put him out again."

"Damn, between you two that's one fairy that will have one hell of a headache when he wakes up," Sebastian said.

I saw Sadie peeking out from behind a warrior, her eyes shining with tears. I walked over and kneeled in front of her and took her hand in mine. "What are you crying for? You were right. When it came down to it. I created the fire that killed the monsters in there."

"Since you killed them, I guess you'll have no more use for me and I'll have to go back to the vampires."

Still holding her hand, I stood looking out over the water toward the lonely dark outline of the island in the middle of the bay. "We aren't done yet, Sadie. We may have killed these creatures, but we need to find the succubus before she creates any more of them. So, I guess you're stuck with us."

Sadie wiped the tears away from her eyes. "Thank you, Sin"

22

Aezriane lurched to her feet. Cold fury radiated from her center as she felt her sisters die in the hot flames of the dragon's fire. Their screams filled her head as the heat consumed them, knocking her to the ground as she fled the graveyard.

Now looking back up the hill, she could see the glow of the dying fire. She took two steps back toward where her sisters had met their end when self-preservation kicked in. Going up that hill wouldn't accomplish anything except maybe getting herself killed and then how would they wreak vengeance?

No, there were easier ways to get at the dragon and the fairies around her. The same way she had taken the gifts from the Were and the vamp; through dreams. Yes, that is what she would do. Visit the dragon in her dreams and kill her that way.

It amused her to think how she would walk into the dragon's mind once she was asleep and find the one thing that would torture the dragon the most. They all, humans and supers alike, had something hidden deep within their subconscious. Something that frightened them, or they were trying to hide. Yes, they all had something, and she knew this dragon wouldn't be any different.

Rose put a hand on my shoulder. "What do we do now, Sin? We need to find the creature that caused all this mess."

Everyone's eyes were locked on me like I knew what to do. "Me, Rose? Why are you asking me? With Fallon out, I figure you're the ranking fae on this mission. Besides, I'm done for the night. I'm going home. You fairies can do whatever the hell you want."

"I think the queen would want you to be in charge with Fallon down and out."

"Rose, screw your queen and the horse she rode in on. I'm done with this job. Come on Sadie and Sebastian, we're out of here." I turned and walked back down the hill toward the city below us. I could hear the grumbling of the fairy warriors behind me.

"Shut up, she's right. We're done here. Two of you grab up Fallon and let us depart this cursed place," Rose said.

I could hear the warrior's grunts as they hoisted Fallon off the ground and moved out behind us. I was glad that Rose was coming back with us, not that I would have told her that. After the day we had, I wasn't too keen on walking through the city on our own.

The trip back didn't take as long as it had going up the hill. We were almost to the docks before we knew it. It had been a quiet march. I was tired. I was thinking of my nice warm bed back home when I felt a quick tug on my hair. "Sin, are those the two fairies that ran away from the crypt?"

"What was that, Sebastian?" The group stopped as we took in the two forms lying in the middle of the road. "Damn, break's over, people. Everyone spread out and let's start paying attention to our surroundings again," I said noticing how we were all clustered together. Shit. We must all be tired if seasoned warriors like these were getting this sloppy.

Rose scanned the adjacent buildings. Her quick eyes darted back and forth between the darkened windows and the two bodies. "What do think happened to them?"

I eyed the nearby shadows. "I'll tell you in a second." Sadie made as if to follow when I waved her back. "You stay here with Rose."

"I can help you, Sin. I'm not some helpless child you know. When I was younger, I was a warrior. I could fight just as well as you."

I couldn't help but smile. As tiny as she was it was hard to remember she was older than me. "Hey, I need you to watch my back and keep an eye on these fairies for me. You know how they can be under fire, right? You're the only one I can trust."

Rose snorted but Sadie was unperturbed. "Okay, Sin, I'll watch your back for you."

"Thanks."

Sebastian eyed the two dead bodies. "Well since she's the only one you can trust, can I stay here? You know, since I don't know how to watch your back. Oh, and have the kid here protect me too."

"Nice try, Sebastian. You know I trust you too so suck it up because you're coming with me, partner."

"Damn. I knew you would say that, Sin."

We moved deliberately over to the bodies lying in a pool of light, thrown off by a single lantern hanging from an old pole. Kneeling beside the fairies, I could see that whoever had killed them had stripped all their weapons and armor. Sebastian looked around the buildings before tapping me on the shoulder. "Sin, this is not good; not good at all."

I knew my partner was right. The two warriors lay splayed out, their cause of death obvious—two large bullet holes between their matching blue eyes. "Few human weapons could make an entrance wound that size."

"You know we've seen these wounds before, right?"

"I remember the ogre that attacked a young human girl. What was it? Two years ago? The one that ate her."

"That one. We never figured out who killed him and no one came forward to collect the bounty on him either."

"I know, but I still think you were way off base on that one. Where would a human get a weapon like that? When the fairies took over, they destroyed all human weapons except for a few they kept for themselves."

"If the fairies got rid of them all, how did you get yours? From the fae council, Sin, but where did they get it from?"

I glanced around at the buildings and several shadowed alleyways once again before standing up and brushing the dirt off my pants. "Okay. Good point, but still. Humans wouldn't have the knowledge or skill to make shots like these. I mean they're dead center, Sebastian. Whoever did this is an expert marksman."

Out of the corner of my eye, I caught the flicker of light off metal at the entrance of a dark alley. "I'll take that compliment coming from a—dragon, right?"

Damn, I was more tired than I thought. I hadn't heard a thing while we were looking over the two bodies. Inching my hand toward my holster, I heard the low click of a safety being released. "I wouldn't do that if I was you, dragon. My men would like nothing better than to kill more supers. Not that I couldn't take you out myself."

I moved both my hands slowly away from my side as I turned toward the alleyway. "Who are you and why did you kill these two?"

"These two? Well, we killed them because they killed some good people back down the road."

Rose was getting impatient. "Are you alright, dragon?"

Turning my head so I could keep half an eye on the alleyway, I waved at the group. "Yeah, we're fine. Just stay there for now. We seem to have a slight problem."

"Okay."

Turning my full attention back toward the alleyway, I could just make out the outline of the creature in the dim light thrown off by the lone lantern. "So, you told me why you killed these two, but you didn't tell me who you are."

"You're right, I didn't, dragon."

Sebastian pointed at the creature. "Sin, did you see that weapon he has slung over his shoulder? Even the fairies don't have anything that sophisticated."

"I saw it." I took in the long barrel with the attached silencer as the shadow moved ever so slightly. "Are we just going to stand here all night, or what?"

"That depends, dragon."

"Depends on what?"

"On what you and your masters are here for?"

I heard the imp on my shoulder whisper, "Oh, crap." I caught him slapping his hand to his forehead as I took a step forward. "Oh, we're in deep shit now."

"The fairies aren't my masters, asshole. I work for myself as an independent bounty hunter."

The click of more safeties being released in the night stopped me like I had hit a brick wall. "Don't sweat it. If I had wanted you dead, you all would have been dead long ago. I have more important things to do than kill a dragon and some fairies that have done nothing to the humans living around here. Unlike those two."

"Okay then, what are you after?"

"I'm looking for my sister. Oh, and the creature that stuck some supernatural baby in her against her will. Know anything about that, dragon?"

"Sin, the succubus. His sister was probably one of the ones she stuck a Were baby in or ... Oh, shit."

"Or what, dragon?"

I stared at the outline of the human, figuring that our lives rode on my answer. "When did you last see your sister?"

"This morning, just before she took off for parts unknown. She told me that some creature knocked her up. When I told her we would get rid of the bastard in her, she freaked and took off on me."

That was comforting, at least to us. I figured this girl was one of the ones carrying the mixed Were children. "Your sister is carrying a Were baby put in her by a succubus. The fairies and I are trying to stop this creature from killing other supers and creating more of these children."

"Why would she be doing this? I mean this succubus. Why would she be impregnating humans with super sperm?"

"From what we gather, she is creating more of her kind. By using supernatural creatures as donors, she can make monsters that are harder to kill."

"So, is that what you and the others killed up at the graveyard? These monsters? And the women that were carrying them?"

"She impregnated those women with vamp sperm. From the minute she did that, they were dead. There was no way to save them."

"And when you find my sister? Do you think you'll do the same to her as you did to those women up the hill?"

I could hear the anger in the human's voice. I didn't blame him. Ever since the takeover, supers treated humans as slaves at best. "Listen, those with the vamps inside of them were already turned before the babies were born. We had no choice. Your sister will be different."

"Yeah, I'm sure it will be, dragon. Now hear me. You supers keep away from my sister and let us hunt down this succubus. We'll take care of her. Just as we did that ogre a couple of years ago and others of your kind that screw with humans."

"Listen, I can't—" I stopped talking to the empty space between the two buildings. I turned back toward our group.

"What are we going to do, Sin? You know we can't let some rogue humans go off on their own and kill one of our kind. Why they would even think they can kill something when they are having trouble finding it, I can't fathom. See that kind of arrogance is why they lost this world to us."

"I don't think it's arrogance, Sebastian, as much as experience. Remember the ogre."

"Well, yeah, but—I guess, but one kill—"

"Think, partner. Do you really think that was their first kill?" He sat quietly on my shoulder, not arguing my point. "Yeah, I don't think it was either."

By then we were back with the group. Rose was looking put out when I heard Fallon's groggy voice. "What is going on here, dragon? Why are two more warriors dead? Who were you talking to?"

"Nice to see that you are finally awake, fairy. Just in time to head home."

Shaking off the two warriors that had been helping him stand, Fallon staggered before he caught himself and stood within inches of me. "I asked you questions, dragon, and I expect answers. Especially after what happened up on that hill. You are treading on thin ice after killing someone in the royal family."

I stared into those cold, blue eyes wondering for a second how everything could have gone so wrong between us so fast. "Edge was already dead, Fallon. Along with every other creature in that crypt when I torched that place. So, you can go suck it."

We stood like that. Neither of us giving an inch as Rose stepped between us. "Listen, Sin, why don't you tell us what happened to those two warriors. Okay?"

Stepping back, I tried to calm myself before telling them about the human in the alleyway. "And you let him go? Just like that? My mother was right, you're worthless. I wonder why I ever thought you could help us find this creature. I wonder what I ever saw in you in the first place," Fallon said.

It took all my willpower not to swipe that smug look off his face. Fallon had definitely not been thinking with his big head when he suggested working together. That brought on another round of melancholy for what I had lost these past few days. I swallowed my anger. "Fine, fairy, you're right. You don't need me. So, I'm going home." I turned to the female fairy and gave her my best smile. "See you, Rose. Have a nice life with dickweed here."

I grabbed Sadie's hand and turned, walking toward the nearest fairy gate to get me home. Behind me, I could hear Fallon and Rose arguing as we turned a corner. We took a few more steps when I heard Fallon's voice echo off the walls of the buildings around us until it faded to nothing. "THIS IS NOT OVER, DRAGON! NO ONE WALKS AWAY FROM ME OR THE QUEEN! DO YOU HEAR ME, DRAGON? THIS ISN'T OVER! NOT BY A LONG SHOT! I'M GOING TO MAKE YOU PAY, WHORE!"

23

Aezriane shuddered as she gazed at the creature lying on the bed. She had tried to peek into the dreams of several of the higher-ranking supers in this part of the world. As luck would have it, this orc was the only one deep in sleep. With another shudder, her mind rebelled at the thought of collecting this creature's seed, especially when his ripe body odor ravaged her nose.

No. Oh, hell no. There was no way she was going to even touch this creature. Even for her lost sisters, this was too gross. She grabbed her bag off the end of the bed and waved her hand to disappear when a low voice rumbled around the room. "My daughter, what do you think you are doing?"

Aezriane froze as the orc rolled to one side, bodily gases from his northern and southern regions permeating the bedroom. "Mother, please let me find another's dream to invade."

"Oh, my daughter. You will not find another dream to enter tonight, only the one belonging to this creature."

Aezriane's hands clutched at her sour stomach. "But Mother, why? Why are you doing this? How have I displeased you?"

"You ask me this after you let your new sisters die? After you spend your time having sex with those humans? Letting creatures that killed my children escape, when you should have been protecting your new sisters. When you should have been doing your duty to me. How dare you question me."

The succubus collapsed within herself as she sank to the floor of the orc's bedroom. "I'm sorry, Mother. Please, please forgive me and give me another creature's seed to collect. This creature is an inferior and will not serve your purpose."

A low hiss burned within her head. "How dare you question my commands? You will do this, my daughter. You will collect this creature's seed and bring it to me to be blessed." Aezriane shuddered at the pain that rippled through her body.

The pain stopped almost as soon as it had started. The succubus held her head to the floor, tears streamed down her cheeks. "Yes, Mother, I hear you and obey your command."

"Yes, I know you do, my daughter. That was only a taste of what lies in your future if you fail me again." Aezriane grabbed the edge of the bed as she staggered to her feet. She gagged as the orc released another cloud of noxious odor. "Oh, and daughter—"

Aezriane cringed, wondering what other hell her mother had planned. "Yes, Mother?"

"When you are done collecting what is mine, I want you to kill the dragon. Do you understand me?"

The succubus nodded eagerly. "Oh yes, Mother, I was going to do that. I was going to punish all of them. The fairies and the—" A blinding flash of pain raced throughout Aezriane's body dropping her to the floor again. She whimpered as she clutched at her head, her eyes squeezed tight against the ripples of agony beating inside her.

Once again, the pain stopped. "The fairies and others are of no importance, my daughter. They will be dealt with later, but the dragon. Yes, that dragon is the dangerous one. The one that could destroy everything I have planned. Do you understand me?"

"Yes, Mother. Please, no more. I understand perfectly. Please, no more punishment. I promise to never fail you again."

"Very good, Daughter. Now get up and collect the creature's seed. It is unseemly for one of my family to be on her knees like that."

Aezriane gathered herself from the floor and stood on shaky legs. "Yes, Mother. I will get this seed and bring it to you to bless. Then I will destroy the dragon as you commanded."

Orb was rudely woken from a sweet dream that involved him and two female elves. The hand over his mouth pressed down, cutting off most of his air as a sharp point at his throat kept him from moving around.

He looked into a pair of dark green eyes set in a face framed by blonde hair so fine he could see the ends flutter with the slight breeze of the creature's breath. His eyes went wide as the creature above him pushed the point of the blade against his throat. The burn from the blade told him it was iron. "You felt that, orc, right?" Orb nodded. "Good and you know that it is iron I hold at your throat?" Orb nodded again. "Good, good, just so we understand each other. Now I'm going to take my hand from your mouth and you will not make a sound. Understand?"

She removed the hand from Orb's face. "Who—who—are—"

Leaning over him, the creature's eyes went darker. "I told you not to make a sound, orc."

Orb nodded as his stomach grumbled for a few seconds and ended as a long stream of gas issued from his body. "Sorry." His eyes bulged as his hand darted to his mouth to cover his lips.

Aezriane's eyes watered. "Oh, Mother, give me strength." Orb sniffed the air wondering what the problem was. The creature swiped a hand across her face. "I want you to kneel on the bed, orc. Just remember, I'll slice your head from your body if you make any funny moves.

Orb nodded, moving around so he was kneeling on the bed in front of the creature. She reached into a bag that sat on the end of the bed and pulled out a golden bowl and set it in front of the orc.

Orb glanced at the bowl and then back into those green eyes. "What am I supposed to do with that?"

The creature laid the knife against his throat once more. "I need you to fill it with your seed, orc. Now no more talking. Get busy."

Orb sent several glances back and forth between the golden bowl and the creature before he held up his hands. "I'm sorry, but I don't have any seeds on me. We're, I mean orcs as a whole, not really farmers, you know."

The knife flashed from the orc's neck down to his crotch, the point digging below the overhang of his belly into the tip of his manhood. "This seed, idiot. The seed you carry down here."

Aezriane poked the knife even harder into the orc, causing him to yelp. She wondered just how damn dumb this creature could be. Finally, she saw the light go on behind the orc's eyes. She moved the knife back up against the orc's throat. "Do it. Do it now."

She watched as the orc's hand moved to his shaft, grasping it with two of his fat fingers. After a few jerks, he looked into her green eyes and pleaded. "I can't do it. I need something to—well, you know—turn me on."

The orc's eyes drifted between her eyes and her chest. "Oh fine, just don't move." She reached behind her and released the ties that held the top of her dress. As it fell, her breasts were exposed to the orc's greedy little pig eyes.

He licked his lips. A tiny drop of drool ran down his chin as his hand began a rapid movement below his belly. A shudder of revulsion ran through Aezriane at the sight of the creature playing with himself. One minute later the orc's eyes went wide as he spilled himself into the golden bowl between his legs. As the last dribble hit the receptacle, he closed his eyes with a smile on his face.

Aezriane shoved the iron knife through the orc's throat, pushing him backward so it pinned him against the headboard of his bed. She watched with some satisfaction as his fat legs kicked in death. After the last shudders stopped, the succubus grabbed up the golden bowl, her bag, and waved her hand taking her from the orc's dream.

Stalking over to the altar, she slammed the bowl onto the stone surface. Some of the piss yellow liquid spilled over, running slowly down the side of the bowl and splashing on her hands. She wiped the liquid off on the hem of her dress. "Mother, I have brought you this gift. Please bless it."

A dark cloud gathered as the bowl sat untouched. "Very good, my daughter. Now, I want you to go out and do as I told you. I want the dragon dead."

Aezriane gazed at her mother. "But—but aren't you going to bless this seed? I will need to insert it in the hosts before I kill the dragon."

Laughter rang out into the room. "Oh, my daughter, I had no intention of using such inferior seed to make more of my daughters."

"WHAT?" Aezriane swiped the bowl from the altar where it smashed against the wall, the yellow liquid slowly dripping down the stone. "I did exactly what you wanted me to and you're not going to even—NOOOOOOOOOOOOOOOOO!" The succubus' legs gave way from the pain. She had thought the suffering that racked her body in the orc's room had been bad, but it was nothing to what was coursing through her body now. She felt as though her soul was being shredded into a thousand pieces.

After a million years, the pain subsided. "I told you, daughter, you were being punished by collecting the orc's seed. Now I would suggest you follow my orders and kill this dragon like I told you. Without any more hysterics, do you understand?"

"Yes."

"Yes, what, my daughter?"

"Yes, Mother."

"Very good. See you don't fail me again. Or next time, I won't be so lenient with you. Do you understand?"

What little light there was in the room reflected off the bloody tears streaking the succubus' face. "Yes, my mother. I understand perfectly."

24

Hours later we were home. I had figured we would have trouble traversing the fairy gates since Fallon seemed so hellbent on making my life miserable but lucky for the fairies controlling the gates they let us through with no problems.

The three of us were dragging our feet. Well, at least two of us were since Sebastian had hitched a ride on our shoulders. The imp had been quiet the whole time which was unusual for him. Quiet that is until we got within spitting distance of our front door. "So, Sin, have you thought about what we are going to do now?"

I fumbled in my pockets looking for the front door key. "Yeah, I think that making a dragon fire as big as I did really kicked my ass. I'm going to bed and sleep for a few days, Sebastian."

"It's bound to kick your butt. That much fire takes a lot of energy. What I mean though is what are we going to do in the long run? What are we going to do about bounties? It's not like either one of us can survive on our good looks and it seems like you burned a few bridges with the fairies tonight."

Sadie tugged on my sleeve. "Uh, guys—"

"Hold on a minute, Sadie," I said jerking my arm out of her hand. Yeah, I know, I'm not nice, but I never was in the best of moods when I'm tired. I patted my other pockets wondering where I had left that damn key. "Screw you, Sebastian, speak for yourself. Just because the only thing that thinks you're good looking is a female imp doesn't mean we're in the same boat. Besides, there are plenty of other people out there that will pay bounty money. The fairies aren't the only ones needing our services."

"Like who, Sin? The vamps? The goblins? Oh no, wait, I know, maybe the orcs will pay us to find out who killed one restaurant owner."

"Uh, guys—"

"Just hold it a second, Sadie. Now, where the hell is that damn key? And as for you, partner, there are other creatures out there that will pay."

"Yeah, right, they'll pay, dragon, but not in gold. And we all know that."

Sadie stomped her foot on the dry ground, dust puffed up around her. "GUYS! YOU REALLY NEED TO SHUT UP FOR A SECOND AND LISTEN!"

I stopped patting my pockets and turned to look at Sadie as the imp hopped from my shoulder to hers. "Fine, Sadie, what's so important that it can't wait until I unlock the door and we get inside?"

"I've been trying to tell you that the door is already unlocked and open, Sin."

It took a few seconds for her words to register in my sleep-addled mind. My eyes swept over to the door and, sure enough, it was cracked open just a hair. I whipped out my weapon as I pushed Sadie to the side. "I thought you said that no one could get through your alarm system, Sebastian."

"No one can, Sin," Sebastian said as he leaped to the top of the doorframe and fiddled with a black box. "This is impossible. I mean, there's no way they could—"

I kept one eye on the door and another on the surrounding area all the while listening to the imp cursing and mumbling to himself as he hit buttons and switches in the box. Finally, after a few minutes, he stopped and looked at me his eyes wide, his mouth hanging open. "Well, you just going to sit there like that or are you going to tell me how someone got by your fail-safe security system?"

"I'm telling you. No one should've gotten past my system. It's all green lights and the power stone is fully charged."

"Yeah, but obviously someone did." The imp shook his head as he glanced down at the black box, and then back up at me. "Now the question is are they still inside?"

"I can't tell."

"Fine. Can you at least tell me who bypassed your brilliant security, partner?"

Sebastian's face fell. "Sorry, Sin."

I didn't want to say anything that would bring down the imp's confidence any further than it already was. The little guy prided himself on knowing more than any super about security. To have someone get past his best work. It had to be killing him inside. "Alright then, there is only one way to find out if our visitors are still in there. We do it the hard way. You and Sadie stay here, while I clear the house. Okay?"

Sadie got a stubborn set to her eyes and her lips pouted. "But I want to go with you. I can help you find anyone in there."

I flashed the 9mm in her face. "You know how to handle one of these?"

"Well, no."

I pulled a knife from the back of my belt. "I didn't think so. Take this and stay right here with Sebastian. I can clear the house faster by myself."

"Fine, Sin."

"Thanks, Sadie. Sebastian, you know what to do in case someone tries to get around me."

"Yeah, I was planning to stay our here anyway. It's not like I would be stupid enough to volunteer to go in there with you, dragon."

I eased the door open and moved into the dark beyond it. I stepped to the wall when I heard a whisper behind me. "Sin. Get out the com gear we found last year."

Reaching down to my belt, I pulled a slim headphone from it. I unfolded it, fitting it on my head and adjusting the mic so it hugged my cheek and extended to my mouth. "Sebastian? Can you hear me?"

"I hear you, Sin. Loud and clear. Damn, these things work great."

The imp had found these com units and a dozen of their brothers in an old human military base. It had taken him about three months to fix them up and get them working. This was the first time we had used them in a real-time situation though.

I stood listening for any sounds coming from the house in front of me. It was quiet except for the low whisper of the heater. "Sebastian, didn't we turn off the heat?"

There was a slight hesitation. "Yeah, I did, Sin. Why?"

I moved down one wall of the short hallway. "Because it's on now. I'm going to clear the first room."

"Be careful, Sin."

"Always, Sebastian. Now keep the chatter down so I can concentrate." There was a quick click on the com unit as I reached the end of the hallway. The part of the living room I could see looked clear. Kneeling, I leaned out about waist high glancing into the room before ducking back into the hallway.

Not seeing anything, I stood up when a familiar voice from the dark floated across the room. "Took you long enough to get home, dragon."

"Shit." I recognized the voice from the alleyway. I was trying to figure out how he could have found my house, let alone got here before we did. I tried to center myself before I called my partner on the com unit. "Sebastian, we have a problem." Silence filled the airwaves. "Sebastian? Sebastian, are you there?"

"My men have your two friends, dragon."

"Double damn." I looked back down the hallway wondering if it would be better to go back and rescue my friends or go forward and take on the human in the living room.

I heard a low murmur in front of me and blew out a quick breath as I came around the corner putting two shots where the voice had come from. Dropping to my knees, my eyes bounced across the space when I felt cold round metal touch the back of my head.

My gun hand twitched. "Naughty, naughty, dragon. That wasn't nice at all. By the way, don't even think about it. I know your kind is supposed to be tough to kill, but even you wouldn't survive a bullet in the back of the head."

I slowly laid my weapon down on the ground. "Okay, now what?"

I heard a large group moving down the hallway toward us. "Why, now, we figure out a way to work together, dragon." The gun left the back of my head. "Go on, get up off your knees."

I stood and turned looking into a pair of dark eyes set into a light brown scarred face. "Who are you? And how did you get into my home?"

Sadie with Sebastian sitting on her shoulder came down the hall followed by a mix of eight human men and women. "Sorry, Sin, they caught me unaware," my partner said.

"It's alright, Sebastian. I got caught myself."

The human walked over to an old coat rack and took a small box from behind my best leather jacket. He looked at the coat for a second, examining the two holes where his heart would be. "Nice shots."

I took a step forward, anger bubbling to the surface. "Damn you. That's my best jacket. You know how hard it is to get a good leather coat like that?" I stopped at the sound of weapons shifting behind me.

I slowly counted to ten while I studied the human. He was taller than me, which isn't saying much, but not quite as tall as Fallon. But where the fairy was lean, I could see by the stretch of the black tee shirt he was broader and more solidly built. My eyes traveled down the battered camo pants tucked into well-worn combat boots. Then, my gaze drifted back up to meet those brown eyes.

His eyes held a certain appraising look as they roamed over my body. I felt a flush creep into my face. Whoa, girl, I scolded myself, as I swept that bod again. The last thing I needed was to get hooked up with a human. Especially one who was unexpectedly in my life and I didn't have any idea why.

"I'm Robert, by the way." His voice startled me, tearing my gaze from that bod.

"Huh?"

"You asked who I was in the alley. Now, I'm telling you, my name is Robert."

"Oh, yeah, right, sorry. Just tired, I guess." I heard a strangled laugh behind me. I shot a look over my shoulder, scowling at my partner. He sat on Sadie's shoulder with a grin plastered on his face, one eyebrow high on his forehead as he made a circle with the fingers of one hand and slid a single finger in and out with the other. I felt my whole body flush and swore that once we were alone, I was going to kill that imp, partner or not.

I flipped him the finger before turning back to Robert. "Well, now that we know who you are. Why are you here?"

The smile disappeared from his face. "Like I told you before, I want to find the creature that violated my sister and see if there is a way to get that damn thing out of her."

"You aren't like regular humans, are you? Just who are you? You and these others?"

"We're part of a resistance group."

"Resistance against what? The fae? Where did you get those weapons?"

Robert held up a hand stopping the flood of questions. "We're not against the fae as a whole. We are against the fairies. Or at least the ones that rule this world. We have other supers we interact with and have a common cause with to get rid of the ruling class."

I shook my head. These humans were in for a rude surprise if they thought any fae would let the humans run free in this world. No fae would ever let them destroy it like they had before the supers came out of hiding and took it over.

My thoughts must have been transparent because Robert's face broke out in a predatory smile. "Don't worry, dragon. We humans have no intention of overthrowing one fae ruler for another. But there isn't any reason we can't share this world with your kind, now that we know you aren't just fairy tales."

I heard the imp snort behind me. "And you believe that any fae, Were, or vamp is just going to embrace you with open arms when and if you get rid of the fairies?"

That grin of his grew. "If we can get rid of one ruler, we can get rid of another."

I stifled a yawn as I shook my head at this human. They just didn't understand the bigger picture. The fae and all the rest of the supernaturals thought humans were the most dangerous creatures on this planet. There was no way that any of them would give the humans their rights back. Most likely whoever they were working for would use them to get rid of the fairies and then exterminate the humans after they were no longer useful.

"Since you're not out chasing after your sister, you're here for what exactly, Robert?"

The smile left his face. "I think whatever that creature was—"

"It's a succubus, remember?"

"Yeah, okay, I think this succubus is going to come after you. So, I figured we hang around you until it comes to kill you and then we can capture it."

I nodded. Not bad thinking, for a human. "Well, for one thing, it isn't an it. It's a she. And for another, do you have any idea how you'll capture it? I mean her?" Goddess above I was tired.

Without saying a word, Robert raised his weapon as the band of humans behind me laughed. "Yeah, that won't work, humans," Sebastian said, cutting off the laughter.

A man next to Sadie shifted the big assault rifle he held. "And why, pray tell, won't our weapons work, imp? She's fae. We have iron-tipped ammo. Seems simple enough to us."

"It won't work because when a succubus comes to kill, she comes in the person's dreams. We need to go into that dream and capture her in a mirror, then you can kill her."

"So what? You're telling me you have a plan to capture this creature, imp?" Robert said.

Sebastian flew off Sadie's shoulder and landed on the back of a couch. He stood there, hands on his hips as he glared at the human. "You're damn right I do. A better plan than some half-assed humans can come up with too."

Robert met the unflinching gaze of the imp before he nodded. "Okay then. Let's hear your plan and capture a succubus."

25

I looked between the two for a second fighting back another yawn. "What? Just like that, you're going with his plan?"

Robert glanced between the two of us. "Aren't you partners?"

I looked over at Sebastian who had a wide shit-eating grin on his face as he wiggled his eyebrows at me. "Well, yes, we are partners."

"So, you telling us you don't trust your partner?"

"Yeah, don't you trust me, Sin?"

I was just too damn tired to fight anymore. I had a sneaking suspicion I would regret whatever plan was pinging around in Sebastian's little mind. "Fine, give me the quick rundown of your scheme so we can get some sleep."

"Well, first of all, you and the human here need to sleep together."

I must have been more tired than I thought as it took a few seconds to register just what my partner had said. My head whipped around as I stared daggers at him. "WHAT?! Are you out of your fucking ever-loving mind."

Robert's eyes roamed up and my body bringing a flush to my face and a gush of wetness between my legs. "Okay."

"Okay, my ass. There is no way I'll sleep with someone I just met. I'm just not that kind of woman." The imp cleared his throat, one eyebrow raised as a foot tapped on the back of the couch. "What? Well, I'm not."

"So, how many dates did you go on before you and that fairy bumped uglies, Sin? If I remember correctly, it was on the first date, wasn't it?"

"That was different. It was love at first sight.."

Sebastian held up a hand with two claws in the air. "And then there was that Were. The same night you two met."

"Yeah, but we—I mean, we connected, and—"

"And don't get me started on the Byer twins," the imp laughed as he held up two more claws in the air.

I heard muffled laughter behind me. I stomped my foot, as anger overrode embarrassment. "Listen, you little piss ass. You know I didn't know they were twins, and that they had a bet going between them."

My partner sobered up. "Yeah, you're right. I'll give you that one, Sin. Even though I did win five gold pieces off that bet."

"Well, alright then, Sebastian. Hey, wait a minute. You and I are going to have a talk about that bet later. And I'll have you know, I went to bed with those others on my terms. Not because you came up with some crazy plan for me to have sex with a human."

"Sin, I said nothing about having sex with him. I just said you need to sleep with him. You know climb in bed, close your eyes, and snore away."

My anger died as the embarrassment returned tenfold. "For your information, I don't snore, Sebastian."

Robert's face went serious. "I wasn't all that keen on having sex with a dragon either."

"Hey, wait a minute, human. I'll let you know I'm damn good in the sack and you said 'okay' pretty damn fast there." Sebastian shook his head as one hand rubbed his forehead. "What? Well, I am pretty damn great in bed and he did answer quick."

The two ignored me as the imp walked back and forth along the edge of the couch. "I need someone strong to keep Sin grounded while she dreams and to help distract the succubus so I can trap her."

"So, why me? Why do you think I can help the dragon with her dreams?"

"Because, for a human, you have a very strong life force and a vested interest in helping us capture this creature. And I can see that your auras are well-matched."

"You can see our auras?"

"Well, yeah, I'm an imp. It's what we do."

"Like I said before, I'm in."

"Wait a second, you two. I never said I was in with this idea." The imp stood on the end of the couch tapping one foot again with that damn eyebrow raised. The human stood behind him; his arms crossed over that broad chest of his. "Fine, fine, whatever. I'll go along with it as long as I can get to bed before I fall down."

"Great, Sin, you won't regret this at all," the imp said as he took off from the back of the couch and landed on Sadie's shoulder.

I grabbed Sadie's hand to lead her to my spare bedroom. "I wouldn't take any bets on that."

Sebastian peeked around Sadie's head. "What was that, Sin?"

"What? Oh, nothing. Nothing at all. Let's get Sadie settled and get your brilliant plan into motion." I headed across the living room stopping just outside another hallway leading toward the back of my house. "Oh, by the way, Robert, I only have two bedrooms. So, your group will have to find somewhere else to sleep."

The human swept one arm toward the hallway. "I know how many bedrooms you have, dragon. We all crashed here while we were waiting for you to come home."

"In my bed?"

A tiny woman with glasses wearing a shit-eating grin spoke up. "We slept in your bed since it was the biggest and could hold Ralph with no trouble." I looked up and up at the biggest human male who looked sheepish and thought, yeah, he would need the room that my king-size bed had. "Oh, and change the sheets before you get in bed." Ralph turned an even brighter red.

Images floated in my head as I took in those two. I winced as I tried to figure out the logistics. I opened my mouth, then wisely shut it. Nope, didn't really want to know. "I'll do that."

The tiny woman's smile stayed as she shrugged. "Sorry, it's been a while."

I ignored her half-assed apology. As far as I was concerned, this conversation needed to die. "Come on, Sadie. Let's get you to bed."

Sadie stumbled down the hallway, half asleep. "Okay, that sounds good. I'm not sure how much longer I can keep my eyes open."

An hour later I had the sheets changed on the beds. Sadie was down for the count in my spare bedroom wearing one of my old sleep shirts. Sebastian had disappeared, mumbling something about needing to set up the trap. I was finally in my room changing into another of my old ratty sleep tees.

Throughout this process, I could hear Robert giving orders to his unit. I still wasn't all that sure my partner's plan was one hundred percent foolproof. Of course, part of it could be I wasn't totally happy at setting myself up as bait. But I figured if the human was right, the succubus would be coming after me since I had thrown a wrench in her plans. It might as well be on our terms.

I was standing, one leg on the floor the other through the leg of a clean pair of panties when a loud knock on my bedroom door startled me. I caught my foot in the material, yelping as I hopped around until I tipped over hitting the floor with my bare ass.

My tee was bunched around my hips as I struggled to right my panties when the door burst open slamming against the wall and Robert came charging into my room. His eyes darted around taking in the space before they fell on me.

I gave up trying to put on the underwear and just tried to save what modesty I had left by getting my tee tugged down far enough to cover my bottom. I have to give him some credit. As he took in the sights displayed in front of him for the briefest of seconds, he turned a deep red and averted his eyes. "Sorry. Sorry. I thought I heard something drop in here."

I couldn't help but feel a tad bit sorry for him as his eyes bounced everywhere but on me. Finished adjusting my tee, I tossed the tiny piece of cloth in my hand onto my dresser. "It's alright. It was just me being me. You would think being a bounty hunter I wouldn't be as clumsy as I am sometimes."

Robert reached down and helped me to my feet. We stood chest to chest as Sebastian came flying into the room. "Was that you, Sin? Falling on your ass again? Man, I don't know how you survived as long as you have, girl." Robert and I glanced over at the imp as he hung in the air a puzzled look playing across his face as we both broke out in laughter. "What? What's so funny you two?"

I stopped laughing as felt a familiar heat coming off the human. Gazing into his warm eyes, I noticed they had a fire smoldering deep within them. A small gasp escaped my lips as I was lost in their depths. Then Robert let go of my hand and took a tiny step away from me as the laughter and the heat left his eyes.

The imp stared at the two of us for a few more seconds before he cleared his throat. "Yes, well—Uh—If you two are ready to get this plan in gear, we should get started."

I nodded as Robert took another step away. "Yeah, let's get it going, imp. I want to find a way to fix my sister."

I deflated as the human's eyes looked everywhere but into mine. Well, fine then. I guess this dragon was just too repulsive for his taste. Then I got mad at myself since only an hour ago I was bitching about going to bed with him and here I was mad because he wouldn't jump me.

"Well, all righty then. Your people know that they need to stay out of the way for this to work, right?" Sebastian said.

"Yeah, they know. I gave them orders to keep an eye out for any intruders and for Cindy-Lou to reset your alarm system."

"Cindy-Lou? Which one is she?"

"The one who shared your bed with Ralph."

I flushed as I glanced at the pile of dirty sheets in the corner. "Oh, right. Uh—" I turned to Sebastian wishing I had taken the dirty clothes out of the room instead of just throwing them in the corner till morning. "Yeah. So how do we go about this plan of yours?"

The imp smiled wide. "Well, first the two of you need to get naked, Sin."

"Partner, you had better not be screwing around, because if you are I swear you will live just long enough to regret it."

The imp put his hand to his chest as his lips trembled. Oh please, I couldn't believe it, I actually thought I saw the slow trickle of a tear slide down one cheek. "You wound me, Sin. I'm just trying to help you two capture this bitch before she kills any more supers or humans. Besides, she is giving demons a bad name."

Robert shook his head at the imp before he whipped off his shirt. "As the dragon says, imp, you had better be on the level with this."

"Listen, you two. For this to work, I need full body skin-to-skin contact. Okay? Trust me. Have I ever steered you wrong before, Sin?"

Robert was unbuckling his pants when he stopped and glanced over at me, one eyebrow raised high. "Yeah, you really don't want me to answer that one," I said as I reached down and rid myself of the one piece of clothing I wore.

The human's eyes went even wider as the tee I was wearing hit the floor. He hesitated for a second, his eyes drinking in every inch of my exposed body before he loosened his pants and let them drop to the floor and stood up straight. "Oh, sweet goddess above," I whispered as I took in my own eyeful of the human standing in front of me.

The scars that ran along his face ran down his neck and onto a chest that looked like it was made of granite. His clenched hands hung at a waist that narrowed, then splayed out into hips and legs that were as muscled as the rest of his body. I dragged my eyes back up his legs stopping between them taking in his size as I felt a light shudder shift through my body and a gush of wetness between my legs.

I heard the imp's voice bounce around my head as though from a million miles away. The tiredness fled as all I could think about was getting Robert in bed with me and not just for sleeping either. "Sin—Sin—Earth to Sin."

I tore my eyes away from that hot body and looked over at Sebastian. "What—I—what were you saying?"

"I said, I should get you guys settled so I can do what I need to do for this plan to work."

"Uh, right, sure. No problem." I turned and leaped toward my bed; wondering just how I would get any sleep with Robert there too.

I moved over to the other side of the bed as I watched Robert steal across the floor like a panther hunting its dinner. I could see those dark eyes smoldering as they roamed my body as if I was the main course.

"Okay, now, I need the two of you to spoon together with Robert laying behind you, Sin."

"Okay." I turned my back to the human and scooted to the center of the bed. There was just the slightest hesitation then I felt Robert's body engulf mine from behind. His hardness pressed up against me. One hand slid under my head and I laid it back down on the hard muscles of his arm as his other hand rested on my belly.

We shifted a bit against each other, then settled down. "Are you sure you're comfortable, dragon?"

I could feel his hardness pressing against my back as his hand traced a slow circle on my stomach. "Uh, yes. I couldn't be better."

Sebastian fluttered near our bodies, the breeze from his wings brushing against my hardened nipples sent delightful bursts to my center. Of course, he was oblivious to the effect he was having. "Good. Glad you two are finally set. Now, I don't want you to move until I finish drawing the runes I need to make this magic work, understand?"

Laying perfectly still wrapped in Robert's arms was going to be harder than I thought.

26

I giggled as the bristles from Sebastian's paintbrush made me squirm in Robert's arms. The giggles turned to a gasp when I rubbed against his hardness. "Will you please stay still, Sin? I need to make these runes accurate for them to work and you moving around is not helping. If I make even one little mistake, I can't guarantee the results."

"Sorry, Sebastian, I'm trying, but you know that I'm ticklish across the ribs."

"Yeah. And on the arms, the feet, your ass, and we won't even talk about your—"

I blushed as a quiet chuckle sounded behind me. "If you finish that statement, I'll kill you right here and now, partner." Robert's amusement died a quick death as I slammed an elbow into his ribs.

"There. You're done, Sin. Now lay perfectly still so I can do the human's runes. They need to line up with yours. Think you can do that, girl?"

"Yes, Sebastian."

"You won't have any problems as I'm not ticklish like the dragon, imp."

"That's good. Then it will only take me a few minutes to finish this and she can get to sleep and we can set the trap for the succubus."

Sebastian started working on Robert's runes. I had to lay still but my mind was working overtime and still fuzzy on parts of the plan. "So how is this going to work?"

"It's very simple. These runes will connect you together so that when you're attacked, Robert will be able to talk to you in your dream and hopefully keep you grounded in this realm."

"Hopefully? What do you mean 'hopefully,' partner? What happened to a plan you just knew would work?"

The imp hesitated for a second. "Just trust me, Sin. This plan is foolproof, okay? Now let me finish these last runes." A couple of quiet minutes later, time I had spent wondering about 'hopefully working' and trust, Sebastian crowed, "There, all done."

Looking over my shoulder, I saw our runes did seem to flow from one body to the next. I looked the imp up and down trying to see the painted runes on his body. "Don't you need to paint the same things on you?"

The imp flew over to my dresser, dumping a tiny brush and paint jar on it before turning back to us as his eyes dropped to the floor. "No way, Sin. You and I have known each other so long I don't need runes to enter your dreams."

I stared at the imp, a sneaky suspicion on my mind. "And you know this how?"

"Uh—well—You see, I may have—Well, you know—"

"I think what your partner is trying to tell you is that he has been in your dreams before."

I dug another elbow into his ribs hard enough to bring a blast of air that blew across my hair. "Thanks, dipshit, I figured that out for myself." I turned my attention back to the imp who still kept his eyes glued to my bedroom floor. "When this is done, Sebastian, you and I will have a long talk about privacy. Do you understand me?"

"Yes, Sin," he said before he flicked the light out and darted out the door, closing it behind him.

Robert and I shifted a bit until we were once more comfortable. The darkness of the room surrounded us. The quiet of the night broken only by the soft breathing of the two of us lying on the bed.

It was quiet for a long time. I closed my eyes trying to will myself to sleep. It shouldn't have been all that hard. I had been barely awake when we came home only an hour or so ago. The heat of Robert's body against mine though was too distracting. I tried shifting a bit being careful not to break the lines of the runes when I felt the human's hot breath on my neck. As one finger traced the lines of my wings. "Do all dragons have this tattoo?"

"It's not a tattoo, it's my wings. It's part of dragon magic."

"So how does it work?"

I flexed my shoulders a little bringing out the tips of my wings, then relaxed them so my wings disappeared. "See? Dragon magic."

In the quiet, I squirmed around trying to get comfortable sharing my bed with an unfamiliar body. "Are you okay? You're being fidgety, dragon."

"I'm fine. I guess I'm just too keyed up to sleep."

"Maybe I can help relax you?" Robert said as his hand slid up and cupped one breast, running his thumb back and forth on my nipple. I sucked in a breath as the nub hardened under his rough hand. I hissed as his hand dropped to the other nipple, repeating the movement on it as his lips caressed the back of my neck. "That's not helping to relax me, hu—"

I stopped talking as the hand dropped from my nipples and slid between my legs and inside the wetness there. The slow back-and-forth movement of his hand had me climaxing in seconds. My legs shook as I hit peak after peak.

When I finished coming, I felt Robert open my legs. Taking the top one, he lay it back over his. I was just going to ask what he had in mind when I felt the tip of his shaft penetrate my wet center. A low animal groan escaped my lips as he slowly slid inside me, hitting depths that even Fallon had never hit before.

"Ooooooooooh, mmmmmmy godddddddddddddess." Then, I lost all ability to speak. Robert kissed and bit the back of my neck and shoulder. His movements picking up speed as I pushed back against him. We were both lost as I felt him spill his hot seed in me, making me come even harder than before as his teeth clamped down on my shoulder. The pain and pleasure sent me even higher into the climax racking my body.

After what felt like a never-ending high, we both came back to the world. My leg slid off his trapping his length within me. I felt Robert gently adjust our bodies so that once again the runes aligned. His hand cupped my breast, his thumb lightly rubbing along the tip of my nipple. "Are you sleepy now?"

I felt a slight prickling of heat rising again. "I'm fine. But if you keep doing what you're doing with your thumb, I don't think either of us will get any sleep and that would defeat the whole purpose of this little exercise."

He slid his hand down to my belly and snugged me closer to his warm body. "Well, we wouldn't want that now, would we? Especially since the imp went through all that trouble of painting us up for the succubus."

I nestled back against him, fighting now to keep my eyes open. Surprising how a hot little quickie can tire you out like that. "No, we need to capture her so that— that we can—"

I could feel Robert's lips brush the top of my head. "Just hush, dragon. Sleep. I'll be here when you need me."

I fought the sleep that was overwhelming me. "Call me by my name, please. I mean after what we just did." I wanted to explain about Fallon and how he always called me his dragon and how I wanted Robert to use my name, but I gave up as the darkness overtook me.

Robert lay listening to the pleading in the dragon's voice before she drifted off into the deep rhythm of sleep. Looking at the dragon, her light green skin against his brown, he wondered just what he had gotten himself into. Leaning down, he kissed the top of her hair. "Someone hurt you bad, Sin. Someone will pay dearly for that." He settled next to the dragon and closed his eyes to rest.

Aezriane looked into the black stone bowl. A bowl that had the likeness of humans and supernatural creatures carved along the rim. She ran a finger over one of the figures on the side. She smiled into the murky depths as a mist rose in the shape of the dragon. "There you are. Yes, sleeping after such a long tiring day."

The smile faded as the figure took shape. The succubus hissed in annoyance as another figure appeared right next to the dragon, a human. Well, well, now isn't that interesting. First the prince of fairies and now we're slumming with humans. No matter, she could invade the little slut's dreams without waking the human. Yes, it will be interesting to see the human wake next to the dead dragon after she was done with her.

Slowly taking a bottle from the table the bowl rested on, Aezriane poured a dollop into the container before taking a sip of the liquid. Setting the bottle down, she could feel the liquid burn itself into her system. She closed her eyes and bowed her head. "Mother, allow me to enter this creature's dreams. I do this in your name." Opening her eyes, the succubus felt herself drawn away from the room where she stood and into the dragon's dreams.

I slowly came awake. Some sixth sense told me something was off. Through slitted eyes, I could just make out the features of my room in the darkness. A room that was mine, but wasn't. There was the same furniture. The same clothes hanging out of the dresser drawers, but the shadows in the corners were wrong. They were deeper, darker. They told me this wasn't my room.

As the sleepiness fled from my body, I felt the cold of the iron that encircled my wrists and ankles. No, we definitely weren't in Kanas anymore, Toto. It was a line I remembered from one of the human children's books I had in my library. I lay as still as I could, trying to clear the sleep from my mind. I tried to extend my senses out without making any movements and alerting whoever could be in the room with me.

"Nice try, dragon, but I know that you are awake. You can stop trying to pretend." I lay as still as I could fighting to keep an even breathing pattern when I heard movement beside me. Rancid breath stirred my hair. "You don't want to piss me off any more than you already have. You would do well to stop this farce. We have so many things to do before daylight comes."

I opened my eyes taking in the green eyes staring at me and laughed. "Screw you, bitch. I think you need anatomy lessons if you think you will get any baby batter from me."

Her hand trailed from my face, ran along my neck, and up one side of my breast. There, she sliced her fingernails across my tough hide, opening four deep furrows. I hissed, stifling a cry as blood ran down my chest and pooled in my cleavage. "I see, my dear, that we need to learn our place," she said as she licked the blood from the tips of her fingers.

"Oh, honey, after the last few days I know exactly where I stand in this world, believe me. I don't need some murdering sex psycho to show me anything."

"You are lucky I don't have any more of the undead seed with me. I was feeling bad implanting it in those humans, but with you? You, I would enjoy putting one those creatures inside of you. Watching it tear you apart as it ripped itself out of your still warm body. Yes, I think I would take great pleasure in that."

Remembering the creatures that had crawled out of the humans in the crypt, I couldn't stop a little shudder bringing thunderous laughter from the succubus. Her amusement stopped short as I spit. "Well, I guess since you felt bad about those women you didn't mind that I barbequed the creatures."

The creature wiped the spittle from her face. I felt her nails slash across my cheek, knocking my head to the side. "THOSE WERE MY SISTERS! YOU KILLED MY SISTERS AND WRECKED MY MOTHER'S REVENGE."

Blood dripped down my cheek as I gazed at the creature. Fear reared its ugly head. Damn, she shouldn't be able to hurt me this easily. Hell, I had been pounded on, beaten on, and thrown across rooms by bigger creatures than this and never shed a drop of blood. That's when I heard a voice from far away. "Sin. Fight her, Sin."

The succubus looked around the room. Her eyes scrunched up, before looking at me. "Did you hear that? That voice? How is this possible?"

"Hear what, you psycho bitch? What? Now, you're telling me you're hearing voices too?"

The succubus glared at me, her fists opening and closing as my blood dripped off her fingertips. "Do not mess with me, dragon. It should not be possible for anyone to connect with you in this dream, but me."

I watched as the succubus spun toward the figure materializing behind her. She backed away, hitting the edge of the bed. Sebastian kept moving forward, holding the full-length mirror in front of him. Runes inscribed along every inch of the frame as he invoked the spell. "INSIDIA DAEMN CONITATUM." Instantly, a light flashed from the mirror and the succubus was gone from the room.

Robert looked at Sin as she struggled in her sleep. He wrapped his arms tighter around her as she whimpered in pain and slices appeared across one breast, splashing hot blood across his body. "Damn, what the hell."

He started to get out of the bed. "NO! DON'T MOVE, HUMAN!" The imp popped into the room behind a mirror. "You need to stay connected to Sin. Talk to her and distract the succubus so I can get into the dream."

Slashes appeared across the dragon's face coating the human once again with her hot blood. Looking between the imp and the dragon for a split second, Robert gathered her body close to his and leaned down to whisper in her ear as the imp disappeared. "That fucking imp had better be right about this or I'll kill him."

What seemed like hours later, Sin opened her pain-filled eyes as the imp popped back into the room with the mirror. Robert breathed a long sigh of relief just as the door of the room burst open and Ralph came stumbling into the room. "The damn fairies stole the girl."

27

I sat on the edge of the bed; a sheet wrapped around me as the unit medic stitched my facial wounds. I half listened as Ralph reported what had happened while we were in bed capturing the damn succubus.

The fairies, with Fallon in the lead, had used a portable fairy gate to enter my spare bedroom and take Sadie away with them. Seems that damn fairy had planted the device in my house the last time he was here. At least everyone was being tactfully quiet about how the device had gotten into my home.

I winced as the woman tugged on the last stitches and tied it off. "There you go. That's the best I can do. Sorry, but it will leave scars."

I figured a few scars weren't going to matter all that much in the long run since we had bigger problems brewing than my looks. Not that I had been what you would have called beautiful before, anyway.

Robert walked over and took my chin in one of his big hands and moved my face from side to side. His expression showed nothing of what was going on in that mind of his. "Thanks, Doc. It looks almost as good as the work you do on me."

I felt my stomach drop even though I had told myself that scars wouldn't matter. I couldn't figure out why I should care what this human thought anyway. "Oh, so she's the one who's been putting you back together?"

"Why, Sin? Are you going to try to match me, scar for scar?"

My heart skipped a beat at hearing my name from his lips. My eyes darted to his bare chest, taking in the crisscrossed marks. "I think I'll pass on that, Robert. Seems like you have enough for both of us."

Robert leaned over, his warm breath stroked my hair as his lips brushed my forehead. "Remember that next time, Sin. I like that green skin of yours unmarked."

I blushed as his hand slowly slid down my neck and along the top of my breast, just above the sheet. Our eyes locked together. I wondered just what was happening here when I heard Cindy-Lou clear her throat. "Uh, any time you two are through giving each other goo-goo eyes, we need to decide what to do about the succubus and the fairies."

We walked over to where Sebastian was leaning next to the mirror, his arms across his chest. One huge shit-eating grin plastered across his face as he nodded at the captured succubus. Her face glowered from the rune painted frame of her prison. "See, I told you my plan would work, Sin."

"Yes, and your partner was hurt during your plan, imp. What the fuck was that all about? She could have been killed by the time you got off your ass and got in her dream to rescue her."

The grin fell off imp's face as he lunged toward the human. "Hey, now, you wait just one fricking minute, human. I got in there as soon as I could."

"My ass you did. If I hadn't distracted the creature who knows what she would have done to my woman."

"Your woman? Why you ignorant, half-assed human."

I stood half listening to the two of them argue as I looked in the mirror. The succubus blew a tiny kiss before licking my dried blood off one finger sending a chill through me. Then Robert's words slammed into me like a sledgehammer. I spun around and slammed my fist into his chest. "WHOA! WHOA! WHOA! YOUR WHAT?"

Confusion played across his face as he looked at where I had hit him. "Your what? What?"

I heard Cindy-Lou laugh. "I think we should wait outside while they figure this out. It might be safer for all of us."

The humans in the room disappeared like a puff of smoke before a high wind as Sebastian flipped off Robert and laughed as he flew past him. "Oh, you are in sooooo much trouble now, human."

I slammed the bedroom door shut. "Your woman?"

Robert crossed his arms over his chest, one eyebrow arched. "Do you really want to get into this while we have to deal with the succubus and your missing friend, Sin?"

I glanced over at the mirror as the creature trapped in it smiled and casually waved her hand. "Oh, don't mind me, you two. It's not like I'm going anywhere. You just go ahead and work out your little mundane problems."

"Screw you, bitch." I grabbed Robert's arm and led him away from the mirror. Stopping by the bed, I let go of him and glared into those brown eyes of his. "Now, listen here, human. Just because we had sex," I stopped as I flushed. "Granted it was hot sex—but anyway—that doesn't mean that you own me. I put up with that shit with that damn fairy and I'm not going to do it with you."

My words were drowned as Robert's lips crushed mine. I moaned as one hand wrapped itself in my hair and the other gripped me to his hot chest. His tongue dueled with mine. All that escaped from me was a low whimper of desire.

Laughter and hands clapping brought me back to reality as Robert broke from our kiss. Letting out a tiny gasp, one hand on his chest, I peeked into those intense eyes. "That still doesn't make me your woman, Robert. It just means you're hot and I'm attracted to you. Understand me?"

He slowly rubbed one finger across my chin. "Whatever you want to believe, Sin. After this is over we can talk about it, but until then you're mine."

His touch and the low growl of his voice sent a shiver down my spine. "Yeah, sure, talk." I wasn't sure this was heading in a direction I wanted to go. It was too soon after the disaster with that damn fairy.

Noises from the mirror caused both of us to turn. The succubus stood in the glass and smirked at us. "You two think this is over? That there will be an end? How cute. In six months, when my sisters are born, it will just be the beginning."

Robert marched over to the mirror, a low sound rumbled in his chest. I'll have to give him credit, the look in his eyes had the trapped creature cringing in her cage. "One of those women you put those creatures in was my sister, you bitch. I ought to kill you here and now for that."

The succubus regained her composure enough to shrug off Robert's threat. "Go ahead, human. Kill me. It won't change the outcome. There is no way you will find all the women I gave the seed to and there is no way to stop the pregnancies either. Not without killing the women."

Before Robert could retort, the bedroom door burst open and Sebastian came flying into the room. "There's a fairy at the door for you, Sin. They have a message and will only give it to you."

"Who is it, Sebastian? Do we know them?"

"Oh, yeah, we know her alright. It's Rose."

"Rose? Why would they send her?" I gathered some clothes together figuring there was only one way to find out. I waved my partner out of my bedroom. "Tell her I'll be right out, Sebastian."

He threw a glance at Robert a grin playing across his lips. "Yeah. Well, make it a quickie, Sin. I don't think she was too happy to find humans in your house."

"Listen, you tiny pervert. I'm just going to get dressed. Now, get your mind out of the gutter and let her know I'll be right out." Sebastian hummed his way out of the bedroom.

Robert was picking his shirt up off the floor as I dug a clean pair of panties from a pile of clothes. "Red is your color, dragon." I ignored his comment but I couldn't stop the blush that painted my face.

Turning my back to the human, I slipped the panties on along with a semi-clean pair of pants. I was trying to get a tee shirt turned right side out when I felt his arms slip around me, cupping my bare breasts as his hot lips played along the back of my neck. I laid my head back against his chest as his thumbs rubbed across my nipples, bringing a sigh from deep within me. "We—we don't have time for this, Robert."

His hand slid down my bare belly and he cupped my covered mound giving it a squeeze bringing a gasp from deep within me as a low growl rumbled against my neck. "Mine, Sin. You are all mine. Remember that."

I sighed again as he released me and walked out of the room. The succubus' voice, tinged with humor, drifted over from the mirror. "Oh, that one is going to be trouble for you, dragon."

I finished putting my shirt on before turning to scowl at the mirror. "Bite me, bitch."

I passed Ralph and Cindy-Lou coming down the hallway. "Robert said we're to keep watch on the creature in case this is a trick. Or the fairies have another way to open a gate into your bedroom." I nodded cursing to myself once again about that damn fairy. I promised myself one day I would neuter him with a dull knife. Better yet a spoon. Yeah, a spoon would definitely make a better impression on Fallon.

Entering the living room, I saw Sebastian had neglected to tell me that Rose hadn't been alone. Three of the queen's Amazon guards were flanking her, their weapons held at the ready. On the other side of the room, Robert and his group had their own weapons locked and loaded. Ready to rock-and-roll. The tension in the room was as thick as porridge. All it would take was one wrong word and bullets would fly, with me in the middle. Sometimes, I wondered how I got myself into these situations.

Rose frowned as Robert came over to stand just behind me. "I see you have new friends, dragon."

I glanced around the room. "That's what happens when the friends you think you have turn out to be enemies."

Her frown deepened. "I didn't know he put a gateway in your house, dragon. I swear on this."

I figured what she did or didn't know really didn't matter much anymore. I was just tired of all the fairy politics and bullshit. Rose was welcome to Fallon and his mother. "So, what is this message you have to give me, fairy."

Rose stiffened. "I'm supposed to give it to you and only to you on the queen's orders."

"I'm sorry, do you really think I give a damn about your queen, fairy?" The guards lifted their weapons but stopped as Rose held up a hand.

"Fine, then how about on the orders of Fallon?"

I laughed as I shook my head at the fairy. "Oh, I care even less what that ass says, Rose. Just give me the damn message and get the hell out of my house." The Amazons' eyes narrowed.

"Fine. You bring the creature you have captured to the castle and you will get your friend back."

Robert stepped to my side. "Not going to happen, fairy."

Rose shot him a look before she turned back to me. "As I was saying. A fair exchange, you bring the creature and you get your friend back." I studied Rose for a few seconds as I gathered my thoughts. There was no way I was going to go inside the queen's castle. Once in there, I knew there was no way Sadie or I were ever walking out of there in one piece. "Well, dragon, what is your answer?"

"Why does the queen want the succubus? Why not let us just get rid of her?"

"She wants the names of the women infected by the creature with the Were seed."

I had a pretty good idea why the queen wanted the names, but I wanted to hear it from the fairy's mouth. "And when she gets the names? Then what?"

"Then we will get rid of them before the creatures are born and destroy us, dragon. You saw the monsters the vampire seed produced. We can't afford any other monsters to be born."

"Yeah, well, I won't do the exchange in the castle. I don't trust either Fallon or your queen. I'll let you know where we make the exchange."

"The queen will not accept those terms."

"Screw the queen, Rose. We do this our way or the succubus dies without you getting the list of names. Take it or leave it. Your choice."

"Alright, but make it quick. The queen is not a patient fairy in the best of times."

"I'll let you know where the exchange will go down in a few hours. Alright?"

"Fine, but if it's any longer than that, I would not want to be your little friend." The fairy signaled her group to follow her out the door.

"Oh, and Rose—"

The fairies stopped, and they all looked back at me. "Yes?"

"Make sure you tell the queen that Sadie better not have a mark on her at the exchange, understand me?" Rose didn't say anything before walking out the front door with the Amazons following closely behind her.

28

It was quiet for about ten seconds after the fairies left then the humans and Sebastian all started to yammer at once. All except for Robert who stood looking at me as I tried to cut through the noise. "Knock it off, all of you. Sin has something to say." Everyone went silent, even Sebastian. Robert winked at me. "So, what's the plan, Sin? You do have a plan, right?"

I rubbed my head as the start of a headache pinged inside my skull. "I have a plan, I think, but first we need to have a talk with the succubus."

"I don't think it will matter. She just doesn't give a damn about her life, Sin."

I didn't say anything as I headed down the hallway to my bedroom. Ralph was standing outside the door, his weapon at the ready. "Well, we going to war or what?"

I ignored him as we walked past him and into my bedroom. The smirk on the succubus' face added to my headache. It took all of my willpower not to reach through the glass and wipe it off. "So, if I understand it correctly, you would die before you gave us the names of the woman you put the Were seed in. That's what you're telling us, right?"

"Go ahead and kill me, dragon. I couldn't care less. In six months, my sisters will avenge me when they are born. With the Were mixture in them and my mother's blessing, they will conquer your kind and send you all to hell."

"And there is no way we can talk you out of the carrying out this crazy plan of yours, right?"

"Oh, dragon, you and these humans cannot scare me. There is nothing you can do that would make me talk. Do your worst."

"Oh, I wasn't thinking about what we could do to you, bitch. I was just wondering what kind of nice things the fairy queen could do to you that would make you talk. What do you think, Robert?"

The smirk she wore died as she turned white. "Knowing the fairy queen as I do, Sin, I'm sure she could dig through her magic spells and find something to break her. Why I once heard that she had a lesser fae screaming out information five minutes after she started in on him."

"You—you wouldn't. You are enemies, human. Dragon, think what that stupid fairy did to your heart. You would turn me over to the queen? His mother? Would you really do something like that, dragon?"

I gazed at the panic building in the succubus' eyes and shook my head. "After what you did to those women in the crypt, you are dead no matter what."

The succubus fell to the bottom of the mirror, burying her face in her hands. "I was only doing my mother's bidding. My mother commanded me to do this for revenge against what the fairies did to my kind."

I let her sob for a few seconds before I kneeled next to the mirror. "You will pay with your life for what you have done. What you have to decide is if you want it quick or—well, I've heard the queen can extend her punishment out for years if she is properly motivated. And believe me when I tell you she is very, very motivated to get her hands on you and find out the names of those humans."

The succubus looked at me. Her tear-streaked face fallen in despair. "You aren't giving me much of a choice, dragon. Have you no heart inside that body of yours?"

"You raped and killed innocent women. And those are the victims we know about. I reserve my compassion for the innocent, succubus. As I said, you will pay one way or another. The choice is yours to make."

She looked past me and at the humans grouped behind me. "Are you just going to stand by and let her do this, humans? You can't just kill me or turn me over to the fairies like the dragon wants, can you?"

"One of those women you put the Were seed in was my younger sister, bitch. You will get what you deserve"

The succubus' eyes darted over to Ralph and Cindy-Lou. The big man hefted his weapon and clicked the safety off. "I say we just give her to the fairies for what she did." The tiny woman chambered a round in her own weapon.

The succubus stared off into the distance for a few seconds before she sighed in resignation. She reached inside her dress and pulled out a piece of parchment. "Fine, dragon, you win. This is a list of the names of the women I gave the gift to."

"You mean the women you raped, bitch."

I gazed at the mirror trying to figure out how we would get that paper when I heard my partner's voice at the bedroom door. "I'll get it for you, Sin."

The imp flew to the floor and reached out for the runes on the lower corner of the mirror when I heard weapons move behind me. "Don't try any tricks or your life will end even quicker than you want it to," Robert said.

I watched a little light die in the succubus' eyes as her lips compressed into a white slash. "Fine, human, no tricks."

Sebastian glanced at the weapons aimed at the mirror and moved to the side before he wiped the runes off of one corner. The succubus hesitated for a second, her eyes locked on the weapons aimed at her before she slid her hand through the glass laying the piece of paper on the floor.

As soon as her hand was back inside her cage, Sebastian redrew the runes. "There, I sealed her back in."

Grabbing the paper, Robert helped me to my feet. I unrolled the sheet with nineteen names and addresses on it written in what I hoped was red ink. The succubus sneered when I glanced at her. Yeah, that was blood alright. Shit.

Sebastian landed on my shoulder and looked at the paper before letting out a low whistle. "Man, these women are spread out all over the human areas. How are we going to collect them all in time?"

Robert held out a hand, and I gave him the paper. He passed it to Cindy-Lou and nodded at the door. She and Ralph disappeared. "We'll take care of getting these women to a safe place."

Sebastian shook his head as the two disappeared. "Those two have a magic carpet or something, human? There is no way they can get to all those women in a couple of hours."

I took in the sly look on Robert's face. "Their group is a lot larger than we thought, Sebastian. Isn't it, Robert?" The human leaned against the wall, not saying a word.

"Shit, what the hell did we get in the middle of, Sin? A couple of days ago we were hunting rogue vamps. Now it's like we're in the middle of a fae and human war. What happened to the nice simple days?"

Robert straightened up from the wall. "You need to realize that life in this world has never been simple, imp. There are layers of crap over other layers. More than what you see. Welcome to the world that we humans are forced to live in."

The human was right. The life we knew as supernaturals had changed. We may have been gutter trash to the high fae, but our lot in life was still better than what the humans endured. It was time we stopped standing on the sidelines and decided what we would do. "Well, partner?"

"You're my partner, Sin. I go where you go. Not going to abandon you after all these years. Besides, who will watch your back if I'm not around? This human and his friends?"

Robert reached out and grazed a hand across my cheek. "What's your plan, Sin, once we get these women?"

His light touch was distracting. I heard the imp gag under his breath bringing my mind back to more important things. "I'll make the exchange with the fairies."

The succubus leaped from the floor of her prison, pounding against the glass. "WHAT! YOU SAID YOU WOULDN'T GIVE ME TO THE FAIRIES IF I GAVE YOU THE NAMES OF THE WOMEN, DRAGON! YOU LIED! I KNEW, I NEVER SHOULD HAVE TRUSTED YOU AND THESE HUMAN SCUM."

I stood there as the creature finally ran out of steam and fell back to the floor of her cage, tears streaming down her face as she slowly shook her head from side to side. "I have no intention of giving you to the fairies. I said we would set up an exchange to get Sadie back. Then you will get what you deserve, quickly and efficiently."

Robert coldly gazed down at the sobbing succubus as though she were already dead. "What did you have in mind, Sin,"

"How good a shots are you and your group, Robert?"

He turned his eyes to me as a certain gleam lit up deep within them. "We're the best, Sin. None better."

Ralph walked into the room and slapped the side of his weapon. "Oh yeah, baby, sounds like action time."

I couldn't help but smile as I looked at the two humans knowing that in a few hours my and Sadie's lives would depend on their confidence. "Okay, but first we need to deliver a message to the fairies. We need to let them know when and where we will meet."

Sebastian flew off my shoulder and perched on the dresser. "How you going do that, Sin?" The imp glanced between the humans and me as all eyes zeroed in on him and no one said a word. The color drained from his face. "Oh, just one fricking minute, girl. I am not going to the queen's castle. Do you know what they will do to the messenger, dragon? No way. No how. Even I'm not that stupid."

"You don't need to talk to the queen, Sebastian. You can contact Igmun and deliver the message to him."

"Oh, yeah, right, Sin. Like that will be sooooo much better for me. I mean that old dragon is only one step below the queen in the bat shit crazy department."

"You're the only one that can get in and out of there in one piece. I have no one else, partner."

The imp hung his head staring at the floor for a few seconds before he sighed and looked up at me. "Alright, Sin, I'll do it, but—"

"But what, Sebastian?"

The imp shook his head as he straightened up. "Nothing, Sin. I'll deliver your message. Where is the meeting and when, girl?"

I looked over at the two soldiers. "All the women will be safe in two hours?"

"Give it four hours, just to be sure," Robert said.

I turned to my partner wondering what he had been going to say. I shrugged it off. It could wait until after we got Sadie back in one piece. I stopped worrying about Sebastian and started thinking about a meeting place. Then I remembered a park we had once been at in the northern human zone. "Okay, so tell Igmun four hours at that park in Bellingham we were at last week. Remember it, Sebastian?"

"Yeah, I remember. Good fields of fire and escape routes. Yeah, that should work, Sin."

"Good. Oh, and Sebastian?"

"Yeah, Sin?"

"Tell that old dragon I want no more than five fairies at the exchange."

"Alright. I'll tell them, but I don't think it will do much good. You know the queen has a habit of doing whatever she damn well pleases."

"Do what you can, partner. Oh, and one more thing. I want Sadie in the same condition she was taken from us. I know I told Rose that, but I want you to impress on Igmun just how important that point is, okay?"

"That's a good call knowing the queen as we do. I'll pass the requests along, but no guarantees they'll listen."

"Just do the best you can, Sebastian. That's all I ask."

"I'll try," he said as he disappeared from the bedroom with a dejected flutter.

Robert watched the imp go. "Will he get through to them?"

I hoped I was doing the right thing by sending him off to deliver our message. "He should be okay if he gets through to Igmun." Still, I felt like I had swallowed a rock.

Robert and Ralph's faces mirrored my own doubt. For a split second, I wanted to take a hammer to the succubus' cage and destroy the cause of all this trouble but knew that would just doom Sadie.

Robert interrupted my thoughts and dragged my eyes away from the still slumping succubus. "Okay, why don't we get you packed and get over to this park and figure out where we will station my people."

Robert was right about packing up. If this trade went down the way we wanted it to there was no way I could come back to my place. I was pretty certain the queen would put one hell of a price on my head.

29

Six hours later, I was alone sitting on one of six picnic tables in an open-sided building. "Dragon, free me and I'll help rid you of these fairies." Well, not quite alone as the mirror with the succubus leaned against the table.

I scanned the empty park once more, wondering what the hell was keeping those damn fairies, or Sebastian for that matter, before turning my attention to the trapped creature. "Yeah, not going to happen. I trust you even less than I trust the fairies, so save your breath."

Turning my attention back to the overgrown foliage around me, I tried for the hundredth time to see if I could see any sign of my human backup. Hell, for all I knew Robert and the others he had called in had all taken off an hour ago and left me to hang on my own.

"Dragon, you know something is wrong. The fairies are already an hour late. Do you think the humans will really stick around to save you since they have what they want?"

Sitting in the quiet of the park, the only sound was the song of some faraway bird floating through the air. I wondered if the succubus had a point. Maybe I was here all on my own. I'd only known Robert a few hours. Great sex does not a relationship make. I've already had my faith in love trashed once and here I was blindly putting my heart out there again.

I heard a tiny pop in the air in front of the building and Sebastian appeared in mid-air before dropping to the ground. I was off the table top in a shot, all thoughts of my love life evaporating. I hopped over the low wall. "Shit. Shit. Shit." I hit the grass kneeling next to my partner as he gazed through eyes buried in a face that looked like it had gone through a meat grinder. "Sebastian, talk to me. Shit, partner, say something."

I stared at him seeing the smashed face, the body that carried slashes across his chest and back and tried to decide if it would be safe to pick him up and carry him back to a table when he forced one eye open and managed a damaged smile through his split lips. "Hey, Sin, I was wrong."

Tears pouring from my eyes as I laid a hand against his cheek. "What were you wrong about, Sebastian?"

My partner let out a low moan that changed to a hacking cough before he could catch his breath. "Igmun. I was wrong about that damn old dragon. He isn't one step below the bat shit crazy of the queen. He has pretty much caught up and passed her."

I felt a rage building up in me as a fiery red haze flashed across my eyes. "He did this to you, Sebastian? That bastard?"

"Oh yeah, Sin, but the good news is that I gave him your message. The bad news is, he didn't take it too well."

His chest rose a grimace plain across his face as a rattle sounded deep inside him. "Try not to talk anymore, partner. I'm sorry that you had to deliver the message, but you did great."

A single tear tracked down his broken face. "Oooooh, I don't feel like I did so great."

I swallowed back the bile that threatened to spill from my throat. "I'll lift you and take you back to the tables so I can fix you up, partner. Okay?" Silently, Sebastian closed his eyes. I gently slipped my hands under him. Cradling him to my chest, I ignored the blood staining my top. Ignored also were the pitiful sounds the imp was making as I crawled over the low wall and set him on the table. "Where are you hurting?"

He let out a low hiss. "I don't think that damn dragon missed an inch of my body. Wait, no, my mistake, the little claw on my left foot doesn't hurt."

I couldn't help the laugh that escaped my lips. The sound, edged by a touch of hysteria, bounced around the empty building before floating out the openings into the night air. I opened the small pouch on my belt and took out the first aid kit. "I need to tend to these wounds, Sebastian."

"Uh, Sin, I have a better idea. How about you just leave me to die right here? It will be less painful than having you do whatever you're about to do."

I threw the kit on the table, thinking about all the times Sebastian had patched me up. Granted, I never remembered me being this bad before, but I would not let him give up and die on me if I could help it. "Now you listen to me, imp. I'm going to fix you, and you will not die on me. I have no intention of being in this crappy world all by myself."

He half-heartedly waved a hand at me as I doused a rag with some disinfectant and cleaned up the cuts on his chest. After a few seconds, he hissed. "Uh, Sin—"

"What, Sebastian?"

"You said I couldn't die on you, Sin. Right?"

"Right."

"Well, can I pass out on you?"

My eyes swept his broken body. "Yeah, might not be a bad idea, partner."

"Oh, good." His eyes closed and his body went limp.

I held my breath for a second before I checked for a pulse. Feeling a strong, steady beat, I went back to cleaning his wounds as I cursed old dragons, fairies, and humans. Since now, I was pretty sure that Robert and his group had left me as no one had come out to help.

"You know, I could probably fix your friend there, dragon. All you need to do is erase these runes around the mirror and I can come out and help you. If you try to do this alone he'll probably die."

"Listen, you crazy bitch. If you think I'm stupid enough to let you out of there, you had better think again."

There was a loud pop outside the low wall and I spun around as Igmun chuckled. "Well, Granddaughter, it is nice to hear you still have some sense."

I glared at the smug look on his face. My hand reached for my weapon. He shook his head. "Don't be stupid. Your weapon will never clear your holster."

My hand stopped as Fallon and five other fairies popped into the park right behind the dragon. Fallon had Sadie in front of him as the other fairies had their weapons trained on me.

Relaxing, I looked over at Sadie and saw the torn dress and bruised face. Her eyes staring at a place far away. "What did the queen do to her, you son of a bitch?"

The old dragon just cocked his head as he clicked his tongue in his cheek. "The queen? Why the queen didn't do anything. I mean she couldn't after her unfortunate accident."

It took a few seconds before his words sunk in. I wasn't surprised, but then who would do this to Sadie? I tore my eyes away from the dragon and locked on Fallon. He had the same smug look on his face. "You? You did this to her, you bastard? Why? Are you that petty, that you would hurt my friends just because I dumped you like three-day-old garbage?" His eyes already cold turned to ice.

"Now, is that any way to talk to the new ruler of all the fae on this continent?"

"Damn, you killed her, didn't you, Igmun? You were her lover, and you fucking killed her. You're one cold-hearted bastard you know that, right?"

The old dragon shrugged as Fallon stepped forward and pushed Sadie toward the low wall. "Here is your friend, my dragon. Now, give me the mirror with the succubus in it."

I took in the hard cold look in the old dragon's and Fallon's eyes. "You're not letting us walk away from this are you, Fallon?"

A tiny smirk that I used to find cute and appealing appeared. "I told you, my dragon, that staying in the gutter would get you killed one day. You should have taken me up on my offer and became my mistress."

"Yeah, and how long before Igmun here decides that you're not needed? Just like your mother? I figure, since he isn't screwing you, you won't last as long as her."

Fallon's eyes darted to Igmun before they came back to me. "Well, unfortunately, my dragon, you won't be around to see what happens. Get the mirror, kill the two bitches."

Two of the fairy guards lunged toward the mirror when both their heads disappeared in a ball of bright red mist and gore. Everything stood still for a flash before I filled my hand with my weapon. I grabbed Sadie by the front of her shirt and pulled her over the low wall of the building.

Sadie lay on the concrete floor, comatose, with me kneeling next to her. "GET THE MIRROR! KILL THE OTHERS LATER!" Igmun said.

Whoever was shooting must have been using a silencer. I never heard the shot that hit the mirror. Igmun stopped yelling as the glass exploded into a million pieces. I threw myself over Sadie to protect her from the shrapnel as a loud shriek and a cold wind washed over us. A sound like a thousand tortured souls screamed in my ears. Looking up, it seemed like time slowed as glass and wood expanded from a bright white light. Then it was as though it sucked all the air in with all the pieces flying outward before collapsing within the white light until it dissolved into nothingness. The monster was dead, she had paid for her crimes.

It was quiet when I heard Robert's voice from the foliage. "You lose, fairy. If you want to live, you and that damn dragon will leave."

I peeked over the low wall and saw Fallon standing with Igmun gripping his arm. All the other fairies were down, lying in spreading puddles of their own blood. Our eyes met, and I felt a chill run down my spine as Fallon pulled his arm out of the dragon's grasp and the two of them disappeared.

I glanced at Sadie before standing and seeing what looked like bushes walking toward me. As they got closer, I could make out the humans in the camouflage clothing. Robert stopped in front of me and looked me over. "Bet you thought I left you on your own, didn't you?"

I felt a tiny blip in my heart. "No, why would you think that, Robert?"

He nodded before turning to the others and started barking orders. "Doc, we got customers for you. The rest of you spread out and set up a perimeter in case the fairies decide to come back."

I watched as the humans moved quickly at Robert's command. The medic hopped over the wall with another creature who I saw was an elf and kneeled next to Sadie. They gave her a quick once over before the medic stepped to the table and started working on Sebastian.

I started over to the table when I felt a hand on my arm, tugging me in the opposite direction. "Let them do their job, Sin. The Doc is the best medic we have. If anyone can fix your partner, she will."

I threw one last look over at the table then tore my eyes away from the sight of the medic working on my friend. I looked into Robert's eyes for a second before I smashed a fist into the middle of his chest. "Damn, you cut that one pretty close, didn't you?"

He looked at my fist before he pulled me close. His lips brushed mine. "I got your back, Sin. Never doubt that. I told you before you're mine, got me?" What could I say to that? Nothing. I rested my head against his chest and closed my eyes as his arms wrapped around me.

30

Three months later:

My eyes opened as the morning sun slanted through the half-open drapes. I snuggled against Robert's chest as his arm tightened around me and he mumbled something in his sleep. Contented, I gathered my thoughts for another day.

Another day of searching for Robert's sister. Another day of trying to figure out what we would do with the half Were–half succubus children that would be born in a little less than three months. Another day of fighting the fairies. Another day of trying to get Sadie to talk.

My mind flashed to Sebastian, when the door burst open and the tiny imp fluttered into the room. He was flying low in a zig-zag pattern since one wing was still on the mend. For the most part, Doc had said he would be back to one hundred percent in no time, but that didn't stop my partner from complaining about his various aches and pains whenever he could get someone to stand still long enough to listen.

Robert grunted in his sleep as I threw the sheet over our bodies. "What is it, Sebastian?"

The imp landed on the edge of the bed. "Sin, it's almost time to get up, and you promised me I could go out with you. Remember? You promised me." His eyes were wide as he held his hands under his chin.

"I said you could go with us if, and I mean if, the Doc okays it."

His face fell for a second before it brightened as he jumped up and down on the edge of the bed, his voice rising on each word. "She'll okay it, Sin. She was just telling me how much better I was. I'm sure she will give me permission to go out with you, Sin."

I put a finger to my lips. "Ssshhh. I don't want you to wake Robert. He just got in from patrol a couple hours ago."

"I'm awake, Sin. Hard not to be with that damn noisemaker coming in our room the first thing in the morning."

"Hey. I resent that. Besides, if you had gone straight to sleep instead of boinking the dragon here, you would have gotten more rest."

Robert turned and rose up on his side with a wicked smile playing across his lips. I slid off his chest and down on the bed. "That sounds like a great idea."

Sebastian looked confused. "What sounds like a great idea? What's he talking about, Sin? What great idea?"

"Why boinking Sin here. That sounds like a great idea you came up with, imp."

My partner fluttered off the bed and headed toward the door. "I'm out of here."

"SHUT THE DOOR BEHIND YOU!" Robert said as Sebastian flew out of the room.

It was quiet after the door slammed closed. I looked into those dark brown eyes, seeing the heat and passion in them caused my stomach to flutter all the way down to my center. "Really, you're going to boink me? I thought you humans had more romance in you. Ooooh—"

I stopped scolding as Robert snaked a hand under the sheets and between my legs. I forgot all about romance in the quick orgasm that racked my body. Screw romance. Getting my brains boinked out was just fine this morning. Just fine, indeed.

Five hundred miles north:

Maria rose from her sleeping bag and crawled awkwardly out of the tent. She stood looking around at the surrounding woods, one hand on her distended belly. She spun around at the sound of a snapping twig behind her. Two men stood at the edge of the tree line. Her nostrils flared at the smell of wolf.

One of the Weres stepped forward, dark humor lighting his face. "Well, what do we have here, Slim?"

"Looks like breakfast, Joe."

"Yeah, I think so too," Joe said as he stepped forward. He stopped as the girl pulled a revolver from behind her back.

Slim took a step to the side. "A big gun for such a little thing. Bet she doesn't even know how to use it. What do you think, Joe?"

Joe didn't say a word as he rushed forward. The report of the pistol was loud in the morning air, bouncing off the trees and echoing down the valley. Joe lay on the ground cursing as the gun swept sideways to cover Slim. The Were stood, his hands extended. His eyes wary.

"SHIT! SHIT! THE DAMN BITCH SHOT ME WITH SILVER, SLIM!"

Slim saw his buddy holding his shoulder as blood flowed through his fingers. He licked his lips. "Listen, girly, we were just fooling about eating you for breakfast. There is no reason to go and be grouchy on a fine morning like this, now is there?"

She patted her swollen belly. "I'm here to see your alpha."

"Oh, honey, our alpha doesn't swing that way. She would have no interest in you at all and she sure as hell couldn't have knocked you up. She don't have the right equipment."

The girl lowered the weapon and pulled the trigger again. Now it was Slim's turn to be rolling around on the wet ground, his hands wrapped around what was left of his knee cap. His screams drowned out the echo of the second shot.

Maria looked at the two Weres and calmly took out the two spent casings and put two new bullets in their place like her brother had taught her. She walked over to the first Were she had shot and kneeled next to him. "I need for you to take me to your alpha."

Joe stopped moaning at the quietness of the girl's voice and the sick smile that painted her face. "Why do you want to see our alpha? Did one of our pack knock you up? I mean if that's the case, she really won't care."

Joe stopped talking as the girl cocked the pistol and pointed it at his face. "This baby I carry isn't some wolf bastard. She is a gift from the gods."

Joe gazed up the barrel of the pistol, it looked as big as a train tunnel then further up into the strange light in those brown eyes. "Uh—sure—whatever—you— say—girly."

"Good, let us go find your alpha."

Joe sat up and looked over at his partner who was now passed out. "Uh, listen, I don't think we can go right now. Slim is pretty hurt and it will take him a little time to heal up."

Another shot echoed through the valley as the other Were's head exploded. Joe spun back to the girl. "What the hell, girly? What did you do that for?"

The girl stood, the pistol now pointing at his head. "We don't have time to wait. I need to see your alpha so she will protect this gift from the gods."

Joe's eyes shot to the ruined head of his partner and back to the girl before he slowly stood. "Okay, girly, I'll take you to our alpha. It's this way." He headed back toward the wood line.

Maria gave one last look back at her tent and, ignoring the dead Were, followed Joe into the trees.

ABOUT THE AUTHOR

Robert is the author of multiple young adult fantasy and sci-fi stories populated with strong female heroes and intriguing creatures pulled from his imagination. His characters are based on drawings and doodles that he has worked on since he could pick up a pencil. Robert has traveled the world and met many interesting people but now lives in Bellingham, Washington with his wife and youngest child. Bellingham and the surrounding areas are often the settings for his many novels. For more information on these enjoyable books please visit witchwaybooks.com or stop by the Witch Way Books page on Facebook.

Made in the USA
Middletown, DE
21 February 2022

61579559R00126